SPARROW

The Water's Edge

T.T. McGil

www.PurposePublishing.com

Sparrow: The Water's Edge

ISBN: 9781732683259
Library of Congress Control Number: 2018967504

Cover Design by Justin Greene
Editing by Camika Spencer and Frank Kresen

Printed in the United States of America.

Purpose Publishing
1503 Main Street
Grandview, MO 64030
www.PurposePublishing.com
To learn more about T.T. McGil, visit the website
at www.TTMcGil.com

SPARROW

The Water's Edge

T.T. McGil

Thank you God for the breath of life, and the courage to step out on faith. And most of all the love that you have shown me and given me. I marvel at how you aligned my steps and so honored that you chose me to birth visions to encourage others.

I thank my family for their unyielding love and support. I am honored to be a wife, a mother, a daughter, a sister, a cousin and a friend. This journey is "our" journey, and it is a privilege that I will never take for granted.

I challenge each and every reader to find their very own Water's Edge, where they are able to be quiet and in the presence of the almighty. That is where your strength ends and God's truly begins and where the mystery of life is unveiled.

T.T. McGil

Medical Disclaimer

The data contained in the Sparrow Mystery Series book, including the text, images, and graphics, are for informational purposes only. THE BOOK DOES NOT OFFER ADVICE, AND NOTHING CONTAINED IN THE CONTENT IS ANYTHING OTHER THAN ENTERTAINMENT. This book is strictly for entertainment purposes and should be deemed solely as such. T.T. McGil ("Company") accepts no responsibility for the likeness of any characters, scenes, locations or names based in whole or in part upon the use of this Web site or books.

The Sparrow Mystery Series is a work of fiction. Names, characters, businesses, places, events, locales, and incidents are either the products of the author's imagination or used in a fictitious manner. Any resemblance to actual persons, living or dead, or actual events is purely coincidental. Although great care has been taken in compiling notes, research and checking the information given to ensure accuracy, the authors, publisher, their employees, the sponsors, and their servants or agents shall not be responsible or in any way liable for any errors, omissions, or inaccuracies, whether arising from negligence or otherwise, or for any consequences arising therefrom.

Preface

This book is a result of reflections about the full capacity of knowledge that is received from all the people we encounter. There are some individuals we meet in a brief, fleeting moment that leave an everlasting impression on our souls. And there are some souls we have known all our lives that impress only a minimal or even a negative, scarring impact on our well-being. The choice is solely up to us as to the impact that any personal interaction will have on our life.

This story will take you on an adventure like no other. Its characters are fictional, but the message that the story is intended to impart is a very real one — a message of self-discovery, promise, mystery, faith, forgiveness, resolution, and insight. This book brings to you the textures and true grit of day-to-day life, while leaving your creative mind to visualize the characters' lives and the life they were called to live. My hope is that, while this book can entertain and enhance the senses, it can be a call to action to challenge each and every one of us to truly engage in each moment we encounter and live the best possible life we can, despite our circumstances.

Chapter 1

When most people think of true friendship, they think of a comfortable place to exist, but not me. I cannot relate. My journey with my best friend was not pretty; it was raw, jagged, and downright horrifying at times, erasing all possibilities of comfort.

It was what it was.

I grabbed my jaw as it throbbed with pain. I often thought it was a myth of being hit so hard in the head that stars appeared. However, I was seeing them now, as the taste of blood flooded into my mouth. My feet were unsteady from the strong blow to my face. I tried to catch my equilibrium by planting my feet firmly into the white, powdery sands that seemed to evaporate under my feet.

Can this be happening to me? And at whose hands? I asked myself in pure disbelief while falling with outstretched arms, as gravity pulled me toward the ground.

This was so unlike me, as I prided myself for being in control at all times. For the first time in a long time, I was not in control; I was at the mercy of the unknown.

The white sands splashed into my face, softening my fall.

How in the hell did I get here? I pondered.

I lay there with closed eyes while infinite granules of sand rested easy on my tired eyelids and my mind propelled back to how this day had begun, at the Miami Airport. It started unlike any other day I had ever experienced. "Rough" is the word that comes to mind.

I can't believe I am doing this. Should I be out here, all by myself? I thought to myself with my arms raised while TSA patted me down in the closed airport security section away from the long line of passengers checking in; my carry-on bag had triggered the security alarm. The security team escorted me to where the "suspicious" people go to be checked out further before being able to board a flight. A guard conducted a thorough search of my bag *and* my person. I was annoyed, but they were doing their job, making sure the airport was secure. I waited impatiently while my stomach began to seriously growl.

Damn, I'm hungry. I need get to get to a food court for some breakfast before my flight. They need to hurry this shit up, I thought while still presenting a perfect, non-threatening smile to the security guards, trying not to show how irritated I was and to forcefully be on my best behavior.

The last thing I need is a damn headline all over social media: "Dr. Sparrow Mack, physician and soon-to-be-best-selling-author, arrested for assaulting airport security!" That's the last shit I need to disrupt the mission that I am on! Stay cool, Sparrow. Stay calm, I had to tell myself over and over again.

The security guard who meticulously combed through my belongings turned toward me and asked with a curious look on his face,

"Dr. Mack, why will you need steel-toed boots in the Bahamas?"

I took a big breath, let out a sigh, and calmly replied,

"A lot is being renovated in my life right now."

The guards looked at each other, nodded and released me; I was free to go. I finally made to the food court that was on the opposite end of the airport from my boarding gate. Thank goodness the line was short, so I was able to order quickly and take a seat, ready to devour my breakfast.

"Umm, this is so good," I said out loud with no shame while I sank my teeth into the delicious egg-white-and-turkey-bacon sandwich, toasted to perfection and garnished with a slice of avocado. This was my "go to" breakfast, and the taste of this wonderful distraction made me forget about the irritating run-in with security.

Sparrow, you know you shouldn't be eating all of this, I thought while adjusting the waist of my pants, but I needed this nourishment and satisfied my appetite mouth first. *Damn the calories.* I looked around at my fellow airport passengers also attempting to get their first meal of the day, while keeping an eye on the clock so they would not miss their flights.

In between bites, I yawned aimlessly, since restless nights seemed to be my new normal. And it did not help that my curiosity had gotten the best of me last night, while I turned page after page of the leather journal I'd found in the closet until late into the evening. There appeared to be clue after clue jumping out at me and catching my attention, which prompted me to take this bold step into the unknown and venture to the islands.

I carefully sipped the freshly brewed chai tea that the cheery barista had meticulously made for me. She was charming as she took the extra effort to create a heart-shaped foam design on the top of my tea. I really needed that simple gesture of love today, and I hated to cover up that example of sunshine with the lid, but I did. I tried not to burn my lips as steam billowed from the to-go cup as I drank.

This is so delicious. Luke would have loved this, I thought. Luke was my best friend, and this was his favorite morning beverage. Luke, a connoisseur of chai tea, had introduced me to the beverage when we used to meet at the Big Gulp Coffee Hut across from the medical center long ago, when I was a medical student and he would come by to hang out with me during my study breaks. If Luke were sitting here with me drinking this, he would have slipped a shot of Jack or Bailey's in his. I smiled in that reflection. How ironic was it that I was sipping Luke's favorite morning drink and headed to the islands to try to figure out why he was now dead?

My cell phone began to ring. I put it in silent mode, adjusted the tone to vibrate, and turned it face down and continued to consume my breakfast.

"I need a break", I said as I looked around continuing to people-watch. Besides, it was too early for a telephone conversation — the sun wasn't even up yet. I stretched my legs and rubbed my overworked calves to give them some relief. My phone began to vibrate across the table.

Maybe I should take a look. This could be my agent or one of the clinics calling. I considered flipping the phone over, because in my current real life, I was in the process of transitioning out of my clinical practice at the same time that I was in contract negotiations with my publishing house to get my first novel, *Step 1,* on the best-sellers list. Even though I was preoccupied with Luke's death, I had put in a lot of sweat equity into my own goals, and I couldn't neglect taking care of that business. I put my big-girl trousers on, took a deep breath, and slowly turned the phone over: "Unknown Caller."

Who could this be? I don't have time for this. I am really being tried today. First, I'm hemmed up by security, and now somebody is playing on my phone, I thought as I took another bite and chewed, intensely annoyed, and ignored the call. Then my phone pinged with a text alert. It was a text message from my agent, Tabitha. As I picked up the phone to read, I thought to myself, *Geez, not again. I can't deal with any extra demands on me right now, Tabitha! I had signed off on all of the paperwork with the publishing house. Besides, I have a plane to catch!*

The text read, "Sparrow, please look at your email and review the itinerary for the book tour. Review the contracts for your upcoming appearances! I need your stamp of approval on them ASAP!"

I responded while swallowing another bite of my sandwich and taking a sip of my chai tea:

"Tabitha: Yes, I got the documents in your email last night. Sorry, I've been swamped. You will get my response by the close of business today! You are the best! Ro."

I did not want to tilt my hand and tell anybody, even Tabitha my new plan to connect the dots of what happened to Luke. And even though I was a little irritated by Tabitha's bossiness, I chalked it up to my sleep deprivation, irritation over how my day had started, and the recent tragedy — I was more than a little on edge these days. Tabitha was always on her game. She makes sure that every single "i" is dotted and every "t" is crossed as my agent and broker, and I appreciated her for that.

When I finished responding to Tabitha's text, I sent a heart emoji to my husband. I had already called him early that morning before I left the hotel, to check on the baby and pray. That was apart of our morning routine, minus the fact that was flying off to the islands to put on the cloak of being a detective. My husband thought I was scheduled to be in Miami submerged in book signings and appearances, and he would just not understand my need to dig deeper into what really happened to Luke.

Thinking about my family and the uncertainty of what I was up against made my chest warm with anxiety and angst. *Man, I miss them something awful. What the hell am I doing? I can't believe I'm out here all willy nilly trying to figure out what had happened to Luke. I am not a damn detective!* I took a deep breath and fanned myself with a napkin.

I said — out loud — in my own space at the food-court table, to counter the fear that was welling up inside of me, not caring if anybody could hear my self-talk, "Sparrow, you really need to get yourself together and get focused! Get your shit together right now, girl! There's too much riding on you — your family, career, the book, the tour, and now, Luke's ongoing issues, from beyond the grave!"

God, please help me. I can't do this alone! I thought as I lowered my head. Suddenly I felt God taking some of the weight off of my shoulders. And I knew that God would help me bear all my issues, my family's issues, and my friends' issues — but now I knew I wasn't alone in bearing all of those crosses.

Looking at my watch, I realized I had about an hour to board the plane, so I turned my phone off after responding to Tabitha's text and placed it into my oversized bag, drank the last bit of my chai tea, and held the remaining corner of my uneaten breakfast sandwich. I reached into my bag for the leather journal to investigate its contents a little more, when suddenly I heard,

"Somebody, help! Somebody, please — help us!"

Abruptly standing up, I threw down the little bit of my breakfast sandwich that was left, and I took a panoramic scan of the area to see where the scream was coming from. The commotion was behind me, about fifty feet away, toward the seats at Gate 37. The blood-curdling calls for help continued and increased in intensity, making the hairs on my forearms stand on end. These days, when people scream in an airport, many people run away to secure their own safety.

But not me. I grabbed my stuff and ran toward the cry for help. This was definitely not a part of my plans today. I was supposed to be focusing on catching a flight to the islands to get to the condo to map out why Luke's final residential address was in the Bahamas. However, beyond my control I felt that someone in this airport needed my help as well. I curiously pushed my way into the deep pack of on-lookers that was growing by the minute. This had a strong possibility of being a medical emergency, based on the intensity of the cries for help and my natural medical instinct and intuition. I went into full doctor mode and became a little more aggressive in making my way to the front, propelling myself forward through the thick crowd.

compressions. My necklace began to swing and caught on my chin, distracting me with the chest compressions. I reached up and tucked it into my shirt to immobilize it, an eerie reminder of Luke's ever presence.

I was in deep, full-throttle CPR mode, when, to my left, I saw something irritating — I couldn't believe it. Standing right behind me, someone was live-streaming this horrible incident.

"Here at the Miami airport, a man lay in distress, as we all try to help him stay alive!" a young blond-haired man arrogantly stated, smiling into his phone as if he was reporting the morning's breaking-news.

"Can you believe this guy?" I said as I continued to compress, hoping that he would overhear me and stop this heinous act of insensitivity, but he continued to film while Mr. Meyers lay still and I attempted to bring him back to life. I looked over and made stern eye contact with live streamer as I counted off in my head the number breaths and compressions to give. I couldn't take the lack of respect from this guy any longer. I had to say something.

"You — in the black jacket live-streaming this! Yeah — I'm talking to you with the blond spiked-out dated haircut. Yes — you! Call 911, right now, and get security, before I really give you something to live-stream!"

The entire crowd turned toward the young man and gasped and shook their heads disapprovingly; his face flushed with deep embarrassment. He quickly turned his phone from live-streaming mode and dialed 911, with his hands now shaking with concern and worry. Once he got the dispatcher on the line, he approached me, bent down, and said in a terrified tone,

"Hey, doc. I got 911 on the line. What do I tell them?"

While continuing cardiopulmonary resuscitation protocol, I instructed him,

"Tell the dispatcher that we have a sixty-plus-year-old man who is unresponsive. He has likely suffered a cardiac event, and I'm not able to detect a pulse. I am a doctor performing CPR, and there is no AED in sight! Tell them we need an ambulance here — stat — at Gate 37, across from the food court, in the Miami airport! I will continue to work on him until they arrive. And please hurry!"

He repeated everything to the dispatcher just as I had instructed. While I continued to work on Mr. Meyers, out of the corner of my eye, I saw the black-jacketed, blonde-spiked-haired man disappear into the thick crowd. He headed toward a door marked "Security" that I had not noticed before, on this side of the food court.

I felt a little guilty. Maybe I should not have been so hard on him. I knew that I'd be thinking about this all day — if I'd hurt his feelings. I am such a pushover. If I get the chance later, I will apologize – or maybe not since he had the audacity to livestream. Who's to say? I need to stay focused.
"Can somebody go find an AED — a defibrillator — for this man?" I yelled to anybody in the crowd still standing around, pleading to anybody willing to help.

While I worked on the patient, the lady continued to hold his hand. She was a brunette with tight, pale skin. She was wearing bright-red lipstick and a pungent, aromatic, floral perfume that was near nauseating as it hit my nostrils. I was inhaling deeply to muster up the strength to give meaningful chest compressions after giving another set of breaths. She continued to cry, and her mascara ran in long strides down her face that was sealed beneath a matte foundation finish, leaving streaks that revealed her true skin complexion. This experience appeared to be aging her by the minute, and I tried to calm her, reassuring her that I was a doctor who was going to do everything I could do to make sure her husband was okay until the ambulance arrived.

"Doctor, he is not my husband! I don't know this man!" She trembled as she continued to hold his hand tight.

"What?" I responded while continuing CPR.

"Please allow me to explain. I was seated at the gate next to him. His phone rang, and he got up and began to have a heated conversation with someone on his cell phone. As his voice got louder, it caught everyone's attention. Then all at once, he grabbed his chest, and down he went, collapsing onto the floor," she said. The telling on upset her more because now tears flowed out of her eyes like a fountain.

"Doctor, I didn't know how I could help him, so I begged and pleaded for someone to please help! And then you showed up, thank God!" she continued to share. She was obviously horrified by this experience, as her whole body appeared to shake as she knelt by his side.

"Ma'am, just try to remain as calm as possible. I am going to do everything in my power to make sure he is okay."

Although I was far from perfect, I had grown in my spiritual walk and had learned to use my voice, to speak things into existence, I introduced myself to this diminishing soul and prophesied over this man clinging to life while pushing down diligently on his chest, willing myself to press life back into him.

“Mr. Meyers, I am Dr. Sparrow Mack. God is working through me to make sure you are going to be restored. Now, you come back here and finish out what the Almighty has planned for your life!” I commanded divine intervention, as I knew it was the only way we could get through this situation.

I turned my head around and looked for an AED once again, thinking that I’d possibly missed it in all the excitement. I didn’t see one anywhere, which was strange. An AED would be crucial for this man’s survival, and there should have been one in obvious sight.

“Can someone see if there is an AED around here?” I yelled out again, as the crowd continued to thicken and stand around. I was working alone, and my arms were getting more rubbery from the consistent, methodical compressions. Sweat beads rolled down my temples, and I was beginning to get a little concerned because my own personal strength was fading fast. I knew my human spirit, by itself — although well meaning — was not enough to bring this man back to life.

"God, please help me revive this man, if it is your will!" I pleaded out loud unafraid of how my walk with the Lord might be perceived.

A lady dressed in denim from head to toe forced her way through the crowd, knelt across from me on the other side of Mr. Meyers, and announced herself.

"I'm a nurse; how can I help?" she stated with boldness, breathing hard while looking at the patient up and down doing her own visual assessment of the situation.

"I'm Dr. Mack, Internal Medicine. Yep — I need a breather. I will continue to do compressions. I have sent someone to call for the ambulance."

"I got it! I'm Jennifer, an ICU nurse. You got an extra mouth piece?"

"Yes," I said as I pulled another disposable plastic mouth protector from my bag and tossed it to her. She removed my mouth protector and placed a new one on Mr. Meyers' lips, which were now cyanotic and turning blue.

Jennifer gave him two breaths, and his chest rose upwards. During those breaths, I took the opportunity to stretch my arms and hands. Then I placed the heel of one hand on the center of his chest and placed two fingers at the tip of his breastbone. I put the heel of my other hand right above those two fingers on the side that was closest to Robert's pale face. I used both of my hands in that fixed position, with my elbows locked, to give deep, consistent, forced compressions with all my might.

We continued with the breaths and compressions as we counted off in unison, a team practicing medicine in the trenches on the Miami airport floor. Who would have ever thought that I was headed out today to find out the mystery behind Luke's death and end up on the Miami airport floor trying to save a life?

"I know there should be an AED around here. I yelled out for one before you arrived, and no one has shown up with one yet!" I said while compressing Robert's chest. I looked around as Jennifer gave her next set of breaths, and then she also looked around also and replied,

"Yep — there should be one, but I don't see one, either." In that moment, an airline gate attendant walked over to us, dropped an AED down, and asked if we needed any assistance with the device.

"Thank you. What a blessing. This is exactly what we needed. Please, make sure the ambulance knows where to find us!" I said, as severe fatigue set into my arms.

"I'm on it. They have been dispatched and are en route. I'm going to open the secured doors, so they can get in quickly when they arrive." She walked off, disappearing into the crowd toward the security door.

I opened the box containing the AED, and Jennifer asked,

"Doc, have you used one of these before?"

Making his way back to the front of the crowd, where the still-limp body of Mr. Meyers lay, was the twenty-something, blond-spiked-haired man. He said, while huffing and puffing as he bent over to appear as if he were assisting the good doctor and the nurse in the field, "Doc, security is right behind me, and the ambulance has been dispatched!"

"Great. Thanks!"

"What else can I do?" he asked.

"Pray," I responded. His eyes closed as his shaking hands came together; he clasped them and slightly lowered his head in agreement.

"And yes, Jennifer. I know how to operate an AED. I trained and certified physicians on how to use these devices in my clinical practice," I replied, as I turned the AED on; Jennifer went right in and kept CPR going while I got the AED ready.

"God is so good!" Jennifer replied and smiled as she compressed Robert's chest.

The green light indicated that the AED was ready to work. I attempted to open Robert's shirt properly; it had small buttons all down the front. But proceeding button by button was taking a bit too long. I had to act quicker. I took both of my hands and ripped the remaining buttons off this fine, starched, and obviously custom-designer dress shirt, with his initials embroidered on the cuffs. The skin on his chest was not hairy, which was a good thing, however, it was wet from his profuse sweating and diaphoresis, which was not so good.

"Does anybody have a towel, napkin, or something for me to wipe Robert's chest? This part of his body has to be dry for me to apply the AED pads!" I screamed out in panic and desperation.

The lady holding his hand gave me some napkins as she mindlessly explained they were from the coffee shop that Robert had dropped on the floor when he collapsed. I wiped his wet chest as best I could. I attached the AED pads to his chest. I followed the visual and audio prompts of the AED device. I looked at the connectors, and, fortunately, with this

AED system, they were already plugged into the AED box.

I prepared to analyze his heart rhythm and deliver the charge, as I ordered everyone, "Stand clear!"

My finger was on the "Analyze" button, and I was getting ready to push it, when an older lady who'd appeared out of nowhere, knelt down at Mr. Meyers' feet, and begun to rub his pant leg. I turned toward her. "Ma'am, you need to stand back now!

"But I'm praying for him!" she replied.

"I understand that, however, everyone has to stand back and stand clear, which means do not touch this man! We must analyze his heart rhythm and possibly shock him. With you touching him, I can't do that, and it could hurt you. Pray over him, but do not touch him! This is to help him and protect you." I looked around him once again and made sure there was no one touching Mr. Meyers. "Stand clear!" I commanded the crowd at the top my lungs.

I scooted back a little from him and repeated, "Stand clear!" Assured no one was touching him, I pushed the "Analyze" button, which allowed the AED to scan Mr. Meyers' heart rhythm. It indicated that a shock be delivered. I pushed the "Shock" button, the AED machine counted down, and the shock was delivered. Robert's body pulsed upward and shook quickly, but no change; he remained still.

"Come on, Robert! Come on, brother! Come back to us!" I yelled over his lifeless body. I checked his pulses, and they remained absent. My head hung down in despair as we prepped for the next cycle of compressions.

"Come on, doc — you've got this!" a voice yelled out from the crowd.

And suddenly, there was a small blip of rhythm on the AED monitor. I frantically rechecked his pulses. They still were not there.

"What should we do, Doctor?" Jennifer asked, her eyes big with concern.

"I figured this would happen. I presume that he is experiencing PEA or pulseless electrical activity. This is treated similar to a systole or flat-line. It is not really a functional heart rhythm, so we need to do our best to reset the rhythm of his heart. Okay, I need everybody to stand clear and not touch Robert. I'm clear, you're clear, we are all clear!" I commanded again as I pushed the "Analyze" button. The AED machine recommended another shock.

"Everybody clear!" I yelled out.

The shock was delivered. Robert's body heaved off the floor with more force than before. He rebounded and landed hard.

All at once, a huge gasp escaped his throat and he began to cough.

"Yes! Praise God!" I yelled out. That cough was like music to my ears, and my eyes began to mist a little with joy. He groaned and gargled up copious foamy-white secretions that oozed from his mouth. While his eyes were open wide and he appeared alert, I didn't know if he was going to regurgitate. So I had to act quickly.

"Let's roll him on his side," I said to Jennifer. He then spit out a large amount of foamy saliva. With the napkins that were near, Jennifer wiped the foam out of his mouth. And then he took a clear, deep, strong breath, and the color resurfaced in his face. He was back!

The EMS team arrived as we were placing Robert on his back, and they took over. The crowd of onlookers began to disperse.

Once the emergency-response team got Robert stabilized and on the gurney they took down our names as the individuals who'd coded this man in the field.

As I sat there a moment, collecting myself, I realized that, once again, God had put me in a position to be a vessel of service to help someone.

I wish I would have been able to help Luke, just like I helped Mr. Meyers today, and was able to save his life, I thought to myself as I dusted off as I stood beside Jennifer Marx. She was an Intensive Care Registered Nurse who lived in Wyoming, headed to her Texas hometown for her grandfather's funeral after being in Miami for a nurses' convention. I realized how unique it was to have met her at this critical time. This is a true testament of what can happen when two people come together in a divine connection.

We made a proper introduction, I gave her my condolences for the loss of her grandfather, and we embraced and laughed in hysteria about the craziness of what had just happened. We dubbed ourselves the "divine code team" — especially since our patient had survived! We exchanged information and parted ways. I grabbed my bag and began to walk away to go toward the ladies' room to wash my hands and freshen up before my flight, when I heard my name called.

"Excuse me, Dr. Mack. Can you come here, please?" It was one of the ambulance workers motioning for me to come over to where he was.

"Sure. I'll be right over," I replied.

"Good work here today, Dr. Mack. You were spot on with your resuscitative efforts. If it had not been for you being in the right spot at the right time, this man would have surely died. And if it is okay with you, Mr. Meyers would like to speak with you for a moment."

"Sure — it would be an honor," I said as I attempted to pull myself together by adjusting some loose strands of hair and straightening my clothes.

I approached the now-smiling and tired, but alive man who now had color back in his cheeks. Mr. Robert Meyers was sitting up with his torso strapped to the stretcher. The heart monitor beeping, showing normal sinus rhythm. I was so glad to see that rhythm, appearing like a long lost best friend. Oh, the relief. I let out a huge sigh. Mr. Meyers reached his hand out to me and said,

"I heard everything you said, Doc. My lady, you are a bossy little thing, aren't you? I had no choice but to come back!" he chuckled and rubbed my hand with a gentle caress. He went on to say, "Seriously, thank you. I have a lot of things in my life I have to make right, and by you saving my life, I will be alive to do just that." His eyes began to well up with tears.

"Mr. Meyers, I cannot take all the credit. God was here today, and there was an ICU nurse who helped me revive you! And I trust that you will use this second chance to the fullest."

"Yes, I believe that. I've never really believed in miracles, but now I do!" Robert said as he wiped his eyes.

"Okay, we have to go. The ambulance is awaiting us!" the ambulance worker said as they unlocked the wheels on the stretcher and began to roll Robert away.

As he headed toward the open security doors, I told Mr. Meyers to promise to take care and that he would be in my prayers. Also, I apologized for single-handedly destroying his nice shirt, and I offered to buy him a new one.

"I will have no such thing." He waved as he approached the security doors that led to the waiting ambulance.

As I walked away from the scene, I got several pats on the back and "Way to go, doc!" accolades while walking toward the restroom. I smiled and kept my head humbly down. The spiked-haired young man and the lady who'd been holding Robert's hand were long gone as the crowd of travelers dissipated, hurrying to catch their flights. And now in the airport, it was back to business as usual. As I walked to the rest room, it was more evident than ever that I was divinely supposed to be here at this time. Although I was here by chance to catch a flight to the Bahamas based on the information I found in the closet, journal, and bank lock box in correlation with the untimely demise of my best friend, there clearly was a bigger plan here, and I had to acknowledge it. I went to the restroom and washed my over-worked, life-saving hands. While I was drying them, I noticed my watch. I had totally lost track of time!

Oh, no! My plane should be boarding right about now!

Just then I looked up as I heard the overhead system announce boarding for my flight to the Bahamas. I ran out of the restroom full speed ahead, still drying my hands off with the paper towel as I ran through the airport.

I was weaving in and out of people from gate 37 all the way to gate 15, my boarding gate.

"Excuse me, excuse me, pardon me, and pardon me," I said over and over as I bumped into people and accidently stepped on a couple of toes of fellow airport patrons trying to get to their gates, like I was. Running as fast as I could, I was a mess, as my hair flew in every direction, my carry-on bag flopped at my side, and my necklace charm kept swinging up and getting stuck on the tip of my chin with each step. I was breathing hard, trying to keep a long stride, so I would make it to the gate in time and not miss my flight. Even though I had just saved a life, I am sure they were not holding the airplane from leaving just for little ole me. Finally, I arrived at my gate. I reached into my carry-on tote, and my hand blindly scrambled around, all of its contents, until I grabbed my boarding pass. Handing it to the boarding agent, the realization that I'd made it just in time sank in. I was in line behind vacation-ready passengers dressed in linen, flip flops, tank tops, and shades, ready to get their vacations started on the islands. I walked down the jet-way; my heart was still pounding hard and the adrenaline was still racing through my vessels.

Wow, I just saved a life! Sparrow, you are one bad chick! You are a child of God, wife, mother, doctor, author, and, now, you've just saved another life. Girl, if you could just get your whole self together, and figure out what in the hell happened to your best friend, you would really be the bomb! I thought to myself.

Chapter 2

"Thank you, Lord!" Anyone who knows me knows my favorite place to sit on a plane in a window seat. I had come across an open one. Despite the residual adrenaline still racing through my veins from saving a life — mixed with the sleep deprivation from the turmoil that was trying to infiltrate every fiber of my being surrounding the mystery of Luke's death — my fatigue won out hands down. I was exhausted. Normally after I got in my seat on the plane, I would eagerly raise up the window shade, put my face close to the window, and gaze out in awe beholding all of God's glory at thirty thousand feet, flying along the horizon and admiring the shapes of the clouds and the hues of blue of God's global canvas.

However, today was different and not like any other day. As soon as I sat down, I looked out the window and saw the ambulance, with its sirens blaring and its cherry-red beams blinking, speeding off to get to the nearest hospital. I felt a peaceful settling in my spirit and knew the dear soul that I just helped save would be just fine. As the ambulance drove away into the distance, I took that as my cue to pull the window shade down, put my earplugs in so that my ears would not hurt from the barometric pressure change, and get some much-needed rest. I leaned deep into my plush gray neck pillow, pulled my matching fuzzy travel blanket across my body, and sank deep into my seat. My hope was that the pilot would immediately dim the cabin lights, so I could close my eyes and go to sleep. I needed to be well rested when I got to the condo so I could methodically lay out all of the information I had found after Luke's home-going. I had to try to figure out the "how" and the "why" of the clues leading me to our family condo in the Caribbean. I snuggled deeper into my pillow and pulled my blanket closer to my neck wanting to cocoon myself away from the world. The rest of the passengers were boarding the plane while I was headed toward slumber land.

"Excuse me, Miss. Is this seat taken?"

I peeked my head from under my blanket and pulled one of my earplugs out. I turned to look toward the way-too-cheerful voice that had asked the question. It was a middle-aged, tanned petite lady who was standing in the aisle, with her bright beach t-shirt matching her smile; she was holding up the rest of the boarding passengers. Giddily, she stood in the aisle facing me, while she awaited my response to her question. Meanwhile, the passengers waiting behind her sighed in discontentment and frustration, attempting to get to their seats, so their vacations could commence.

"Come on, lady. Will you grab a seat already!" an irate passenger yelled out behind her. This was a row with three seats, and I was perplexed; truth be told, a little irritated that she would dare disturb me and engage in a conversation about the empty two seats that were available. I did not own this plane, all seats were fair game.

I put on the face of courtesy for the perky lady and responded,

"This seat has your name on it."

She sat down, put her belongings below the seat in front of her, and hummed as she did so. I was in deep hope that this was the last dialogue I would have with her for the entire flight — or, for that matter, with anyone else on this plane, including the flight attendants.

"No beverage, peanuts, or pretzels for me. I'm out. I need some rest!" I said to myself. I leaned back into my space of comfort to get a nap and get my head right. Before I knew it, I felt a gentle tap on my shoulder.

Oh, no she didn't! I thought to myself.

By now, my eyes were truly heavy. I opened them, wiped them, and turned toward my seat neighbor with a raised eyebrow. Despite my expression, she proceeded to talk.

"Howdy. I'm a teacher, and my name is Sally. I'm headed to the beaches for some 'me' time. I am going on vacation, and I cannot wait. I tell you that's what being in a classroom full of third graders will do to you. What about you?"

From her enthusiasm and eagerness to engage in conversation, I knew I needed to lay down some ground rules. However, I do have home training, so I politely said,

"I am a physician and author, and my name is Dr. Sparrow Mack. I am going to the island to take care of some personal business. Ma'am, I am exhausted. Nothing personal, but I need some rest. So, I am going to take a nap for the duration of this flight." I gave a half smile and politely turned my entire body toward the window, pulled my seat tray table down, used my sanitizer wipes to clean it off, and put down the magazine I was looking through earlier. I figured that, after I caught a nap, I could finish reading the article about how bookstores are trying to make a comeback in the technological age. As I began to put my earplugs back in and found the section where I left off earlier, then my seat neighbor said,

"You're a doctor?"

"Yes, ma'am," I responded and nodded as I dog-eared the magazine page.

"Well, did you hear about the man who almost died at the airport?"

"Yes ma'am, I sure did." I did not want to offer up any more information to spark any additional conversation, so I kept my response short.

"'Sparrow' — now that is an interesting name. So that's what that is around your neck, huh?" she said while pointing to my charm necklace.

"How did your parents come up with that?" she asked.

Rolling my entire body toward the window and tucking my necklace with the charm back into my shirt, without turning back around, I replied,

"It's a long story." Now my upbringing had to take a back seat. I wasn't up for talking to chatty Sally. This time, she got the message.

The plane took off; we had a few rough bumps due to wind shear during ascent into the horizon, but after we reached ten thousand feet, I dozed off. The plane's engine hummed in my ear while my pillow leaned against the plane window had returned me to a dream-clouded womb.

"*Sparrow*? How did you get a name like that?" was a question that I'd been asked all my life. Thinking back as far as I could remember, it was kind of cute how Luke always made a big deal from the uniqueness of my name. He even saved up enough money during one summer while he worked a paper route to buy us matching sparrow necklaces at the local mall. This made me think back to when Luke and I were kids, when he showed me the necklaces that he purchased for *us*. I remember him excitedly showing me the necklaces and he was taken aback by my less-than-enthusiastic response.

"Luke, this is crazy. Why did you buy us matching sparrow necklaces, when 'Sparrow' is my name and not yours?" I asked him when we were kids.

"Because that's what you do for family — you sacrifice for them. Besides, it is a great name that I would name myself if I could."

I can hear him saying that to my face like it was just yesterday, and I always thought his response was kind of odd, but that was my Luke – the free spirit — and we were family. Later, when I had time to reflect, I realized how insensitive I must have appeared to him, because he had taken all of his savings and honored our friendship by making that purchase, which was a huge sacrifice for him. And from that day forward, I've never taken that necklace off even to the present day, to show him I didn't take his act of love for granted.

You see — I was the one who made it out and made something of myself. By society's standards, anyway. But Luke did help me equally, but in ways that I chose to forget and put in the recesses of my mind. In my slumber on the plane my thoughts went back a little further. I reflected on how Luke was so fascinated by the story of how I got Sparrow for a name. When we were children, Luke was over to our house a lot to escape his volatile home setting, and he would ask my mom to tell "the story." We would both smile as my mother shared with us the special meaning of my name and the miracle surrounding me. That story was ingrained in my soul and made me feel so special. Luke seemed equally as enthusiastic about its origin as I was.

As the story goes, it was a cool fall day, and my parents had decided to ride out on my dad's freshly purchased Yamaha motorcycle. Newly married, they were still in the honeymoon stage of their romance and loved to go riding together on the weekends. What better way to hang out with the one you love than go riding into the sunset?

On this particular day, they decided to go see some of my dad's friends in a southeast neighboring town about an hour and a half away. Under her helmet, my mother's beautiful long, thick brunette hair bounced in the wind as they rode down the highway. With platform shoes, bell-bottomed jeans and jackets to match, straddling my dad's freshly washed and waxed Yamaha motorcycle, they were a sight to see. Midway down the highway, something unexpected and horrible happened. Control of the bike was lost.

My mother awoke with the taste of dirt and pavement particles mixed with her own blood pooling out of her mouth. While she was face down on the road, her new husband was nowhere in sight. She floated in and out of consciousness. She could remember looking down at the dark ground after flying through the air and landing on the asphalt headfirst. She struggled to stay awake. Intense alarm shot through her mind and body when she realized she could not move. Alone, somehow separated from her husband, who'd been driving the motorcycle, she lay unable to move. The one thing she did know was that she was hurt and that she needed help.

The longer she lay there, she knew beyond the shadow of a doubt that she needed a miracle — and she needed that miracle real fast. A strong, cool, brisk breeze flowed across her head, stinging her scalp where her helmet was supposed to be. She imagined it was the breath of God, attempting to comfort her or possibly welcome her home. Surely, her husband or someone would come to help her soon. As she lay cold, hurt, alone, and afraid on the highway, she felt the life attempt to seep from her body. Her vision tunneled to black, and she began to fade in and out of consciousness. She kept calling out quietly, saying, over and over, with her eyes closed,

"God, please help me! Please help me!" hoping that her voice would echo to heaven above.

Suddenly, she felt a small peck on her left cheek. Her eyelid slowly opened slightly and then closed again. Once again, she felt a small, constant peck on her left cheek.

Peck.
Peck.
Peck!

It kept occurring on that same cheek in the exact same spot with increasingly intense pressure. The peck was persistent enough to keep her awake. In fact, it was the *only* thing keeping her awake.

Meanwhile, the other side of her face was pressed firmly against the pavement of the highway, becoming a part of her skin. Her eye that was facing toward the brightly shining sun opened slowly, with hesitation, and looked at the source of the pecking. She saw a bird. It was looking with both of its beady, small obsidian eyes directly into her hazel-brown eyes in such an intense way that she never forgot it.

The bird was not only a sparrow — it appeared to be a *baby* sparrow. Every time her vision would start to fade to black again, that little sparrow would peck her cheek with great intensity. This kept up until the paramedics arrived. And just as mysteriously as the baby sparrow had appeared, it disappeared. My mother attributed the reason she was able to fight to stay alive to the sparrow's pecks on her cheek.

Arriving at the hospital, she learned something miraculous. Not only did she have just a couple of bad scrapes and bruises, but neither she nor my father, who was retrieved from a ditch more than 100 feet away from the wrecked motorcycle, had suffered any broken bones or fractures. All this despite my mother's helmet being broken into two pieces when she'd landed on her head. However, the most profound miracle that revealed itself was that she was pregnant with me.

The miracle continued when she went on to tell us the other part of the reason she named me "Sparrow." Nine months later, when she was getting ready to deliver me in the hospital, something interesting happened. She went into labor on a Wednesday, and the labor continued for forty-eight hours; the doctors were contemplating a cesarean section. When the doctor left the room after telling my mother the troubling news, she was tearful and anxious about the impending possible change in plans surrounding my birth.

My mother read her Bible, dried her eyes, and looked toward the window of her hospital room. There on the window ledge was a baby sparrow. Seeing that sparrow on the window ledge brought her comfort and reassurance that everything was going to be okay with the baby and her. Just as miraculously as the baby sparrow appeared, when I was finally born by a natural birth and arrived into the world, that sparrow left, never to be seen again.

The nurse wrapped me up in a pink blanket to prepare me to meet my parents for the first time.

"Please hand me my little Sparrow," my mother told the nurse, as my father looked on, and the rest was history. I have forever cherished the vision of Luke and I sitting on the porch while my mother shared that story with us. And I know that Luke did, too. With my family, Luke felt a sense of belonging and a true sense of trust, loyalty, and love. I awakened on the plane as felt the barometric pressure changing as the aircraft began its descent, and those memories of my origin and the meaning behind my name, and the good old days with Luke, were left above the clouds at thirty thousand feet. I had to leave them there, because I was being thrust back into the reality of what was bringing me to the islands in the first place and that was the pursuit of the truth surrounding Luke's demise.

"We are making our initial descent into Nassau, Bahamas. Please place your seats and tray tables in the upright position. It was a pleasure to serve you on this flight. It is a nice, clear 75 degrees, with balmy winds out of the west. Enjoy your stay on this beautiful island, and we look forward to serving you again in the near future."

I pushed my seat upward and began to put my tray table in its place when the magazine I'd placed on the tray fell to the floor of the plane. As I picked up the magazine to put it in my bag, my still-smiling-never-went-to-sleep neighbor brought to attention that I had dropped something on the floor as she tapped my arm and pointed. I thanked her and reached for what appeared to be a random piece of paper. I was still trying to wake up and focus. The paper was a piece of loose-leaf that had fallen from the journal. I picked it up, and my eyes skimmed across it. I was stunned, as this is what I was supposed to have read two weeks ago at the funeral:

Luke, we love you and miss you. We will solve the mystery of what happened. Until we meet again, see you later, and rest easy. Love, Sparrow.

I clutched the paper for dear life as the plane descended. I wanted to make time rewind and stand still — I wanted the paper to have never existed, then Luke would be alive. This was the first time I'd read it since I'd written it. Without warning, my eyes welled and a single full tear rolled down my face and landed on the journal entry clutched in my hand. I looked down and saw the tear landing squarely on the word "Love," and, with its fluidity, expanded over it, causing a halo around the word. The transparency of this was overwhelming: Love was the reason I was on this plane, the love for my friend.

I had to keep my composure. This was so not like me to be overly sensitive. I attributed it to the sleep deprivation, the intensity of the emotions of the day of saving a life, and the recent loss of a life. I folded the paper in two, put it back in the leather journal I had found at Luke's house, and tucked it away in my carry-on. My "seat neighbor" noticed my tear, attempted to be neighborly, and handed me a Kleenex from her purse. I raised my hand to decline her generosity and collected my faculties.

Come on, Sparrow — get it together. Come on, girl — you have a lot to get done and a short period to do it. You do not have time for this! God, give me the strength! I thought.

I put my neck pillow and blanket away; while doing so, my hand hit my boots. I blindly moved them out of the way in hopes of finding my makeup bag. Digging a little deeper, I found it, pulled it out, unzipped it, and got out my bronze compact mirror and concealer. I opened it up, and I could see puffy bags under my eyes.

I can't touch down and get off this plane looking like this!

I patted concealer under my eye to lighten the tired, swollen bags and then smoothed it out with some foundation. I grabbed my coral lip-gloss I'd gotten from Dean Baby and moisturized my dry, stressed lips with this refreshing color that was melon infused.

"At least my lips can be on point!" I said as I did a hair check, corrected the loose strands around my edges, and ran my fingers through my tresses in an attempt to freshen my appearance. With those adjustments, I looked a lot better than I felt. I'd gotten in a little nap, my puffy eyes were concealed, and my lip color was nice. I felt more focused than I had felt in the last couple of days. I was ready to land.

Chapter 3

My first stop before heading to the condo, as always, was the beach. The moist ocean breeze was clear, cool, and crisp. My freshly painted full-coral lips were wide and in awe of the familiar breathtaking sight. As I closed my mouth, my tongue ran smoothly across them. The salt from the misty droplets of the ocean air rested heavy on my melon-infused lip-gloss, making my lips taste like sweet and sour candy.

Man, I got to remember to send Dean Baby a thank-you note for giving me this fantastic lip stain.

It made me feel beautiful, which was rare — and very nice.

I walked down the length of the powdered white-sandy beach, gazing as far as my view would stretch. I had to bring this magnificent familiar scene into more focus, as I always do. In that attempt, I held my right hand over my brow shading the sun for more distance. Although this was a sight all too common to me, a second home of sorts, my hazel-brown eyes glistened and twinkled with surprise as if this were a completely new experience.

There were beach chairs up and down the shoreline, some full of people enjoying the balmy Caribbean sun, and other empty chairs awaiting vacationers to start creating unforgettable memories. Usually, this beach was bursting at the seams with crowds of people, however, strangely, today it was more quiet than usual, which was nice.

Standing there peacefully, I noticed that with each wave of the tide, the beautiful breeze blew through me, and I closed my eyes and let the wind tousle my chestnut-brown hair. The foaming ocean and the tides appeared to be fuller than I remembered or had ever seen. I smiled, and then, all of a sudden, the corners of my mouth became tense as a flashback of being at the graveside, standing by Luke's casket, flashed in my mind. I realized that I was in a physical and emotional paradox. I felt relaxed and tense.

I took a deep breath and exhaled hard and long, as the island air evaporated from my lungs into the horizon. I loved just being in this mystical place. The waters beckoned me as I walked closer to the beach's edge. This was the part of the shore where I can view all the beauty of the island. I can see every peak and every valley, every palm tree, and every area of white sand landscape. If I turned just right, the water appeared to be an infinite body of water that extended to the edge of the earth.

It was just like a scene from a brilliant puzzle — the perfect picture of paradise. This view reminded me of the postcard that I'd found in Luke's belongings. And on the back of the postcard, he had written the word "home," and home was what this place felt like to both of us. Being at the water's edge today reminded me of Luke's oneness with this place.

"Sparrow, let's go up to the water's edge, girl!"

I could hear Luke in my mind, just like it was yesterday, speaking those words as soon as our plane would touch down on the runway.

This was Luke's favorite place to come to on the top beaches' shoreline; he felt this point in the island was the perfect place to steal away for isolation. When we would walk up here, he'd get really quiet while we stood on the rocks in our flip-flops, and he would say,

"God is here. This is the place where our work ends, Ro, and God's mercy begins. Don't you ever forget that," while he would look out into the endless, infinite waters. I can remember that, on one of our visits up here, he attempted to paraphrase the story of the fishermen in Luke 5:2-11.

"Ro, this water's edge reminds me of the story in Luke, when the fishermen were distraught because they had not caught any fish after casting their nets for a long time. They listened to the word of Jesus that instructed them to cast their nets into the deep water. When they listened and went deeper, they caught so many fish they did not know what to do, and their boat began to sink. Then Jesus beckoned them to become fishers of men. So, they pulled their boats up on shore and left everything behind and followed him."

"Yes, Luke. I know that story very well," I replied.

It was so good to see that Luke was becoming engaged with the word of God. I had never seen him like that before. I was happy about it, but it made me a little concerned to think there was possibly something going on with him that he was not sharing with me, to make him talk that way. Drawing closer to the Word is usually something we do when our life meets the challenge of change.

"Luke, is everything alright?" I would ask.

"Ro, I'm good!" he would say, reassuringly.

About six months ago, on the last visit to this exact spot, Luke shared with me that he really wanted to work on his walk with the Lord and become that person in whom the world could see Christ.

As I was standing here alone today, I, too, could feel God in this exact place. In my mind, I pondered those final conversations I'd had with Luke.

I planted my feet on the smooth black rocks lacing the crumbled sands like a black-beaded onyx necklace that adorned the beach, separating the innocent powdered sand granules from the infinite, roaring body of water. One by one, the waves continued to roll in. They had a life of their own as they pulsated and morphed bigger and bigger, rushing toward me and crashing along the black rocks on which I stood. With each cycle, the waves would become one with the beach as they took colonies of the native island sand with it back into the ocean of uncertainty in anticipation of the next breaking wave. This cyclical motion seemed to parallel the flurry of emotions I was feeling. My mind was whirling and whirling, pulsating and pulsating, just like those waves. I stood as still as I could in that matrix.

The waves began to be a bit too much for me, and my feet began to slip off of the black rocks, as they became slick. I slowly and carefully walked back down, keeping my eyes transfixed on the infinity of water before me. Now, standing firm, my feet not in flip-flops like I usually wear on these white sands, but in steel-toed black leather combat boots that had barely made it through airport security in my oversized purse. I felt like a convict on the run when those boots triggered the airport security to do a full body check in a private security room.

I watched the water roar and rush in centimeter-by-centimeter and now inch-by-inch. My boots were sinking into the powder-like white sands from the heaviness of my firm stance. The beach, just like I knew it would, embraced me with familiarity, welcoming me back home.

Oh, how I had missed the islands. We'd frequented this part of the Caribbean because of the inherited timeshare from my Uncle Cyrus. Those memories are multiple and bountiful — all of us hanging out on the beach with the sand between our toes, sitting in the beach chairs, and talking through the night into the early morning hours. We would laugh and relax while sipping seasonal cocktails while eating fine island cuisine. I smiled while remembering when my crew and I, especially Luke, danced along the shoreline as the sun set with the tiki lamps flaming, lighting up the orange and red-glazed Caribbean sky, as we partied on the shore. Our hips would move as the locals played the steel Caribbean drums and sang the native songs.

Even now, I could hear the tinkering of those drums as clearly as I had when the native men would pound their hands onto their calfskin drums, expressing themselves through song. I closed my eyes and felt at peace with the rhythm of those memories. It seemed like yesterday that Luke and I would venture out from the condo to get a taste of the island culture and hang with the natives. Down to the docks we frequently would go to buy fresh Snapper or Rock Lobster and bring it back to the condo to cook.

As I would approach the dock, I would hear the chuckling of the locals when I would walk through the market and hear them call out to me,

"Here comes our Sparrow!"

The island people were my people; they had accepted me and become like an extended family.

And most of all, this was a place where Luke and I had prayed and reflected on our lives, in this very spot — the water's edge.

The realization sank in that this trip, to one of our favorite destinations, our home away from home, was definitely different this time. I was here for a different reason, for a battle of sorts — a fight for the truth. The hairs on my forearm began to stand on end as the anxiety intensified throughout my body. Warm all over, I had a flushed feeling that overwhelmed me. I believe it was a combination of the Caribbean sun and the anxiety that was building regarding the discovery I knew was coming to pass.

I thought, *my goodness, what have I gotten myself into? I wish things were like they used to be, and I could just get out of here right now and go back home.* There was no doubt that I was, justifiably, on edge, as my eyes scanned the beach up and down, searching to find an exit sign that promised, a way out so could I be free from this nightmare.

These were the thoughts that infiltrated the cornices of grey and white matter in my brain.

The reality was that I could not get away. I had gotten in too deep and there was no turning back.

Looking at my watch, I realized, *damn — time really got away from me.* I had done what I'd come down to the beach to do — survey the perimeter and venture up to the water's edge. Now it was time to get back to the condo, unpack, and lay out my next step. But first, I had to touch base with Weston, in order to keep his suspicions at bay. I knew in my heart of hearts that Weston would never approve of what I was up to — attempting to find out what had happened to Luke. I could just imagine him now saying,

"Sparrow, babe, it is not in your best interest to do this!"

And deep down, I'd know he was right. Truth be told, in the last several years, Weston felt that my friendship with Luke was a little too much.

"Babe, this dude is toxic. Every time there are issues with him, you get stressed out to the max and drink to deal with it. How many times are we going to get calls late at night to post bail — to rectify and get him out of those situations? How many times are you going to use our connections to rescue him from his bad business decisions? His presence in our lives has been truly overwhelming and has put a dent into our savings account." This was the conversation Weston had with me about a week before Luke's passing.

Luke was a loyal childhood friend who'd became an adult friend — one who'd put a strain on our marriage. After his burial, it was as if Weston had a sense of relief that Luke would no longer interfere in our lives, cost us money, and bring grief to our doorstep. Although he'd never said it out loud, I could feel Weston's consolation with Luke's passing. And it kind of pissed me off. If Weston knew I had ventured off to the islands, based on clues in a journal, to figure out what had really happened to my best friend, he would come unglued. Especially that I came alone, with no protection and no one to have my back.

I looked down at my watch and realized time was getting away from me and that I needed to get to the condo and continue to study the journal. I had to get some answers to assist me in mapping out my plan.

Taking one step backwards away from the breathtaking scene of the white-foaming ocean, I was abruptly stopped. A deep pressure in the back of my skull halted my motion as if I had bumped the back of my head on something hard.

What the hell? I thought to myself.

The object was firm, solid, and frigid, and, without seeing it, it felt like cold steel pressing against the base of my skull. It hit the occipital part of my head with such force that the back of my hair swung around and hit my right cheek. I stood frozen as every bit of momentum in me was locked in place, and the waves from the foaming ocean seemed to go motionless. With the feeling of impending doom, my eyes dilated, and my heart skipped a beat in deep terror. To say the least, I was afraid. My feet wanted to move, my mind took over, especially since no one was around, and the beach was strangely empty today.

What if this thing pressing into the back of my skull is a gun, and I am about to die?

What if this person is going to blow my brains out all over these beautiful white powdery sands?

And most importantly, will I ever see my beautiful family again? Damn! Weston is going to be sad and disappointed in me.

Those thoughts rang through my mind, while the hairs on the nape of my neck stood on end. Then a hollow voice came from behind me and whispered into my right ear,

"Hello, Sparrow. I knew you would be here, but this is way sooner than I thought."

I could feel the heat from the person's moist breath in my ear. The synapses of my brain acknowledged that I had heard the intonations of this person's voice before, but I needed to hear more, to be 100 percent sure of the perpetrator. And obviously, they knew me, and I felt absolutely no comfort in that. The pressure eased up a little from the back of my head. And at that moment I could not prevent my natural instinct to boldly turn and face my assailant, especially if I was going to die, anyway. I clenched my fist tightly, turned around slowly, and raised my hands, now balled into fists. The trembling gun lowered, we were face to face, and our eyes locked. I knew those eyes.

The first time I'd seen those eyes was more than thirty years ago. I was in the fourth grade in Mrs. Fulton's class. I remember those eyes on this fragile young boy. He was so frail he looked like anybody could knock him over if they sneezed. Ah choo! — and he would have been blown to smithereens. Mrs. Fulton introduced us to the new student, Luke Armstrong. He stood right next to the teacher, dressed in a red shirt, red shorts, and red sneakers, and appeared to shiver as she introduced him. He was instructed to take one of the empty seats quickly so Mrs. Fulton could get the fourth-grade lesson underway. As the class newbie, he walked down the aisle to find a seat. I looked at him in his pitiful state and shook my head.

This kid does not stand a chance in this classroom! I thought, as he walked with his eyes down and a timid aura all around him. I knew he would not last long in this tough fourth-grade fight-cage, otherwise known as a classroom. By the time he'd been assigned this class, the hierarchy had already been established. Tall for my age in the fourth grade, and as a transplanted girl from one of the toughest areas in the city, I was not a young girl to be messed with. I was known to be smart tough pretty girl with braided hair and a sweet disposition, but don't let the pigtails fool you! I had to constantly be on guard and stay ready to defend myself, especially with a name like "Sparrow." I had developed thick skin early on. I always had to respond, with hands on deck, to kids taunting me with,

"Here comes the bird girl."

"Here comes the bird girl."

I knew how to handle myself. But this one here, on the other hand, was a new fish, waiting to be preyed upon, in this big, unforgiving pond. And all at once, he turned his thin face toward me, and our eyes locked. And then his 9-year-old self, with his big, bright, fearful doe-like eyes, came over and stood right beside me, bypassing the obviously vacant seat that was right in front of me, and said,

"Hello. Can I sit next to you?" with a quiver in his voice.

"Yep, you can. My name is 'Sparrow,' but my friends call me 'Ro.' You can call me 'Ro,'" I replied out of pity for the poor soul.

I felt obligated to extend kindness to this young man. By letting Luke sit next to me, it provided a protective shield around him from the probable harshness of this tough fourth-grade class. And besides, I did not want him to be prey for Tommy, the school bully, who also happened to be in our class. I could tell, by the piercing glare in Tommy's eyes, when Luke walked down the aisle to find a seat, he had already made Luke one of his targets. In true Sparrow fashion, I was there to save the day.

Or rather, that was the first day of so many eventful days to come in my life with Luke. And one of many times I had to save Luke. He had an Army father and was living on the local military base. His father chose to be stationed on the base because it was close to his mother, Luke's grandmother, Mrs.

Elizabeth, who lived in my hometown. Fast forward years after we'd met in primary school; his father would be killed in the line of duty while deployed. This left Luke and his stepsister, Lucinda, in the custody of his grandmother, Mrs. Elizabeth. Luke never had a relationship with his biological mother; she was never in the picture.

And now, here I still stood, on the beach with white beautiful powdery sands beneath my combat boots, looking down the barrel of a gun in broad daylight on the beach, face to face with my best friend's eyes. And the reality was, beneath the disguise, this was Luke holding a gun firmly and pressing it now into my forehead with deep intention. Although his hand quivered just like that little boy I first met years ago, he was steadfast.

Luke began to rattle off a list of demands; this was so uncommon of him. Of the two of us, he'd always been the meek and quiet one. As kids progressing into young adulthood, I often found myself speaking up for him. However, with the gun, it appeared that, with each word, he'd summoned authority. This Luke was now strong, confident, powerful, and in control. This was in complete contrast to his natural self I knew.

"Ro, you are going to help me! And you are going to listen to me. And most of all, you are going to forgive me. Isn't that what the good Bible says?" he asked while he repositioned the wig on the top of his head and held the gun in his other hand.

I couldn't believe what I was hearing as the gun's barrel edge pierced my forehead. I stood still, but the adrenaline pulsated into every fiber of my muscles, adding to the anxiety I experienced from this morning's events. It was too much for me to be quiet. I blurted out,

"'Forgive you'? Are you serious? Are you kidding me, or have you lost your ever-loving mind? I can't believe that you had us crying and laying your ass to rest no less than two weeks ago, while you were still alive chilling in the islands. And now you have the nerve to stand in my face, dressed in drag, with a gun to my head after all I have done for you?" I said as my hands balled into fists — like my fists were any match for a gun.

I never knew Luke to have this much craziness and aggression or boldness. His eyes looked empty, as if he did not have a soul. There was a moment of confusion that he blinked away. He looked as if he had not slept in two weeks. He pushed the gun more and more force into my forehead. Not listening to a word that I'd said, he forced me backwards, until I fell with my legs kicked out from under me, and I landed on my backside. I had no idea he had walked me so far backwards that we were now in the area where there were beach chairs. With me now seated, Luke slowly lowered his gun wielding arm, pulled his other arm back, swung it forward full force, and struck me across my lower jaw; I fell out of the beach chair. I plummeted to the ground and was immersed by the soft, white granules of sand.

"Shut up, Ro. You have always talked way too damn much! And I am sick of it!"

"Aw, shit!" I said as I grabbed my jaw. My mouth was full of blood. For a moment, I had been knocked silly from the powerful blow to my lower jaw; I was actually seeing stars and trying to catch my equilibrium enough to get back up.

Can this be happening to me — and at the hands of my brother?

He glared down at me as if I were a stranger, as he paced near me, not bothering to help me up. He finally settled into sitting in an adjacent beach chair to my left. I sat up slowly, held my jaw, wiped my lip with my hand, and spit out the blood on the white beach sands.

I got up unsteadily, taking my time to resituate in the beach chair. I turned to him, infuriated, and said as I held my jaw, "If you didn't have that gun, it would be game time — right, Luke? You know where I come from!"

"Ro, just stop! And here — wipe your damn mouth!" he responded while handing me a white napkin from a wicker beach table.

"Stop, nothing! I came here for your ass, to find out some answers to some questions surrounding your death. I was not expecting to find you alive. Luke, what the hell is going on? I need you to come clean!" I wiped my lip, and the small white cocktail napkin was wet with the beautiful melon-infused coral lip stain mixed with my blood. So much for the sweet and salty. Now, all I could taste was the bitterness and feel the swelling.

"Ro, stop! Just be quiet! I need to think!" Luke said as he continued to hold the gun; then he rested it on his thigh as he sat back in the beach chair, leg quivering.

"Girl, just like always, you run your mouth without thinking. Always trying to fix the world and figure out every damn thing. You should have just let some shit go!" Luke spoke those words with a disdain of me that hurt my feelings. And this definitely was not the Luke I knew.

Most people would think it a gift from God, a miracle of sorts, to see someone they thought they had lost and would never see again. This, however, was not that type of miracle. Instead, this had turned into a horrible nightmare. And who knew how this was going to end?

In the past, Luke and I had visited these islands together, as best friends, or rather, brother and sister hanging out. We would tear this place up. On these trips we would eat too much and party above and beyond. We did the things that best friends do together. We would laugh and talk into the wee hours of the morning. Our conversations were about all of our aspirations and all that we desired and what would come our way. Love, money, success, and, of course, us growing old as friends. And the icing on the cake was swimming and hanging out in the hot tub in the condo, with fruity cocktails at poolside. That was the life. Even after I was married, Luke and I made this trip often. In the past, Weston, gave his approval because he knew that Luke was the brother I never had, until right before Luke's death. Although Weston did have his concerns about Luke's lifestyle, his decision-making, and his integrity, Luke was family, and he got a pass.

With our history and kinship, and basically being siblings after all that we had been through together, I was sitting here today right next to him with an unusual, disproportionate awkwardness and silence between us. This was a first. At the forefront of my mind, I was surprised that he still had one hand on the gun and, moreover, that he'd hit me. My Luke would have never done that. Surely, he was not going to shoot me. He couldn't — I was his sister. Despite the brunette wig, ruby lips, and lashes that he wore, I had to touch his face, reaching for something to make this situation really real for me.

I put down my blood-soaked napkin, slowly reached out my right hand and touched his cheek. "Luke, it's me, Ro!" I ran my hand across his smooth skin, and, sure enough, there was the scar on his jawbone back by his ear that he had gotten when he'd lost the battle with trying to pop a wheelie when we were kids. That mark let me know that this was definitely Luke. He also had a new scar on his right temple, which appeared to be a healing flesh wound that I did not recognize. However, he was alive. Despite the gun, and the current circumstance. My eyes welled up with tears of joy and immediate forgiveness as I clutched my heart with the closed fists that, moments ago, were ready to come to blows. I couldn't help but be happy to see him again after the massive loss that I'd felt with his unexpected "passing."

The hole in my heart I never thought I would fill with another friendship of that magnitude was now whole again. My heart was full but my trust was tainted. Luke was the person who knew me best and I no longer could say the same for him. This was Luke, the person with whom I shared all my secrets, the only male maid of honor in my wedding, and my son's Godfather. Luke was alive, in the flesh, and I could feel him, touch him. We were breathing the same air and sitting in the same space. It was a resurrection of sorts. Although I was happy he was not dead, he had a lot of explaining to do.

Luke steadily held the gun and with his opposite hand grabbed a walkie-talkie out of his beach cover-up. He pressed his polished lips into the device and beckoned for the order of drinks that he'd apparently pre-ordered. As he placed the walkie-talkie back into his pocket, his shaking hand reached into the beach tote that he had placed on the small wicker table and pulled out a small, black, rectangular object. It was a book. When he laid it on the table, I saw it was a Bible. It was like the ones that are generally given away for free. It was weathered; the cover was faded black leather, like it had been exposed to too much heat. The words "Holy Bible," in golden lettering, were chipped and crackled.

Luke brushed fine, powdery granules of white sand off the top of the Bible ever so gently with his manicured hand. He treated the Bible as if it were a priceless treasure; handling it with such care as if it were the most precious item he owned. The Bible sat peacefully on the small wicker beach table that was between us. The Bible's presence caused the atmosphere to shift, and you see could it in Luke's face and demeanor. The Bible appeared to provide

Luke with a comfort that gave him invisible permission to relax and let go. God's word was present, and I too, all at once, felt undeniably safe as I unclenched my fist and sat with my arms on my thighs while I leaned forward, facing him. We both welcomed the silence that floated between us.

For the first time since he pulled the gun on me, Luke appeared comforted and at peace. It was as if the life had been drawn back into his distant, big brown eyes by the presence of the Word. His shoulders were now relaxed, and his head fell back into the white-and-teal striped beach chair. He was calm — so much so that he placed the gun into his small beach tote.

A young boy with perfect Caribbean skin, who appeared to be of teenage years by his petite stature and a pep in his steps, approached in a giddy fashion, with beads of sweat rolling down his temples that caused his silky black, thick, shaggy hair to stick to his skin. He had what appeared to be a white t-shirt wrapped around the crown of his head tied in four knots, two in the front and two in the back. It was a self-made ball cap to help shield his young skin from the rays of the scorching heat. He wiped his brow with one hand and held a tray with four shot glasses filled with amber-colored tequila with the other.

Turning toward Luke, he stated, *"Ms. Lucinda, aqui es su tequila!"*

"Gracias, Carlos." Luke stated.

"Su Amiga es Bonita," the young boy stated, and then he turned his head toward me and winked.

Oh, no, he didn't, I thought as I pulled my neck back. I couldn't even absorb what I guessed to be a compliment from this child delivering tequila, which there should be a law against. *This young fool sees me with a busted-ass lip, and he's trying to flirt?*

Moreover, I was in shock as Luke portrayed our interaction as if we had gone on a weekend getaway and were chilling on the beach post spa treatments.

And did I hear him correctly? Did this boy just call Luke "Lucinda"? Has Luke transformed himself into what I am seeing now — a gun toting, best friend hostage holding man in a wig pretending to be his dead sister? My mind was whirling. I needed to lie down.

And besides that, why are we speaking Spanish in the Bahamas? This is too much! I thought.

I looked around, and there were no other beach-goers in sight, just empty chairs lining the shoreline.

I usually liked being one of the only beach-goers relaxing in the sun, so I could have dibs on where I sat. However, in this moment, when my life was at stake, I welcomed anyone who could help me out of this nightmare. And with my Spanish being subpar, I did not feel that this young man would be of much help to communicate my need for assistance and help. And besides, he was so puny that my infant son could probably take him down. I decided to wait this thing out and find out as much information as I could.

Carlos placed the tray with two additional shots on it on the table between us. He didn't know it, but he'd placed the tray right next to the beach bag with a sawed-off shotgun and a Bible nearby. Luke took two of the shots off the tray and slammed them down on the table. Then he picked up the shot glass full of tequila closest to me and shoved it into my chest, forcing some of the tequila to spill on my shirt. He held the other shot into the air as if making a toast. As Carlos retrieved the tray off the wicker beach table, Luke ordered the shots to keep coming. As he signaled to Carlos for the refills, Luke accidently knocked the beach bag with the gun in it off of the table and onto the sand. I jumped, raising my knees up toward my chest to protect myself, thinking that the gun would go off inside the tote and kill us all.

When the bag hit the sand, Luke looked at me and said, "Don't worry, Ro — the safety is on." He reached down, grabbed the beach bag, and placed it back on the table, tossing it as if it were an empty plastic sack. My jaw was throbbing, and my heart was pounding in pure anger and confusion. I grabbed another napkin next to the bag and wiped the blood off my lip, which continued to drip.

Just as quickly as he'd appeared and delivered the shots, off Carlos went. He took his tray and appeared to tiptoe on his tanned bare feet through the deep white sands, sinking with each step toward the condo's *Cocina,* where the bar was. He faded into the sunset that was now approaching. It was as if time stood still and sped up simultaneously. With silence between us, we sat on the beach for hours.

Every time I attempted to ask another question, the only response I got from Luke was,

"Shut up, Ro! Let me think!"

I obliged, and we sat still as the ocean waves continued to roll in across the white, powdery sand. As time passed, wisps of yellow and red began to filter across the Caribbean sky, reflecting off the rolling waves that abutted the beach line. The sunset and a calming breeze cooled the atmosphere. Luke turned toward me and commanded, "Ro, drink the tequila!"

"You know me, Luke. You know the trouble this stuff has caused me. I don't drink tequila — it messes with my head, and it makes me have heart palpitations. And besides, I am cutting way back on alcohol. Man, hanging out with you, I came close to needing a sponsor, but God delivered me, Luke. I stopped drinking and you know this. Why are you tempting me? The struggle is super real. You are supposed to be my best friend."

"Ro, you not drinking? Since when, honey? Don't tell me you done found God again! Your grandma would be so proud," he said sarcastically. "Girl, drink the shot — *now*!"

"Gun or no gun — watch how you speak to me, Luke. Keep my grandma's name out of your mouth! You don't want none of this," I spit back.

"Drink the damn shot, Ro!" he commanded, as he grabbed the gun inside the tote and freed the safety. It was as if Luke had been doing this for days. He put the shot glass to his cherry-red lips, threw his head back, and swallowed. I watched him as his Adam's apple rose and settled midway in his neck and the curls of his wig bounced. He sighed with relief and slammed the shot glass on the table. He leaned into me and whispered as if there were someone else around who could hear us,

"You're going to need it for everything I am about to tell you. So, drink, Ro — drink!"

I felt that if I did not drink, there would be consequences. I followed his orders, not knowing the real state of mind Luke was in and questioning what he was truly capable of. I threw my head back and downed the shot of tequila.

"O-M-G — it burns!" I could tell it had been a while since I'd had any alcohol, let alone tequila, because that one shot sent me over the edge warming everything in me. I think I may have taken it in way too fast. My throat was on fire, my head swooned, and the cut on my lip seared from the alcohol. "Damn, Luke! Why did you make me do this?" I said as I held my head.

For that moment, I forgot all about my current situation. My head reclined onto the beach chair, and my mind traveled back to the National Authors Convention when this all began and I first got the news that Luke had passed away. That was fourteen days ago.

Chapter 4

Two weeks ago before we laid Luke to rest and before the violent confrontation on the white sands of the Caribbean, my life was on the precipice of a new beginning. My family was good, my career was excellent as a physician transitioning out of clinical practice and into writing full time, and my life as an up-and-coming author was making a vast imprint on the literary world. I truly felt it could not get any better than this as I entered the green room of the National Authors Convention. It was the first time I had ever stepped foot in a green room. Silly me — I thought it would be a room that would actually be green. It wasn't.

However, it was so much more! I hated looking like a novice at the NAC, but I found myself looking around, my eyes big and in awe of everything around me. Truth be told, I felt a little awkward and out of place among these accomplished celebrity authors sharing the green room. And to be very transparent, there were some who were trying to block the blessing of me being in this space. Case in point, Jasper Cummings, the President and CEO of Grace Publishing who questioned my talent and readiness to be placed in this category, but God had other plans.

My friends and family always saw me as a "Plain Jane." They'd say I might come off as "professional and classy," but not *well refined*. I was not into any elite type of lifestyle; I was just really a humble chick who was about God, family, and business. With my medical career going so well, I had graduated to some of the nicer elements of life; I felt I was walking into my purpose. And now, it appeared that I might be catapulting to more VIP living through my literary work. But "Thank God" is all I can say! This writer's convention was an exclusive event, to which only the national best sellers are invited, and they'd invited me. I was not yet a national best seller, but there was talk that I was close. I *claimed* this!

I didn't want to appear over-excited, but my eyes got bigger and bigger as I looked around at the expanse of grandeur. All around me were well-known authors in their finest couture, engaging in profound dialogue, sipping their mimosas and rocking their bling, which haloed the room. This was definitely an icebox, with all the diamonds up in here. It put the four-carat rock on my finger to shame. Photographers were capturing their candid conversations.

And the *food*! The gastro envy was fierce. If any of my friends had seen the spread lying before me, they would have fainted. There was a table tiered with satin linen with Swarovski crystals sprinkled around high-end china loaded with stacked jumbo grilled shrimp, lamb chop kabobs, and chicken satay. If that did not suit your fancy, there was an array of kosher gourmet deli meats and block cheeses. A rainbow of lovely fruit trays with giant strawberries, grapes, pineapples, and mangos was spread across the tiered crystal towers. I grabbed the tongs and went right in.

I can't believe this! A dessert table that is out of this world — mini-cheesecakes, strawberries dipped in chocolate, and petit fours next to a candy table. To top it all off, there is a mini-bar with a beverage table that could quench any palate with wines and cocktails galore! I'm going to have to run ten miles to burn all of this off! I thought to myself.

My hands were full, so I decided to take a seat and then come back for my drink. Before I could get to my table, a nice gentleman, apart of the greenroom wait-staff, approached in a starched white shirt, white pants, and white apron.

"Ma'am, may I assist you?" he asked.

"Oh, thank you," I replied. He took my plate, escorted me to a table, and pulled my chair out with one hand for me to sit. He laid a linen napkin on my lap and then placed my plate on the table. I found myself thinking, *I could really get used to this.*

"Ma'am, what would you like to drink? Perhaps the signature mimosa, house-brewed coffee, chai tea, or southern-style lemonade with a sprig of mint?"

"I believe I saw a Riesling, a Chateau?"

"Yes, as you wish."

I couldn't help but blush; I was already getting spoiled just being there. I was truly trying to cut back on my alcohol intake. But this was a time to celebrate so one drink wouldn't hurt.

I would have loved to be able to share this moment with Weston; however, he was home taking care of the baby so I could follow my dream. And my best friend, Luke, would have been off the chain up in here. I wished I could have experienced this with him, as well. I paused while I held my fork; I missed Luke because we had not spoken in a while. He had been blowing up my inbox and leaving multiple messages on my voice mail, but I didn't have time for his drama. Besides, knowing Luke, he would have said or done something to get us kicked out of this elite space. I chuckled to myself. I didn't wait on my wine; I quickly dove into my delectable plate. While eating, I noticed for the first time the swag table that was flooded with couture grab bags.

I will check that out after my makeup and hair, I thought to myself.

The adjacent room was an area for makeup, hair, and wardrobe, separated by a black-curtain partition, and per the itinerary that Tabitha had texted me, I would be going into that area to get all glammed up before heading out to my appearance as a new, up-and-coming best-selling author.

"Your wine, ma'am"

"Thank you." It was chilled, just as I like it.

As I sat alone, with each bite, I looked around and saw so many fabulous authors whose work I admired and whose career paths I would happily try to emulate. It was humbling to be in their presence, and, truth be told, a little intimidating.

I questioned my own strength and ability to stand and be in the same space as these people in that green room. *Do I really deserve to be among this dynamic lineup?* And just as quickly as those doubtful thoughts entered into my mind, God stepped in and whispered to my spirit,

You would not be here if I had not put you here!

That confirming word from the Lord crushed every bit of doubt I had in my mind about belonging. That confirmation made my spirit dance. I relaxed and was a little more at ease being a part of the VIP experience of the NAC.

I'd been waiting a long time for this, my first book signing. Look how God had masterfully orchestrated the way it occurred.

My first book signing was a part of a National Authors Convention, with Grace Publishing as my sponsor and publishing house! *Look at God — won't he do it? This does not happen every day for new authors. It was as if he designed this experience just for me!* I said to myself, pondering over the magnificence of the day and what I was about to experience.

I finished my food, crossed my flatware, put my napkin down beside my empty plate, and walked over to look at the schedule posted on the wall in the encased glass holder, to confirm my plan for the day.

I need to get myself together — I will be going for makeup and hair in about ten minutes. Reading further, I realized I would be going to wardrobe, too — and then, after the panel, for re-touch for the group photo shoot for the national writer's magazine cover. I smiled.

I went back to my table, gathered my belongings, tipped the wait staff for their service, went over to the lounge area, and waited for my turn with the glam squad.

This appeared to be the perfect time to take a mental retreat to read my daily devotional. I usually did this as my morning ritual, after my husband, Weston, and I prayed together, but time had gotten the best of me that morning. So after our remote morning prayer, I had to hurry down into the holding area for brunch and glam. I opened the devotion. It read,

"God is the author and finisher of your faith. No matter what people do to you, God has it all under control. You must change your mind and repent! Your focus should be on God and how He is going to use you to glorify Him in the world. And in order for you to be used, you must operate out of love and continual forgiveness. Continual forgiveness allows room in your life for God to manifest and do His work in you and through you."

Man, God was right on the mark with that word for that day. That word was edifying and confirmed so many things I had been thinking about lately — especially as it pertained to friends, especially my best friend, Luke.

I relaxed my eyes for a moment and meditated on that word. I was getting a little comfy in my chair when my attention was drawn to a uniquely flamboyant-looking man who waltzed through the opening of the partition, motioned to me, and said,

"Come on in, Mrs. Sparrow!" The air this man had put my disposition to shame. His presence alone made me straighten my posture and clear invisible clutter from my throat. I stood up, straightened my clothes, followed his fabulousness, and tried to reflect his manner. Walking behind him, I smelled the deep aroma of hibiscus tea that seemed to swirl around him as he swayed. He did not walk — he glided in high-end slippers, and his clothes flowed as if he were walking into music.

How did he know who I was? I wondered. I looked down at his right hand and realized that he was holding a conference program turned to my bio, with my picture on it.

Oh, that's how. Man, he knows all my business! I thought to myself and chuckled.

"What's so funny, Dr. Sparrow? We've no time for jokes, Missy."

We walked behind the black partition and arrived in his makeshift studio. He motioned for me to sit in his leather zebra print studio chair by tapping on its back.

"Oh, nothing. Just happily looking forward to this!" I said, still holding my devotional while I sat.

"What are you reading, girl? Put that book away. We are on a tight schedule, and you are not going to make me make you late, and have production all down my throat!" he said while opening up makeup containers and jars.

"I love your chestnut-brown hair. It looks so silky, and your ends are so healthy," he commented while grabbing about an inch of my shoulder-length locks and glancing at them with a fierce once-over, scrunching his eyebrows.

"Did Mika color your hair earlier? I know it's going to look even better when she flat-irons and styles it," he added, as he blew off one of his make- up brushes. I noticed his lips had gloss on them.

Baffled by all of the run-on questions, I was kind of taken aback by this individual and how intrusive, bossy, and glamorous he was all at once. I didn't even know how to respond.

"Well, thank you, sir. I do try to keep my hair healthy. And I'm sorry I don't know who 'Mika' is. However, I had my hair color done back home."

"Hold up! Did you just call me *sir*? Sir, shmir! We need to lay out some ground rules here, sis! Oh, no

— it's 'Dean Baby.' Call me that — that's my name!" he said as he placed his immaculately manicured right hand on his hip, showing a beautiful gold pinky ring.

"'Dean,' is it?" I remarked.

"No, everybody calls me 'Dean Baby'! Girl, open up those ears! Naw, for real, though, that was a nickname my mother gave me, and I have gone by it ever since. I apologize for not making a proper introduction at the outset. We have been crazy busy back here this morning," he replied as he smirked and licked his lips.

"Well, Mr. Dean Baby, Tabitha told me you were going to be so nice and so easy on my nerves. All of this glam stuff is still so new to me."

"Welcome to the baller life, girlfriend," remarked Dean Baby, as his perfectly eye-lined eyes squinted and he pulled on my chin to angle my face upward more toward the light, to get a better look at the canvas upon which he was about to apply his artistry.

"Your eyes, Mrs. Sparrow, girl — they are absolutely beautiful. Child, you know I am half Irish, and you get the pretty hazel eyes — please!" Dean Baby said, as he stepped back with folded arms to glare at me. He had a thick, stout build but was of short stature. He had smooth, golden-bronze skin, glowing to perfection, as if he had foundation on. Blemish free. His cheekbones were high. He had the face that most women get plastic surgery and Botox to achieve. His hair was thick, with wild, curly ringlets; the color of his hair was the flawless mix of streaks of cinnamon and blond that was perfectly styled in a wild, small, elegant, curly fro that looked smooth and silky. His being was magnificent. With all of his flamboyancy, he had a bold but gentle air about him.

"How are you feeling today, Mrs. Sparrow?" he asked, as he took a delicate ceramic teacup and sipped.

"Dean Baby, you can call me 'Ro.' All of my friends and family do. And you seem like family already. That smells good; what are you drinking?"

"Cool. Okay — then 'Ro' it is. And it's Hibiscus tea — it calms me. Now back to these eyes you got. Oh, woo, girl your eyes are beautiful. Out of all five of us kids, from our pale-skinned, blond-haired Irish momma, none of us got her deep-blue-sea eyes. Our father was from Africa."

"Well, Dean, your eyes are beautiful as well. And you know now people are wearing contacts, to get whatever color eyes they want."

"I read the other day that there may be a way to get the eye color you want permanently, without contacts. And you know how?"

I shrugged my shoulders, unsure of what he was even talking about.

"Come on, Ro. I know you ain't that much in the dark ages. Well, honey, people have been traveling out of the country somewhere to have surgery on their eyes, child, to make their eyes different colors."

"What?" I replied.

"Yes, child. That shows you that you can love what God gave you and buy upgrades!" Dean Baby said as he twisted his fingers and snapped; he took another sip of his tea, while shaking a bottle of light-tan foundation. Then his eyes zoomed in on my eyebrows, and he said, "Child, what in the world is going on with those eyebrows?"

"What do you mean, Dean Baby?"

"When was the last time you had your eyebrows arched? Girl, you are about one week away from looking like the Bert from Sesame Street doll I had when I was a kid!" Dean Baby looked slightly disgusted.

"It has been a long time," I said through my embarrassment.

"No need to be shame, girl. I got you!" he said as he shaped my brows and then calmed the inflammation down with some witch hazel.

"Thanks, Dean Baby. I promise to do better."

"Girl, you look better already. I'm going to put this primer on your skin; it's enriched with vitamins and proteins to cause a natural glow to enhance your skin before I apply the foundation. And if you let me, I want to try a new eye-shadow color on you; I just got it in yesterday. It's called 'Sincere.' Sounds sexy, huh? I am going to use this on your eyelids. It's like a taupe. Your eyes look like they have little flecks of gold in them. And, for the icing on the cake, I am going to rock you out with this metallic sage, on the lids. You know, this shade of green is all the rage with the celebs. This is going to set your eyes up a notch. Money-green, baby!"

"Sounds nice."

"And when I am done with you, Ro, you are going to be able to hold your own with any of those legendary authors in that green room! And trust and believe, let me know who and what you need to know about around that green room out there, and I got you," he shared secretly, as if he were part of a covert operation. He repositioned my chair around to continue working on my makeup. Then looked me square in the eyes, and said, "And you are going to know all about that fabulous life soon. You are now entering a different type of lifestyle - Lifestyles of the Balling and Famous, baby! I am going to make you a serious ten! Yes, honey — you are going to give it to them tuh-day!" he said, as if he was setting out on a mission of vengeance of his own through me.

"Balling. I know nothing about that. I am just a girl from a small town in the Midwest who is a doctor and who wrote a little book. And by the grace of God, I was blessed. The book is finally getting some publicity and has turned into a big thing — a big thing that I'm not sure I'm ready for. "

"Amen and amen. Well, all I can say is that this is something to get used to with your new book, the tour, and all. Tabitha gave me the skinny on you, girl! You are all over the social media. You are the "it" girl now. You got this, and you have to own this! You'd better seize the opportunity while you can! You have to change your ways and the ways you think about yourself! Sista — you got to bring it!"

Man, that was how Luke always used to encourage me, and I miss those days. It was so easy to talk to Dean Baby, and it made me realize that I missed my best friend. I had been ignoring him over the past several weeks, because I just could not afford to be distracted by his drama in this crucial time in my life. It felt like every time I had something good happen to me, somehow Luke and all of the bullshit he would bring would somehow throw some shade on my monumental occasions.

"Thanks, Dean Baby, for your words of encouragement. You will never know how much I needed to hear them."

"No problem. That's what I'm here for. I see you got your nails done — that color is slamming."

"You like it? It's called Princess Purpose. I got my toes done to match!" I said as I pulled my right foot out of my shoe, extended it, and spread my toes as if to display the color.

"Girl, you sure are country. Put your foot back in that red bottom, girl. Yes, I see you."

"Dean Baby, you are a mess. And when you are finished doing my makeup, I am off to get my hair styled, and then to wardrobe, right? Then to the panel venue, then a touch-up, and then the photo shoot with the other up-and-coming authors."

"Sounds like you got it under control. You are already an old pro at this. Now, are you ready to go all in? Dr. Ro, did you hear me? Are you ready to go all in?”

“Yeah, Dean Baby. I think so. A little.”

“Cool, Ro. But I need you to get on my team. And I need to get you hyped for your signing. Are you ready to do the dang-gone thing?’

“Yes, I am!” I said, with a little more spunk. “Oh, Dean Baby, I need you around me all the time to keep me motivated through the day,” I responded, and we slapped a high-five.

“Ladybug, this is my job, dear-heart, to beautify the world, and make God’s creations manifest into their destiny,” he said as he began to place the finishing touches on my makeup.

He applied the color to my lids, and I dared to ask, “Dean Baby, you don’t think this is too much? I am not used to all of this makeup and what not.”

“Just sit back, and let me do my magic.”

“Yes, Dean Baby.”

“And you know this. I got you, girl. You represent me, and I don’t play around with that!”

"This is such a rare treat. For so many years, I was in college, medical school, residency, a new physician, and then starting a new clinic, and then being a medical director, a wife, raising our son, and involved in all of his activities, and devoted to my very busy corporate-executive husband. And now I am an author, starting this book tour. In this midst of all of this, I have totally lost *me*," I transparently shared with a complete stranger what I had not even admitted to myself.

I got a little choked up and overwhelmed with emotion in the whimsy and intensity of the day from that brief walk down memory lane. Talking about and reflecting on the sacrifices that I had made, and all mothers make on a daily basis, made it all too clear that this was the first time I had actually embarked upon my own dream; my own passion.

"Girl, you'd better stop with all that sensitive stuff. You got me all misty-eyed up in here, and I haven't got time for that. And besides that, I am glad you are taking some *you* time, 'cause you were making me tired with all of that busy academia and what not," he said as he used a big brush and brushed all over my entire face.

"You know, when I was a little boy, I wanted to become a doctor, too. Yep, you would have never guessed it, but I did. Yeah, I had a — what do you call that thing you listen to people's hearts with?"

"A stethoscope." I replied.

"Yeah, that's right — a stethoscope toy. I used to play with it until the cows came home. I listened to my teddy bear's heart, gave him his check-ups, and pretended to do surgery on him. And even to this day, I'm always watching those medical shows. That's my jam."

"Really?"

All at once serious look suddenly came across Dean Baby's face; it appeared as if he were zoning out. Putting his brushes down, he stared off into the distance, as if to relive a moment in time.

"And then my mother passed away, and I had to go live with my uncle, who was my mom's brother. And he used to beat me until I was lifeless on the floor." Dean's eyes had lost the twinkle they'd had before.

"Dean Baby, I am so sorry." I grabbed his hand that was resting on my shoulder to console him.

"Yes, that was my life then. Those childlike dreams were beat out of me, along with my soul. But enough about that — let's get back to business! The only beating around here today is the one that unibrow on your forehead took."

We chuckled.

I found myself apologizing again. "Oops, my bad. I promise I'll do a better job of keeping those brows shaped up. I won't let your hard work go to waste."

"You'd better, girl! I told you, honey: I am in charge here. And it is my job to make sure you can sell that little book of yours. You're going to be so fly, you're going to sell a million copies. And I know that you're going to cut me in on that commission, right?"

"You are too funny, Dean Baby," I replied.

"Can I ask you a question, Dr. Ro?"

"Dean, yes. You can ask me anything," I replied.

His eyes squinted and zeroed in on my neck. "What in the hell is that thing around your neck?"

"What do you mean?" I reached up to my neck, felt my necklace and the charm.

"Is that a bird? Honey child, please say 'No'!" he remarked in disgust.

"Oh, Dean Baby, this is a necklace that my childhood best-friend, Luke got me when we were kids. It's a sparrow which is also my name." I laughed nervously. "There is a whole, long story behind the meaning of my name. I have always worn it. I cherish it."

"Aw, that's a cute story and all. But it looks like that thing is going to turn your neck emerald girl!"

"Dean Baby, the pendant is 14-carat gold."

"That pendant may be real, but that chain is trash."

I looked down at the necklace. Dean Baby was right. What was once gold was now dull and metal-bronze in color.

"I'm just saying, girl. Tabitha ordered up this rack with a fine high-end knit black pantsuit for you to wear, and you're walking on red bottoms. You are rocking some beautiful diamond studs for your debut as an author. You need to keep it clean, chic, high-end, and classy. And you are going to wear this cheap necklace around your neck. Girl, you're going to make me cuss, and I am trying to quit. That necklace is sacrilegious, to the Saint himself. Besides, where is the glam in that? You need to get it right and tight to do your *selfie* before you go out on stage and send out a pic to all your followers. They don't want to see that atrocious thing around your neck, Ro. Give me that thing before I call the authorities, the ambulance, or the animal patrol for that pathetic little bird!"

"But…it's symbolic," I replied.

"Well, Dr. Ro, who bought you that four-carat diamond on your honeymoon finger that's blinding everybody?" Dean Baby asked, as he leaned in, grabbed my left hand, and gazed at it with bugged eyes.

"Man, Dean Baby, you're all up in my business. My husband, Weston got it for me. It was an upgrade from the original engagement ring for our ten-year anniversary. How do you know it's four-carats, might I ask?

"Just call me 'Bugs Bunny,' honey, because if there's something that Dean Baby knows all about, that is them carats — and not the ones you eat. Check out my ears! There are two carats on each of these ears and all canary, glam-fabulous! Now, girl, trust me on this. I'm going to take this lovely sparrow necklace off of your honey-toned and beautiful svelte neck and put it in this nice clean plastic bag. And BAM! You look better already. Okay, now place this in your purse. You, your BFF — 'Luke,' or whatever his name is — and that bird necklace will carry you through this big event from your clutch. But, this off-the-chain love that big daddy Weston has for you, with his four-carat heart on your little ring finger right there, will carry you through and make you look even more fabulous. Okay, put that hand out, girl. You better work it!"

"Okay, Dean. You got me. I do look better without the necklace. You're right."

"You know Dean Baby will never steer you wrong."

Dean Baby stood back behind the chair, with confidence, as if he held all the power.

"Yeah, look at my work. I did that!"

"I do look good. Wow, my eyes have not looked this amazing, since, well, never. I did not see an air-brush, but did you air-brush me, Dean Baby?" In the midst of all the conversation, I had not noticed that he had placed a beautiful deep-coral lip stain on my lips. It tasted like melon.

"Dean, I love this color on my lips. Can I get it from you?"

"Ro, girl, you have a good palette to work with; your skin is so healthy. I can tell you have been getting your water in. And these new colors work well with your tone. My work here is done. And yes, I will order some for you and have it shipped.

I'll get your contact information from your agent Tabitha. But, here — you can have this sample. You taste the melon in it? Yep, I know you do, and the color will stay on all day. Girl, you are rocking it! Mika!" Dean called out, as he put his hand up to his mouth like it was a megaphone. "Your turn. Dr. Sparrow is ready for you."

In walked Mika. She looked like she was ready for war or damage control with her apron full of combs, brushes, and hair clips for miles.

Mika was tall and statuesque; her skin was the color of midnight. She appeared to label herself with her white t-shirt, "Somalian Beauty," in glitter. In her thick, rich Somalian accent, she stated, "Follow me. Let's make this hair talk the talk!"

When Mika finished flat ironing and styling my hair, I caught a glimpse of myself in the mirror. The finished product looked beyond fabulous. My hair and makeup were slamming. I got dressed in the clothes Tabitha had sent to the venue. The high-end knit black jacket, shell, and pants fit me to a tee and really showed off my waistline. Since I'd lost 30 pounds, I now looked fierce — not just on the outside, but from the encouraging therapy session with Dean Baby, I felt confident that my outward appearance matched the talent I had inside. I was starting to feel alive, for real, and was going to enjoy the moment to its fullest.

Chapter 5

Tabitha sent me a text with specific directions on how to get to the holding area, where we would meet. I waited by the elevator, which seemed to take forever, but looking at my watch, it was actually only about two minutes. I took the opportunity to reflect on my wonderful day of pampering and smiled to myself, catching my reflection in the metal elevator door. I had a moment of realization that I needed to take better care of me and spoil myself from time to time— not always put myself on hold or on the back burner. Right then and there, I made a commitment to take 'me' time on a regular basis. The feeling of guilt and selfishness would have to take a back seat for a change.

The elevator opened, I got in, and down we went. Yes, I said "we," because I felt the divine presence of God and the Holy Spirit profoundly in that elevator, and a peace came over me. The elevator door opened; I appeared to be in the basement of the hotel. I stepped off of the elevator, and there were halls that appeared to be without end to the right and the left, just as the directions instructed. The walk was longer than I'd expected, and my feet began to hurt in these heels.

I don't think I'm in the right place, I thought to myself while I looked down at my phone to verify the directions, but there was no signal.

I remembered some of the text. Tabitha had instructed me to go to the left once I got off of the elevator. I continued to walk until I ran into some back doors that appeared to be a service area with swinging doors.

This can't be right. I attempted to call Tabitha, and there was still no signal.

Through those doors came an elderly maintenance man with a nametag that that had Cecil etched across the front.

"How you doing, pretty lady?" he asked.

"Lost," I responded.

"How can I help you?"

"Well, Mr. Cecil, I am one of the authors, and I was told to come this way where I would find a holding area for the authors."

"Well, my dear, you are totally off base. Here — follow me. I can get you back on track."

"I can't believe this. I'm going to be late," I said frantically.

"Oh, no, you aren't, pretty lady. Calm down. Wait here." He went into the swinging doors. I was tapping my foot when Mr. Cecil drove through the swinging doors in a small-motorized cart and told me to get on.

The cart was dusty with splits and tears in the leather seat, but I felt like I had no choice. Cecil was about eighty years old, and I was surprised he was still working. He drove me back down the long cement hallway I'd just walked down, and in that long ride, he told me his life story. He'd worked in this hotel since he'd graduated from high school and how holding this job allowed him to send his daughter to college. His two his sons were in the military and he was a widower with five grandchildren. He was such a delight. However, he drove the cart slow as molasses, and I needed to get to the holding area quick. Finally we were at another, larger elevator, which appeared to be a service elevator. The elevator doors opened up, he drove the cart on, and we rode up to the next floor. As soon as the elevator doors opened, Mr. Cecil got off the cart and motioned for me to get off. He used his elevator key and locked the elevator door open.

"Come on, young lady. We need to go this way."

I got off the cart and followed him. We had a ways to go to the right of those elevators until we reached the holding area, adjacent to the ballroom. And now, in the distance, I saw Tabitha with a both annoyance and concern on her face. She hurried toward me.

"Ro — where in the hell have you been?"

"I have been hanging out with my new friend, Mr. Cecil, who so graciously redirected me from those awful directions you sent."

Mr. Cecil smiled, showing off a gold tooth in the front that I'd failed to see initially.

"I've been looking for you! You're late! I have been texting you! You should have been down before now!" Tabitha yelled, as she grabbed my arm impatiently.

"First of all, you're doing way too much, Tabitha. You don't need to grab me. And if you had given me better directions, we would not be having this conversation, now, would we?"

At that moment, my phone regained its signal, and I heard alert after alert begin to roll in on my phone. Sure enough, there were nine texts from Tabitha, asking where I was and giving me updated information on the directions to the holding area.

I grinned. "Oops, my bad. My phone lost signal, and I'm just now getting the texts."

"You know what? Never mind all of that. You're here now," she said with frustration as she threw up her hands. While I stood next to Mr. Cecil, Tabitha started to straighten my clothes like I was a child, dusting off my knit suit, and adjusting my lapel.

I turned to Mr. Cecil, thanked him, and wished him well with his family. I reached into my purse, grabbed the last large bill I had, slipped it his hand when I shook it, and told him "Goodbye."

Tabitha continued to fuss at me and fuss over me, getting all up into my space and into my hair.

"Girl, haven't I told you not to touch my hair?"

"I'm adjusting some loose strands. Wipe the lipstick off of your front teeth. Here's a mirror; you don't want your photos coming back all crazy, do you?" Tabitha said.

Mr. Cecil walked away and laughed at how Tabitha was fussing over me; he looked into his hand and realized the amount of the tip I had given him; he yelled back,

"Thank you, pretty lady! God is going to bless you!" He put his cart in drive, and off he went.

Although I was a little perturbed by Tabitha, she was what I called my "secret weapon." She was a Mega Barbie type. Nipped and tucked to the tee, in all the right places. So perfect, she was almost plastic. Not a hair out of place. She had a bubbly personality, and best of all, she was brilliant and all business. To sum it up, she was a dynamo agent who could broker any deal; a skill obtained from her grandfather, who was a wealthy businessman.

She would mesmerize the seasoned male publishing agents with her perfect veneered teeth, golden tan, and toned physique. Those good old boys would agree to terms that were unheard of. Tabitha did what Tabitha had to do: lean in on boardroom tables, go out for drinks, show up to bar mitzvahs, be on the front row at a hockey game, whatever it took to negotiate and ink the deal. I didn't always know how or want to know how she did it. I had some ideas, but overall, I was glad she was on my team. She was the bomb. I was truly blessed to have her in my corner. She was a hookup from above.

I'd connected with Tabitha Blanko through my Uncle Cyrus. He was well connected to the upper echelon in Manhattan, NY. Mr. Blanko was one of the wealthiest property developers and venture capitalists along the east coast. Mr. Blanko was Tabitha's grandfather. Uncle Cyrus had worked on a lot of projects with him throughout the years.

And, in turn, my uncle Cyrus was like Tabitha's uncle.

While I was visiting Manhattan one fall for a medical conference, Uncle Cyrus suggested that Tabitha and I go to lunch, and we did. We shared our experiences and challenges of life and had a lot of laughs over a lot of cocktails. She and I discovered we had a lot in common, and we remained connected ever since. It was refreshing to have friendship with Tabitha because it balanced out the dysfunctional friendship I had with Luke.

When I first met Tabitha, she was a pale, bleach-blond-haired young lady who wore flip-flops and sundresses. Unknown to most, she was wealthy beyond words. I'm talking old money, long-legacy wealth. However, she wanted to find her own way and not lean on her grandfather's pocketbook or her inheritance. She pulled herself up by her own bootstraps, with little help from her grandfather, and I truly admired her for that.

After our first meeting, Tabitha and I kept in contact. She kept encouraging me to write down my medical-school experiences I shared with her; she was pursuing internships with some of the top celebrity brokers in the industry. There were many times she was able to add me as her plus-one to red-carpet events, and those were some good times. When I decided to pursue writing full time, I shared it with Tabitha, and she was ecstatic. My husband was on board too, but not Luke. He could not fathom why I would want to write books and become an author after working so hard to become a doctor, but I didn't let him burst my bubble. I figured I could have the best of both worlds; Tabitha volunteered to show me how to make it happen, and she has been my agent ever since.

She has changed a lot since our first meeting; the sweet innocent little nerdy girl was now a bronzed goddess with silky highlights in her hair and adorned in fine, high-end knit from head to toe that glided in the finest of shoes. She rocked the hottest handbags that were the price of an average automobile. Like her or not, she was my "ace in the hole" and she was a force to be reckoned with in this industry, which was very good for me. The only downside in my relationship with Tabitha was that Luke was a bit jealous of my evolving friendship with her, beyond just being my agent. He felt threatened by her influence in my life.

"Ro, do you have to run everything by her?" Luke would ask every time I brought up Tabitha's name or the soon-to-be-released book *Step 1* up in conversation.

"Luke, this is business. And yes, Tabitha is my agent — I have to run everything by her." It seemed apparent, and it was a shame that the mere presence of someone who did not bring dysfunction to my life was a threat to Luke.

But that was then, and this is now, and I was not going to let those thoughts ruin my premier of who God called me to be — an author to share the stories of triumph and victory along life's journey.

Tabitha and I continued to walk toward the end of a long, sterile hallway with our heels sounding like galloping horses in the cement basement of the hotel. We reached a short flight of stairs leading to the ballroom of the convention center.

"Ro, see that room over there? That is where we were supposed to meet. That's the holding area. But we don't have time for that now."

We walked a little further. Tabitha stopped us at the ballroom door, turned to me, looked at me directly in my eyes, and gave me direction:

"Sparrow, now I need you to focus. I know this has been a long morning for you. You just got in from the airport and straight to the hotel to glam. I have everything taken care of. Your bags are in your hotel room. The baby and your hubby are fine. So Ro, I need you to bring your "A" game today — we have a lot riding on this. So, here are your cue cards with the questions on them. Here is the book; I have the chapters marked that you will be reading from.

I've highlighted the paragraphs, and here are your glasses. Water and mints are on the table," Tabitha said while continuing to hurry me along toward the door of the event space.

"Got it. Thanks," I replied, while grabbing all of the things Tabitha handed to me. I began to have a little ringing in my ears, presumably from that long flight and the rapid changes in barometric pressure. I had forgotten my earplugs at home to prevent that from occurring after a flight. I began to attempt to pop my ears as much as I could. An immense pain started to manifest in my right temple, which was quite strange, but I pushed through the pain and poised myself to represent my brand.

Tabitha noticed.

"What's wrong with you, Ro?" as she looked at me concerned yet obviously irritated.

"I'm good. My ears are a little full, and I have some sinus pressure, but I'm good. Don't worry, Tabitha. I got this."

"You better *got this*! Ro, do you know who is out there?" Tabitha whispered, with her manicured hand against her perfect skin. "Your destiny as a super star…"

At that point, I could see her moving her lips but all I heard were muffled words — as if I were underwater. To make matters worse, the pressure in my right temple proceeded to worsen and deepen, causing me to reach up and massage my head in that area. I'd had that pain earlier in the day, but this is the worst that it had gotten.

Tabitha repeated herself again, as if I had not hear her the first time, which was probably true. "Ro, are you listening? Do you know who's out there? You would not believe who's going to do your introduction."

"No, Tabitha. I have no idea. Who is it?" I replied as I rubbed my temple, attempting to relieve the discomfort.

"Wow, Ro — did you not read the updated email I sent you while you were at the airport?"

"No, I must have missed that one!"

"Girl, we have to get you into the new millennium; you were supposed to put your phone in airplane mode, so you could get my texts and emails. Oh, well, I sent you the updated information, as soon as I found out!"

"Who is it, Tabitha?"

"The President and CEO of Grace Publishing!"

"Jasper Cummings?" I asked. I could feel my blood pressure immediately start to rise as soon as I said his name. I stood back and crossed my arms.

"Yes, Jasper. He will give your official introduction, so be on your best." Tabitha clenched her teeth when she spoke.

"Jasper? How in the hell did he get involved in this?" I asked her.

"Listen, Ro, I know Jasper can be difficult. So don't let this steal your thunder. This is your day."

"I know you had to pull some strings and do a lot of behind-the-scenes work to get me here as a newbie, and I appreciate and respect it. But why in the world does Jasper have to be the one to present me? You know this motherfucker tried to halt my career. Let's not forget that shit!"

"Well, he came with the deal! Dammit, Ro! Stop thinking that every damn thing is supposed to be so fucking perfect! Sparrow, you know he's the president of the board, so this should not be a surprise! This is the real deal and everything can't always go how you envisioned it. This is the real damn world girl. And you'd better get used to it. He's doing a simple introduction. No harm, no foul.

Just get your shit together — your little sinuses and ringing of the ears. Get your head composed, get out there, and *do you.* Let the book, *Step I*, speak for itself! And by the way, if you play your cards right, we have 'bestseller' written all over us! Tabitha commanded.

I looked at Tabitha cross-eyed, but knew she was absolutely right. It was my time to shine and walk into my purpose. I was not going to let anything or anyone stand in my way. I had purposefully put Luke and all of his drama on the back burner to focus on my career, and I was not going to let Jasper's hating ass ways or his doubt about me cause me to mess up this blessing that had my name written all over it. And look at Tabitha — she got all in my space, got all gangster on me, and got me in check, real quick.

"Oh, my, Tabitha— you have been around me way too long, you got me told. And yes, I will be on my best behavior," I replied and smiled. She smiled back and nudged my shoulder.

"Are we good, girl?"

"Yes, we're good. Let's go."

We walked in unison with our game faces on and entered the doors of the ballroom. The maroon-and-cream geometric-designed carpet highlighted the black we both wore. The lighting was haloed around the room, making all of the people in the crowd appear welcoming and angelic. As I looked around the room, feeling like a literary gangster, I was in awe of this experience and truly enjoying this moment, with Tabitha on my heels.

My phone rang, from the pocket inside my jacket.

Oh, no — it's my cell phone, I thought and tried to mute it. I thought I'd turned it off. Tabitha abruptly nudged me, smiled, and said between her clenched teeth,

"Ro, turn that damn thing off!" She accompanied her words with a stern glare.

I put the phone in silent mode as we passed by tables on on-lookers. It was probably my husband, attempting to reach me so we could pray. And, truth be told, I was in a little somber mood because he was home taking care of our baby and could not be present for this special occasion.

My phone began to hum in my jacket pocket. There was nothing silent about my cellular devices vibrate feature.

Now that is something Luke would do: call back to back! But I didn't have time for his craziness. I was about to hit the stage.

Tabitha turned toward me, reached out her hand, palm up, toward me, and said, "Better yet, give me your phone!"

I looked at her as if she had lost her mind while she reached into my fine-knit jacket pocket and took the phone away from me as if I were a child she was scolding.

"Oh, *hell* no, Tabitha. You are out of line," I whispered to her, since we were now in public view. Tabitha was one of the best agents around, but we needed to work on some ground rules here. Personal-space boundaries and respect were a must! I shook my head, allowed her to take the phone, and regrouped so I wouldn't knock her block off. I don't do well with people invading my personal space, and she should know me by now. I forced my emotions to fall back. She got a pass on this one because she was the main reason I was there, and she was right: It would be a huge distraction to have my phone go off while I was speaking.

"Girl, it's game time. You look great. Your makeup is slamming, and that color on your lips is fire. Now go represent! I'll be back here," Tabitha said as she took a seat in the back; I walked to the front of the ballroom.

I was honored to be walking toward the long, rectangular dais, with a nameplate reading "Dr. Sparrow Mack" in front of where I was to sit. Behind my seat was a standing poster of my book cover bearing my headshot. I looked at that picture and smiled. It was one of the best pictures I had ever had taken.

A sense of completeness came over me as I sat at the head table while the introduction about me was being read. The National Academy of Writers Vice-President, Belinda Langley, introduced me as an up-and-coming author to be celebrated. She went into my history — a physician by training, a practicing physician, and then a physician who mainstreamed into becoming a journalistic-writer-turned-published-author.

"And now I am going to turn the podium over to the President of the Board for the National Academy of Writers, Mr. Jasper Cummings. Everyone please welcome him to the stage," Belinda Langley belted out, clapping her hands.

"Oh, my! This is going to be real interesting," I said under my breath, as I forced a smile on my face and clenched my teeth. Inside, a sense of dread came over me, crushing all the celebratory feelings of being there and being a featured author I'd felt moments ago in the green room. The anticipation of the words that would come out of this man's mouth caused me to cringe and, essentially, kind of tarnished the moment for me — *my* moment. I looked to the right in the back of the room toward Tabitha to get some type of reassurance. She knew our history with Jasper. Tabitha's perfect smile lit up, and she winked at me, positioned her hands downward, and mouthed the words,

It's okay, Ro. Settle down! In a calm, gentle way from the back of the room. However, I was not completely sold on the "settle down" part. I felt something was up. Not only was Jasper Cummings the President and CEO of Grace Publishing House, he was also the President of the Board for the National Academy of Writers. Tabitha and I had been in serious negotiations regarding renewing my contract with Grace Publishing. We'd gotten a lot of pushback from Jasper. He felt I had not been through the fire enough, proven myself enough, or paid my dues enough to be granted a full book deal. However, *Step I*, my first novel, was on the bestsellers list in e-book and audio book and soon to be for copies sold in print by public demand. So regardless of how Jasper felt about this little girl from the Midwest, whom had not paid the proper dues for a full contract, I was bringing Grace Publishing House major dividends and attention.

Jasper, the numbers don't lie! I am the newest author and among the top five authors you have — platinum status! You are raking in a lot of cash

because of me, I remembered saying in a tense, closed-door meeting with him about two months before. Tabitha, who had sat across from me at the table, had almost fainted by my direct, in-your-face attitude toward the hand that was feeding my debut career as an author. However, I had to get my point across.

But how else was I to respond to a person who came out swinging with direct gut punches toward my writing capabilities and went even further on questioning my talent and literary skills? I think I responded quite well, but Tabitha felt that maybe my delivery of that message was not as polished as it should have been. I remembered thinking after leaving that meeting that he'd really pissed me off with his condescending tone and ridicule. If my Luke had heard Jasper talking to me like that, he would have let him have it.

Later on that afternoon, after that awful meeting and talking to Weston about how I responded to Jasper, I remembered thinking about how I'd behaved and the words that I'd said. It all could have been tailored differently. I should have been a bit more professional in how I handled that issue. Accordingly, I sent Jasper an apologetic email regarding my disposition and tone but still reiterated my value to the publishing house. I never got a response from him.

And now, on one of the biggest days of my life, I was sitting there during my introduction, cringing at what this man might say about me to a room filled with writers and press.

Leave it to Sparrow to speak her mind and mess shit up — damn! I thought to myself about how my previous actions in that meeting months before could really mess things up for me now.

As I sat in front of an audience, there was Jasper, standing at the podium, at what was supposed to be the highlight of my career. The ball was in his court. Was he there to provide some cross words, to darken my shine? I thought, if *he's going to try to rub it in that I wouldn't be getting a full contract from GPH, I'm not having it — this is* my *day. And I don't care if he is talking. I am not going to let him disrespect me or embarrass me.* My heart began to pound harder, and sweat started to gather in my armpits.

I sat on the edge of my seat in an attempt to appear calm — but ready to kick some ass — as he was trying to make his way through some sort of announcement. I waited for a pause to possibly interject in my defense, but none came.

Sparrow, what are you doing? Why are you letting this man all up in your head and stealing your joy? Remember the devotion of today! The words of forgiveness popped into my head from the devotion I'd read that morning, while I was waiting to get glammed up.

I just need to go ahead, calm down, and be still, I told myself, as my defensiveness shrank a little. I felt the Holy Spirit calming me.

Jasper looked toward me, making firm eye contact, while he spoke. I could see his temporal artery pulsating as if someone were *forcing* him to speak well of me. And then he announced,

"Will you all please stand and welcome with me our new platinum author with Grace Publishing House, Dr. Sparrow Mack!" He didn't wait for me to get to the podium. He left the stage and exited the ballroom as the audience arose and applauded in a standing ovation.

I could not believe my ears at what had come out of his mouth. I thought that I must have been dreaming. I was happy, shocked, and puzzled, all at the same time.

Before I knew it, I was at the podium. *I owned this experience*, I kept telling myself, *because these are my words and my thoughts that I have experienced; everything is already all good.* But I was nervous, and my palms were sweaty as I opened the marked pages of the book and began to read from *Step 1*.

After the first sentence left my lips, I felt like the audience was on a magic carpet with me and we were all flying high. It felt like, together, we'd stepped into the book and nothing else mattered. I looked out, and I could see the conference attendees wiping away tears from their eyes while listening to my words and identifying with the experiences I'd written on the pages.

Relating with the stories, I could see the people nodding and agreeing with the challenges that face us all as I read paragraph after paragraph.

"Friendship," "deceit," "bitterness," and "dismay surrounded in faith" were the ideas that informed the book. Beyond the shadow of a doubt, each and every member of the audience understood me and was along with me on the journey. And that is what I had hoped for when I wrote this book. I completed the reading of Chapter 4 of *Step I*, and at the conclusion, the audience stood with a loud, heartfelt applause, as if they wanted and needed more. They were grateful. I was a rock star.

After the crowd concluded their applause, there was a book signing for a limited amount of copies that followed, because I had to go for a glam touch-up and then to the photo shoot with all of the authors attending the conference. After that, there was a new authors' cocktail hour, and I was so looking forward to it. Although I was trying to cut back, I needed a drink.

As the people rose from their chairs and began to form a line to receive my autograph on their purchased *Step 1* book, I saw Tabitha signal me from the back of the room. She needed to talk. I was baffled because I was in the process of signing books, which is what she wanted me to do.

“What’s your name?” I said to the lady who handed me her copy of *Step 1* to sign.

“My name is Maria, and this book has helped me realize the value of true friendship. Since reading it, I have evaluated the relationships that I have with my family and friends and decided to make a lot of changes,” Maria said as she began to tear up.

“Aw — thank you, Maria. I really appreciate your support.” I stood and gave her a hug — she’d tugged right at my heartstrings. It felt like the right thing to do, and she was grateful and continued on about the specific friendships she had evaluated and made some changes. In true Sparrow fashion, I listened and was engaged, not minding the 75 plus people who were waiting behind her patiently.

Abruptly, as I signed my signature after my standard, “God Bless.” I felt my arm being jerked.

Tabitha pulled me up from the table with my cell phone in her hand.

"What's wrong?" I asked in a state of shock at her behavior.

"It's your husband!" Tabitha responded, as she pulled me into the hallway.

I was terrified, especially by the look of alarm on Tabitha's face.

I grabbed the phone from her hand, walked away from her for privacy.

"Ro!" my husband said in a worrisome tone.

"Weston, what's wrong? Is it the baby? What's wrong? Tell me now!" I demanded to know as my heart skipped a beat. My hands were already shaking.

"No," my husband said in a concerned, monotone answer.

I took a deep breath and asked, "Is it our parents?"

"No, but are you sitting down?"

The panic factor had gone from one hundred down to about fifty, now that I realized that it was not regarding immediate family.

"What is it, babe? Don't play. What's going on? I'm in the middle of a book signing!"

"Are you sitting down?" he asked again.

"No, I can't. Dammit, man — there are no chairs in the hallway. Just tell me what the hell is going on, Weston!" I demanded.

"It's Luke," he said.

"Oh, my goodness! What does he want now? Medical advice?"

"No."

"The keys to the condo?"

"No. Ro, listen…"

"Oh, it's money. I see. You had me pulled out of the most important event of my life for another one of Luke's sagas? Just call him back and tell him I will send him some cash tonight and after that I'm done with him! Done! Make sure you tell him the last part." I yelled into the phone.

I had not spoken with Luke in a minute. I had called to verify his new address because I'd heard he was thinking about moving, and I wanted to send Busy, his niece, a gift for her birthday. We had not talked much lately. At this point in our friendship, he called only when he wanted or needed something — that appeared to be his plight in life. Weston sometimes referred him as my "leech." I'd always laughed it off, but over the past year, as I focused more on accomplishing goals in my life, I realized more and more that my husband may actually be right. Luke had been or had become that "leech." Luke had not always been that way, but that was Luke now and I was sick and tired of it.

"No. You're not getting it, Ro. Listen to me! I am just going to lay everything out for you, plain and simple. *Luke passed away. He is dead.* They found him this morning. Mrs. Elizabeth called the house to let you know, and I talked to her myself."

"Dead?" I barely heard myself say it as a cloud of emotions blasted through me: guilt, frustration, sorrow, and confusion.

"Baby, are you okay?"

My knees buckled. Tabitha saw that I was going down, so she braced me as I sagged to the floor.

“What have I done?” I yelled out as guilt took over and weighed me down.

A few people in the crowd looked into the hallway, witnessed me on the floor, and gasped in concern. My body went limp, and my vision tunneled to black.

Chapter 6

My next memory was lying on the hotel-room bed, with my eyes fixed on the ceiling, tracing the lines of the white stucco. It was as if I were in a maze trying to escape this nightmare of the truth. The room was blurred from the tears that had welled up and filled my eyes and from the alcohol I'd used to numb the pain. It had been hours since I heard Weston say that Luke was dead. I stared at the ceiling as if it were a movie reel, and the same, recurring childhood visions of Luke and me replayed in my mind; I could not escape looking at my past.

The memory was that of me as a child, sitting on a piano bench with my grandmother at church while she played at choir practice. Luke sat mesmerized in the front pew, watching me swing my legs sitting next to my grandma as her angelic hands danced on the piano keys and played,

"His eye is on the sparrow, and I know he watches over me," she sang in her strong alto voice.

As a little girl, I remembered being in awe as I watched her and heard her smooth, operatic voice hit each note and wrap around them, elevating to magnificence.

As a little girl, I'd often asked her, "Grandma, what does the song *'His eye is on the sparrow'* mean? And is this song about me?'"

She would pause from playing the piano, look me in the eyes, and would say,

"Oh, baby that means the Lord is always watching over you. And you know what? He watches over all things — the animals, the birds and the fish, and even you, sweetie," as she stroked my cheek and went back to playing the piano.

"Grandma, does he watch over me, too?" asked Luke, in desperation, with his big, brown doe eyes.

And I looked at him in a crossed way and pouting my lips because this was *my* grandma, not his! But grandma, sensing his need for affection, obliged him and said, "Yes, my dear Luke — He watches over you as well."

She reached for Luke and instructed him,

"Come here, baby." And he honored my grandmother's instruction. Luke came over to grandma, and she gave him a hug. That is something he longed for and did not get from his own grandma, Mrs. Elizabeth. My granny was a pure gem, as she would look deep into Luke's eyes and spirit to make sure that he felt special, too. In those moments with grandma, Luke's eyes would light up like a Christmas tree, as he embraced my grandmother like she was his only lifeline. That image of Luke and those happier times continued to play over and over as I looked up at the ceiling. An empty bourbon bottle sat on the nightstand.

"Sparrow. Sparrow — wake up, babe." Weston shook me in the hotel bed, where I lay fully dressed in the same clothes I'd worn for the New Authors Symposium. The visions of Luke, my grandma, and me evaporated as I rolled over and looked toward the nightstand.

"There's that pathetic sparrow necklace that Dean Baby had placed in a plastic bag. Somebody — please cover it up. I cannot bear to look at it," I said in a drunken state as I held my throbbing head.

"Get her some black coffee!" my husband Weston instructed Tabitha.

"It's brewing," Tabitha remarked.

"I thought you were supposed to be taking care of her!" Weston said as he loosened his tie and removed his suit jacket. He put his leather travel bag on the hotel table, coming to my bedside and stroking my cheek.

"I have been, as much as you can a grown-ass woman!" Tabitha tried to say under her breath; shrugging her shoulders, she walked toward the coffee maker shaking her head.

"Excuse me, Tabitha? You say something?" Weston said in an irritated tone.

"Nothing, Mr. Mack. "I'll get her together."

"I'm going to need you to do that real fast; we have a flight to catch early in the morning for the wake and the funeral. They want to bury his remains quickly. Have you notified Grace Publishing House to let them know what happened?"

"I'm working on it," Tabitha said as she watched the coffee grow hotter.

"Are her clothes packed?" Weston asked Tabitha.

"Mr. Mack, no disrespect, but I was just able to get into her hotel room as you arrived. Since last evening, she has been locked up. I was trying to respect her alone time, but when I realized she was not coming out, I had to have hotel management open the door. So, I'm working on that now." She lifted the bourbon bottle and attempted to pour any remaining liquor out, however, the bottle was empty.

"I can't believe she killed all of this. I'd left her for only a moment," Tabitha said as the aroma of the coffee began to fill the room.

"Wes, is that you? When did you get here, babe?" I asked, rubbing my eyes, as he placed a gentle kiss on my check. This scene was becoming all too familiar to him. He is a good man and chose to stay and stick it out to help me fight my demons; they had been recently getting the best of me.

"Babe, I'm here." Weston said as he sat on the edge of the bed, held my hand, and stroked it. I loved the way his strong hands enclosed over mine.

"That feels nice. Oh, no I missed the group photo with all of the authors," I said as I looked up and smiled at the love of my life.

"Baby, you don't worry about that. And Tabitha, you handle the travel arrangements. My mother has little Wes; we're all good on the home front." Weston said. With a reassuring smirk out of the corners of his mouth and with stern eyes, he remarked, "She'll be fine. Let's set her up in the bed and try to get her to eat something."

"I'll order room service," Tabitha said as she sat near the phone and grabbed the room-service menu.

Chapter 7

Our flight was rescheduled twice due to extreme-weather delays from the departing airport to head back home for the funeral. I paced the floor at the airport gate with my arms crossed and my mind in pure dismay as the rain continued to pour endlessly outside the window. Lightning blazed in the dark and ominous sky.

"Weston, we are going to miss the funeral!" I kept saying with tears rolling down my face.

I had forgotten about the New Authors Symposium, my new book, and any and everything about contract negotiations and anything that I thought was so important to me less than 24 hours before. The only thing I could think about was getting back home and being there for my best friend's funeral. It is amazing what can happen in less than twenty-four hours to tilt your world off of its axis and shatter everything you thought was important, and bring into perspective what really is.

"Come here, and sit down, baby, and let me take care of this," Weston requested as he reached for my hand, guiding me to the seat next to him.

Weston had connected with Tabitha and updated all parties involved about what had occurred. I was in a rare space and needed time off, and he had made that happen. Now he was working with the gate agents and the airlines to try to get us on a flight that was not delayed, but the weather was not letting up. All planes were on hold for the time being. We just had to wait for Mother Nature to clear so we could depart.

"Sparrow, I'm going to get you there, babe, as fast as I can — I promise," Wes said as he went back up to the gate counter to see what time our updated departure would be. Although his efforts were sincere and he paid additional fees for us to switch airlines in hopes of getting there on time, due to the weather delays, by the time we landed back home, we had missed the start of the funeral.

"I know we missed the funeral, but we're going to the church anyway!" I said, as we stood at baggage claim waiting for our luggage. I tried to collect my thoughts after what I can honestly categorize as the most turbulent flight I have ever experienced, which absolutely paralleled my life in that moment.

"Sorry, babe. I tried to get you here as quickly as I could," Weston said as we got into the back passenger seats of the black town car that awaited us, while the driver put our luggage in the trunk.

Pulling up to the church, we could see people beginning to leave.

"You know, Weston, honey, this is bittersweet, because I don't think I could have been able to handle seeing Luke in the casket."

Weston held my hand tighter as I leaned my head onto his shoulder. Even though the tears continued to flow, there was less of a lump in my throat because we had missed the actual funeral.

"I know Mrs. Elizabeth is going to have some harsh words for me."

I'd found out through Weston that Mrs. Elizabeth, Luke's grandmother, had wanted me to say a few words at the funeral, and that is exactly what I'd written — just a few words, on the plane,

Luke, we love you and miss you. We will solve the mystery of what happened. Until we meet again, see you later, and rest easy. Love, Sparrow.

I shared those words with Weston, and he said, "Sparrow, don't you dare feel bad about not being there for the funeral or not being able to read your condolences. Mrs. Elizabeth knows how much you have done for Luke — hell, for her and they're whole damn family."

We arrived at the church and sat in the town car behind the hearse parked in front of the church. Busy, Luke's niece was angelic as she walked out of the massive wood front doors down the large, gray stone steps of the church holding onto the rail and walking behind the casket. The gray pewter casket had red roses draped over the top with a sash with red lettering that read, "Beloved Son & Brother." The pallbearers, who consisted of several family members and friends, walked slowly, carrying the casket.

The beautiful flowers — all red roses, to be exact — caught my eye. I remembered that Luke's favorite color was red, as he tried to wear red everything all the time. I smiled briefly, remembering him when I saw him for the first time, scared, standing in front of the class. He had on a red shirt, red shorts, and red shoes, and he was holding his red notebook. He was such a square, but he was my best friend. I cried deeply and mourned my loss. Through the car window glass I saw that Busy tightly held her grandmother's hand with one hand, and, with her other precious little hand, she touched the casket with each step the pallbearers took.

Busy absolutely adored her uncle Luke, who was more like a father than an uncle. Despite all of his flaws, he was devoted to her and would spend his last dime and mine to make sure Busy had everything she needed. He'd taught her practically everything she knew. It shocked me when Luke took an extra job to make sure Busy had tuition to start a pre-kindergarten program because he believed his niece was the smartest girl in the world. He wanted her to get a head start on her education, to be able to "compete in the world." Luke's infinite love for Busy was a beautiful testimony of how someone can come into your life and cause you to want to do better and become a better person.

Busy was the daughter of Luke's stepsister, Lucinda, who'd passed away from cancer. Busy was the only grandchild and Luke's only niece. I believe Lucinda had been pregnant before, but I was not one hundred percent sure. However, I was there with Luke when Busy came into this world. I was there when Busy's beautiful mother Lucinda passed away. And from the day Lucinda took her last breath, Luke had taken on the role of parent for his sister's child. When Luke was with Busy or talked about her, you could tell she was his pride and joy by the pure love that manifested in his eyes. Busy seemed to be the missing puzzle piece to his broken life.

Looking at her now, she was even more stunning than Lucinda. Busy had olive-toned skin and dark, thick, curly, ringlet hair just like her mother and her uncle Luke, but hers was longer — to her mid-back. She was about five years old now. It was so heart wrenching to see her crying and clinging to the casket; her lifeline being cut away. Her grandma, Mrs. Elizabeth, walked slowly behind with a handkerchief in her hands, wiping her weary eyes, trying to be strong for her great grandbaby.

Weston and I decided that, because we were so late arriving to the church, we would not disrupt the procession and remain in the car. We followed the hearse over to the gravesite. Weston held my hand and stroked it gently as we sat in the back of the black Lincoln town car. The driver, Mr. Marcus, was the same one I'd always used when I came back home. We followed the funeral procession from the church to the final destination of the gravesite with our headlights on.

Weston reached over and gently placed my head on his shoulder and held me tight; he could see how hard I was taking all of this. I was so blessed to have him, but he had no idea what burden I was dealing with in my soul, the pure guilt of not being there for Luke — on purpose — when he obviously needed me most. I just could not afford to be distracted in my present space, and that was such a selfish headspace to be in. Although I had recently drifted from him, we had been like family since we were kids. We were like two peas in a pod. We had been through the storms together and had an unspoken promise to be there for each other, no matter what. And when he apparently needed me most, I was not there for him. I had not lived up to the promise. And how dare I behave in that manner?

I felt Luke had reached a point in life where he had become a taker, and I was way too tired of giving. And as of late, it appeared Luke had changed. He could not be happy for anyone because he was so miserable himself. And I'd reached a point in my life where it was okay for me to be selfish for once, focus on my own goals and aspirations, and not be fixated on fixing the world.

"Damn, and then this happens," I said to myself. I sat there crying uncontrollably. I had a torn piece of paper, with torn promises on it, in my purse, and a sparrow charm on a tarnished necklace. How had it all come to this?

Chapter 8

The heels on my stilettos sank in the wet soil at the gravesite. All at once, a slightly cloudy, overcast sky hovered overhead.

"Is it going to rain? We don't have an umbrella," I said.

"We'll be fine. I'll put my jacket over your head if I need to," Weston said. "No, seriously — Marcus has an umbrella in the town car if we need it."

Hand in hand, we approached the graveside, and I could see people nudging each other as we approached; eyes welcoming me and judging me all once. I walked on the green synthetic grass beneath the graveside tent. There was one row of chairs in front of the draped casket. Seated were Luke's grandmother, Mrs. Elizabeth, Busy, and a couple of other relatives I had seen at family gatherings. I smiled and nodded as we made eye contact. The irony is that, right behind Mrs. Elizabeth were people who had given up on Luke long ago, and I knew them by name. The irony.

Regardless of how we felt about how Luke lived his life, we all remembered his straight-to-the-point honesty, his smile, his laugh, and his unwavering love for each of us.

Minister Brown concluded the graveside ceremony and took a small amount of dirt in his hands and sprinkled them on the casket.

"Ashes to ashes and dust to dust, we surrender this soul back to you, Lord." Minister Brown called out to the heavens as the fine brown granules of dirt left his hand and hit the casket, softly rolling down into an endless hole.

"No, no!" yelled out a man standing far behind us. He was handsome, clean cut, with tanned skin. He looked very familiar, but I couldn't place where I knew him. From the angle where I was positioned, it was hard for me to make him out. I needed to see him a little closer.

"Oh, my, is that Lorenzo?" I heard a woman near me whisper to someone near her.

"Yes — that is him, girl. Oh, my — it's about to be on now!" another person stated.

It can't be him, I thought, *not the Lorenzo who'd gone to school with me.*

The man doubled over as another male appeared, who could have been a brother of the handsome man, and braced himself against Lorenzo to keep him steady.

"Could that possibly be Lorenzo?" I said under my breath, as Weston's hand gripped me tighter at the waist.

I pulled out my glasses to bring the man more into focus. I was supposed to wear them all the time but didn't.

"Yes, that was Lorenzo. Wow, he's lost so much weight. I hardly recognized him," I said.

"Who is that, babe?" Weston leaned in and whispered in my ear.

"It looks like this guy I went to medical school with," I replied. I turned my whole body around to try to get a better look at him as he continued to cry uncontrollably. "Yep — that's him, babe. Weston, you remember that guy I told you about who started out in medical school with us but didn't finish?"

"Yes, I think so."

"Remember? I told you how his dad was a big-time doctor, and he just quit school with no explanation. Well, that's him, but he looks a lot different; he looks like a fraction of himself, a new and improved version."

"Why? What changed?"

"He's lost a ton of weight! Lorenzo and Luke were real cool with each other, but I didn't know they were *that* close — for him to be crying hysterically and falling out at the funeral. You would think he knew Luke all his life, like I did."

"Sparrow, did it ever occur to you that other people besides you are taking this loss hard? Look around."

"You have a point, babe," I said as I kissed him on the cheek and returned my head on his shoulder.

Luke had met Lorenzo through me. At one point in time, Luke, Lorenzo, Lucinda, and I spent a lot of late nights out together studying and hanging out. Lorenzo's father, Dr. Ernesto, was a big-time surgeon and had a very well established local surgical clinic. I rotated through his father's clinic when Lorenzo was still in medical school with me. His father wanted him to become a physician and follow in his footsteps. I also remembered that Lucinda was able to get a job as an administrative assistant at Dr. Ernesto's medical office.

In the middle of our second year, when we started our clinical rotations, medical school got really intense. Lorenzo floored his parents when he decided not to follow in his father's footsteps of becoming a physician and dropped out of medical school, which was a huge disgrace in their upper-class world. Lorenzo developed a strong dislike for his dad after some family issues, and he rebelled against the ideas Dr. Ernesto had mapped out for his brother and him becoming physicians. Dr. Ernesto meant for his sons to become surgeons, eventually joining him in his lucrative private practice, creating a continued legacy of wealth and enhancing their family brand.

However, it didn't turn out that way. Only one of his sons followed that path — not the chosen son, Lorenzo, but the younger brother. Lorenzo developed a different vision for himself, and that was to go into the field of information technology. I can remember it like it was yesterday. Dr. Ernesto almost totally disowned his firstborn son when Lorenzo broke the news to his dad that he was dropping out of medical school. I heard through the grapevine that Lorenzo ended up following his dream and became an Information Technology mogul by developing applications and selling them for a profit, even taking his company public. He and his father never really made amends before his father's tragic death.

"Wow, even distressed, Lorenzo really looks great, and not like the pudgy young man who started out in medical school with us," I whispered as Weston shrugged his shoulders. He was lean in a tailored suit that fit him just right, and his acne had cleared up. Lorenzo and Luke had been really close. Even after I moved away, I recall he even tried to get Luke to get his stuff together long enough so he could help him get established in his company. I can hear Luke saying, "Ro, Lorenzo is going to get me into the game. This is going to be my big break!"

And truth be told, I am not sure what Luke meant by "the game" or whatever happened to that notion. Nor did I ever ask.

Minister Brown attempted to speak over Lorenzo's crying as he walked forward, but his severely distraught wails drowned him out. He seemed to be taking Luke's passing harder than any of us, which was quite bizarre. And out of the blue, Lorenzo made his way to the front of the tent near the casket. It seemed really odd and out of character for him to be proceeding in this manner, but he did, and we all just watched in disbelief.

"Girl, where in the hell is he going?" the lady in front of me said under her breath.

"I don't know, child, but he needs to sit down so we can get on with this," another replied.

"Girl, you know when Elizabeth finally found Luke, it had been at least forty-eight hours since she last saw him alive," a different lady behind us said, and

Weston and I both turned our heads to discreetly ear-hustle.

"What, girl?"

"Yes, honey. We all know he was a troubled man with a checkered existence, who was loved by some and tolerated by most."

"Good Lord, you know that's right. He still owed me close to a grand!"

"Shh, girl — whisper. But yes, Mrs. Elizabeth found him burnt beyond recognition. His body was hanging from the tree behind their house!"

"Say what?"

"Yes, girl. It was the tree that they cherished in the backyard of the family home. Girl, I was the one who got home in time enough so that damn fire did not burn down our whole neighborhood. Yes, I called for the fire trucks and saw when they cut his charred body down from the tree."

"Girl, this is too much!"

Weston and I could not believe what we were hearing.

Luke, appearing to be the stain on the fabric of so many lives, had now been blotted out.

Lorenzo continued to cry out, and he was consoled and encouraged to quiet down by someone who appeared to be his younger brother or a man who was related to him.

"I think that is Lorenzo's brother with him," I leaned in to tell Weston.

I had not seen him since he was a little kid. He was about ten years younger than Lorenzo.

"Lorenzo, you are going to be alright, bro!" he stated as he rubbed his back, and they stood next to where Mrs. Elizabeth was seated. Mrs. Elizabeth's eyes rose out of her handkerchief, and she zeroed in on Lorenzo. She quickly stood, slowly pulled her hand back and slapped Lorenzo across the face.

"How dare you disrespect me and my family by showing up here! I can't believe you ….you son of a bitch!" Mrs. Elizabeth stood at attention and squared up on Lorenzo like she was a heavy weight champ as she stated the harshest words I had ever heard her use out loud.

Busy grabbed her grandmother's arm and said, "Grandma, stop! Just stop! You acting this way is not going to bring Uncle Luke back!"

Mrs. Elizabeth did not stop there. She pushed Busy back into her seat.

"Grandma's got this!"

As the commotion was occurring, Weston put his arm in front of me to shield me from the brawl happening inches away.

"What the hell is going on?" He whispered to me. Unfortunately, I had no clue.

As she proceeded to grab the slumped-over Lorenzo by the lapel of his fine, pinstriped imported Italian suit, she drew back her hand again, clenched her fist, and punched him in the face, sending him down to the ground. The crowd gasped in unison. Minister Brown jumped back from the commotion, holding his Bible.

"Now, now! We are not going to have this here! Come on people!" he commanded to Mrs. Elizabeth, trying to regain the order that had been disrupted.

The funeral-home attendants and nearby family members were able to pry Mrs. Elizabeth's hands from around Lorenzo's neck. Lorenzo stood straight up, with blood streaming down from his nose, and grabbed for his pocket square, trying to cup the blood from staining his fine threads. Big tears welled up in Busy's horrified brown eyes as she cried, embraced her grandma's full waist tightly, and hung on for dear life.

"Busy, it's going be alright, baby," Mrs. Elizabeth said as she wrapped her hand around her shoulders, while two big men dressed in suits who appeared to be funeral attendants grabbed Lorenzo and his brother and escorted them from the graveside into a black town car.

"Come on, Grandma. Sit down please!" Busy begged.

"I didn't know that Mrs. Elizabeth had all that in her," Weston said as he and I looked at each other in disbelief. All of the funeral attendees were taken aback at what we had just witnessed. We had gone from prayer and consecrating Luke to the earth, to an outright battle.

In between crying and clutching my pearls, I was trying to figure it all out. "What in the world just happened?" I said, as I bowed my head and said a silent prayer to myself asking God for clarity about what was going on with this family and asking Him to please allow us to bury my dear friend in serenity,

Lord, please bring peace in this moment, for Luke's sake.

The clouds opened up a little, and the sun peeked through. Many of the funeral-goers looked up, wiped their eyes, and smiled a little as that touch of sun began to warm our spirits. The atmosphere had become peaceful despite the angst in the air.

"Okay, let's try this again. Mrs. Elizabeth, are you good?" asked Minister Brown, looking at her as she straightened her wig and dusted off her clothes while her relatives were ushering her back to her seat.

"Come on, Liz. Sit down so we can get this over with," a relative beside her said. Busy gave a half smile while stroking her grandma's powerful arm.

We all heard Mrs. Elizabeth mumbling some words while Minister Brown held up the ceremony so she could get herself together.

"What is she saying, girl?" the lady in front of us said to the lady in her row.

"Chile, she is ranting about the Ernesto family and how they think they run this city. And got Luke all up into some stuff."

"What? This is better than reality TV."

"Excuse me, ladies. Minister Brown is trying to get everyone's attention!" I said as I tapped them on the shoulder and they turned around and looked at me sideways. Weston nudged me in an effort to get me to mind my own business. The graveside service had turned into an outright debacle, just a hot damn mess. We needed to hurry this along. I was ready to get out of there.

Minister Brown refused to proceed with the ceremony until he got a sign directly from Mrs. Elizabeth herself that she was done with her foolishness. He paused with the Bible at his side and looked at her square on. A male family member handed her a handkerchief. She wiped her full, round face and said in a loud, boisterous tone,

"I'm good, Reverend. You can proceed!" Mrs. Elizabeth patted the back of her wig, sucked her teeth, and looked around at the funeral-goers, winking her right eye.

Minister Brown took a deep breath and went on to say, "Lord, there are many questions that we have, that you and only you know the answers to. We surrender everything to you. Please be a comfort to the Armstrong family as we surrender our brother and your son, Luke Armstrong, back to your loving arms."

Minister Brown concluded while glancing over at Mrs. Elizabeth, shaking his head and picking up another handful of dirt from the ground. He sprinkled it over the casket, reciting the standard "Ashes to ashes and dust to dust" monologue that most ministers conclude with at the graveside service.

Those final words seem to redirect attention back to the real reason we were here — to honor Luke.

The funeral attendants began to signal and guide the funeral attendees to walk by the family and friends to say their condolences and pay their last respects to Luke.

Mrs. Elizabeth was now seated again peacefully in the front row, with Busy by her side. As the people filed by to hug and greet the mourning family, Busy got a little restless and wandered off with some of her cousins, skipping around the cemetery, playing tag amongst the gravestones of souls who had been laid to rest.

"Shouldn't somebody tell those kids to sit down?" I said to Weston.

"Not your business, babe. Let it go," he replied.

Mourners passed by to console Mrs. Elizabeth. She looked around to see where Busy had wandered off.

"Where is that child? Oh, there she is. Busy — settle down now!" she said while hugging those who stopped to show condolence.

"Yes, Grandma," Busy replied, as she stopped running, straightened her dress, and dusted off her black-leather ballet slippers, waving to her friends from her Sunday school class who had come to the funeral with their parents.

When it was our turn to walk to the front and pass by the coffin to give our condolences, Mrs. Elizabeth's and my eyes locked when she saw me, and she started to laugh out loud,

"Sparrow — there's my girl! I knew you would get here!" She reached for me, and I bent down to where she was sitting; she stroked my cheeks with her full hands.

"Yes, ma'am. I would not have missed it for the world!"

She hugged my neck for dear life. Being that close to her, as she talked, I smelled a hint of alcohol on her breath. Then she whispered in my face,

"Sparrow, baby it is so good to see you. You are Luke's true friend. Scrap that — you are Luke's sister, since Lucinda passed away. I need you to look into something for me about Luke and what happened to him before you leave. Please, baby — something is just not right. And I know deep down that Lorenzo had something to do with this. Them damn Ernesto's!" Mrs. Elizabeth said with intensity.

I was shocked, and I was sure it was all visible in my facial expression. She reached up to my cheek with her right hand and then let go of the embrace. I stood up and looked down into her eyes, nodded, and said, "I will help you in any way I can."

Her eyes had puffy bags beneath them; they were tired and worried. I knew something had happened, and I needed to help her figure out what it was. I walked away, and I heard Mrs. Elizabeth yell out to me, as other mourners attempted to hug her,

"Sparrow, baby — I'm counting on you!"

I nodded again.

"What was that all about?" Weston asked as we walked back to the car. I felt a pull on my hand from behind. It was Busy.

"Aunt Ro, Uncle Luke is gone. Grandma is not happy about it at all. Will you come by the house before you leave? I've missed you reading me stories," Busy said as she bounced up and down, eager for me to give a reply.

That statement tugged at my heartstrings. I didn't realize she remembered me so vividly. It had been years since I had seen her in person. However, Luke would Face Time me, and I'd read her several of her favorite bedtime stories throughout the years. She loved anything pertaining being a princess. I knelt down and said,

"Your Uncle Luke is always with you, sweetie. And I will always be here for you, too. Let me check with Uncle Weston, and we'll see about coming by before we head back to the airport," I replied.

At my reply, Busy eagerly clapped her little hands, smiled, and ran off, skipping, to get back over to her grandmother before she got into trouble.

Oh, no, I thought. *Those words just came out of my mouth.* I couldn't say "No" to her — she had suffered so much loss. *What have I just committed to?* I really just wanted to go to the hotel and unwind before flying back and getting the heck out of there. Even though this was where my roots were, I needed to get back to my world. I felt a little selfish thinking that, but the truth is the truth.

However, the question lingered. *What happened to my best friend, Luke?* I thought as I bit my lip and shook my head. I needed to find out what Mrs. Elizabeth was talking about. What could make her think Lorenzo — or any of the Ernesto's, for that matter — would have anything to do with Luke's death?

I saw Weston walking ahead of me, as I had been distracted by Busy. Now he and Marcus were waiting for me at the town car. I took a quick moment to look back toward the gravesite canopy, which was now empty. The only things there were empty seats in front of Luke's casket. This was surreal. I was frozen as I watched the caretakers began to lower Luke's casket into the ground. The finality of the moment was here. I felt paralyzed. All of my tears were dried up. The questions surrounding Luke's death from Mrs. Elizabeth's mouth echoed in my brain.

I would never hear Luke's big laugh or have my BFF to talk to about my day or ask me for money. I had taken all of this for granted, and now he was gone. In a brief moment, I realized I was not the friend I thought I was. Something had obviously happened to him, and it was not like me not to know what was going on with Luke. But that was a decision I'd made, and I would have to live with it for the rest of my life. Could I ever forgive myself? And more importantly, could God ever forgive me?

I looked down, and as Luke's casket settled into the ground, I said, "Luke — it's me, Ro. Sit in peace at the water's edge, my friend. If there are any unanswered questions about what happened to you, don't you worry, I will find the answers. I promise!" I grabbed a red rose from one of the bouquets at the site, kissed the rose, and tossed it onto the casket as I hung my head.

"Sparrow! Come on, babe!" Weston beckoned outside of the town car.

Chapter 9

I got into the car, and I felt a buzzing in my clutch purse. I grabbed my phone and there was an alert: I had a missed call and a text. The text read, “Sparrow, this is Tabitha. Call me when you get settled from the funeral. I know you’re not going to like this, but can you stay in town for an extra couple of days? I am lining up a huge opportunity for you while you are there.”

I turned my phone toward Weston and showed him the message. We both shook our heads.

“Damn, doesn’t she get it that I just buried my best friend? She’s always on the grind, and I’m not in the mood for that shit right now!”

“Do what you got to do, babe. I got little Weston. You take care of business. There’s nothing you can do for Luke right now. He is gone, babe. He’s gone.”

Being back home somehow always sucked the life out of me. Ever since we’d been able to set our parents up in condos on the coast, I did not come back this way unless I absolutely had to. It never failed — being back here longer than I was supposed to always resulted in me getting caught up in mess, and now, with Luke gone, I really had no need to come back here. Just as I mentally convinced myself not to stay, the phone rang, and this call could not wait until later.

I answered the phone and put the phone on speaker. "Tabitha, what's going on? I am still at the gravesite in the town car."

"I know this is a difficult time for you, so I won't even ask how you're doing. However, I have some unbelievable news. There is an interview that you've wanted to do with Abigail Lancaster. She just called me personally to request having you on her radio show Tuesday of this week. She will be doing it out of her main studio, which happens to be in your hometown. Can you believe it? The timing may not be the best, but can you stay on a little longer in the city to do the interview?"

"I don't know, Tabitha. Truth be told, I am ready to get the hell out of here. I need time to absorb what happened. I need to regroup, get myself together, and get back to work," I remarked.

"Ro, Abigail Lancaster was a difficult interview to get, girl! She was on our vision board, remember?"

Abigail Lancaster was one of the top book reviewers in the country. If this woman liked a book, it was guaranteed to ride the best-seller's list, not just make the cut. The publishing world called it the Lancaster Effect. In any ordinary circumstances, this would make any new — or seasoned — writer salivate. But at the moment, I was not myself; my head was not right. My game face definitely was not on, because I was mourning Luke and had just seen him being lowered into the ground.

"Girl, I can't get myself together in forty-eight hours and prepared to face Abigail Lancaster. You are asking me to go into the lion's den sleep deprived and malnourished. I'm sitting in the back of this car at the gravesite bawling my eyes out. Is it possible to reschedule, Tabitha?"

"Sparrow, I hear you. Just step back a minute and reflect. I want you to think back to what you told that college literature class you gave the motivational speech to about a month ago. Remember, you told them, 'Always be ready. If you are always ready, your opportunities will find you.' Remember that?"

"I remember," I said in a somber tone.

"Ro, this is what you and I have been praying for, and I know for a fact this is from the divine. Now, I am changing your flight arrangements and will extend your hotel accommodations. Have Weston call me to let me know what his plans are. I will call you later to confirm everything." The call disconnected. In her own way, Tabitha managed me, like she was supposed to.

I looked at Weston, and he wiped the tears streaming down my face with his handkerchief.

"Baby, she's right. You have worked really hard on this and sacrificed way too much not to seize every opportunity God is affording you right now. This is your season — and I know the timing is not the best to do this — but trust in God's will for you, and know that I have your back. My job is to get rid of any distractions in your way. Sparrow, my love, you are ready for this! Now, text Tabitha and let her know you will be doing that interview.

"I'm going to head back home to take care of the baby. Besides, you need to check on Busy and Mrs. Elizabeth to make sure they are straight. I'm moving some money right now, so you can help them out because you know they need it. In the midst of all this external turmoil, do not forget who you are and what divine purpose you are called to!" Weston stated as he hugged me close and massaged my back.

I smelled his cologne, and I felt at ease. *Man, I love this man,* I thought. *He is so supportive and everything I need at every moment.* I grabbed my phone and texted Tabitha to let her know my plans.

She responded, "I am making the arrangements as we speak! I will email you the itinerary."

"Marcus, go ahead and follow the procession of cars headed back to Luke's house!" Weston instructed our driver. Marcus nodded, put the car in drive, and waited in the car line leaving the gravesite.

"But, Weston — I thought we were going to the hotel. Sweetheart, I'm so tired. I need a shower and down time to collect myself, my thoughts, and put into perspective all of these recent events. I have to get ready for the interview in less than forty-eight hours," I said.

"Listen, I heard you when you told Busy we would come by the house for the repast. Besides, I need to figure out what Mrs. Elizabeth wants to talk to you about. I need to make sure you are safe and secure before I get on that plane. Ro — you understand?"

"Yes, babe. I hear you. But Mrs. Elizabeth was drunk at her own grandson's funeral — and commence to give a ass whipping at the graveside. Who does that? I don't have any time for this!" I replied.

"Ro, whether you want to own up to it or not, these are your people! You can't cancel them out of your life just because all is going well on your end and theirs is not — they need you. Besides, drunk or not, I don't know a whole lot about her, but I know enough about Mrs. Elizabeth to see it was out of character for her to sucker punch that dude. We need to find out what is going on," Weston said.

"Marcus, the procession is leaving." I said, as he appeared to be on the phone, not paying attention.

"Yes, ma'am" he said as he put his phone down in the console, sucked his teeth, put the car in drive, and followed the other cars going to the repast with their headlights on. "Yes, ma'am. I got it, Mrs. Sparrow. You and big man just sit back and relax. I have the address and directions. We should be there in about 30 minutes. I have your dark liquor in the cabinet back there. Pour yourself a drink, and sit back. You've had a long day. You and the mister relax and enjoy the ride."

"Marcus, I'm trying to cut back, but you're making it mighty hard," I replied, as I wiped my tears, which continued to flow as I thought of the horrific way Luke had died. Imagining his body burned beyond recognition hanging from their backyard tree disturbed my soul.

With my clutch in my lap, I looked over the beverages Marcus suggested and licked my lips. I wiped my eyes and said to myself,

Should I? I declined. I did not need alcohol adding to the confusion. I reached into my purse, and the first thing I felt was the plastic bag Dean Baby had put my necklace into. *Damn — I can't look at this right now.* It was the necklace Luke had given me. I could not bear to pull it out — maybe later. Right now, I was tired of crying, and I knew that, if I saw it, especially at this time, the floodgates would open up again. I pushed it deeper into the bottom of my clutch, grabbed my compact and lip stain, and pulled myself together. Weston patted my leg to encourage me, poured himself a glass, and took a sip.

"Babe, you sure you don't want a little?"

"No, I don't think it is a good idea. I don't need anything clouding my judgment right now."

We arrived at Luke's family home. Marcus opened the door, and, as we got out of the car, I put my right hand up with the "number one" gesture.

"Only one hour!" I said, signaling to Weston and Marcus,

"Okay, one hour," my husband agreed, and Marcus tipped his hat in silent consensus.

"Baby, I'll meet you on the porch. I'm going to finish this corner of my drink."

I began walking up the cracked walkway toward the front door. Although Luke, Mrs. Elizabeth, and Busy had moved here about four years ago, I had not been physically at this residence since we brought Busy home from the hospital. It seemed strange on my part, since I'd always played the role of supportive friend.

For this address, I have paid many a monthly mortgage and utility bills. Wow — this house has really become run down since the last time I was here, I thought, while trying not to trip on the uneven walkway. Weston saw me trying not to fall in my stilettos. He handed Marcus his glass and rushed to me.

"Babe, wait — don't fall. Here, hold onto my arm."

I grabbed his arm, and, when we got to the porch, I rang the doorbell and waited while Weston went back and finished his beverage. I heard the hustle and bustle of bodies in the house talking and laughing, but no one opened the door.

"I probably should have a key of my own," I chuckled to myself as I beat on the door.

Mrs. Elizabeth is probably making me wait on this porch because I would not give Luke money to pay her bookie three months ago. I was tired of being used and taken for granted by this family. I'd had enough, and I was hoping that this was not one of Mrs. Elizabeth's ploys — to get me here to ask for more money on the light bill or to put on her books.

"When are you coming to visit?" Luke had asked for the last several years, but I'd been too busy. I had too much going on to attend to Luke and all of the bullshit that surrounded him and his family.

"When I get an invitation!" I would playfully remark, to avoid making him feel bad. Our relationship had not been the same in years for a multitude of reasons.

While waiting for the door to be answered, I looked toward the car. Marcus remarked, "Dr. Mack, I'll be out here waiting for you and Mr. Mack. So, take your time." He reached into his pocket and grabbed a pack of Kool's before taking off his hat. He leaned up against the black town car, pulled a loosey from the pack and lit his cigarette. Weston was walking up the jagged walkway with his cell phone to his ear.

"Babe, did you ring the doorbell?"

"Yes. I even beat on the door."

While waiting on the porch for someone to answer, I looked around the outside of the house and saw how the wear and tear had taken its toll. The paint was severely chipped, and the shutters looked like they were going to fall off the house — as a matter of fact, one had fallen off. Someone had placed it against the rotting exterior of the house. As I rang the doorbell again, I if anyone could hear it over all the talking. I beat on the door again. Then I got a ping on my phone from a social media memory. I checked it out, and there was a picture of Luke and me. I was pregnant and big as a house. Luke was rubbing my belly and giving a "thumbs up." Luke looked weary but happy in that moment. I smiled as I reflected.

"Busy, get the door, sweetie!" A voice yelled from inside. I heard someone running toward the door, and it opened. There was Busy, with a beautiful glow around her as the smell of fried chicken and collard greens hit me in the face and filled my nostrils.

"Aunt Sparrow!" Busy said as she stood on her tiptoes to reach up and hug my waist.

"Hi, baby. It's so good to see my girl! I love your dress."

In the doorway, Busy twirled making the dress lift like a blossoming flower. I loved every second of it. "Come on in, Auntie Ro and Uncle Weston! Grandma has been looking for y'all!" Busy had already changed her clothes from the funeral black lace dress with black patent-leather shoes to a beautiful pink linen dress with matching frilly socks and white patent-leather shoes. Her embrace and smile were a breath of fresh air from the darkness of the day. Her coarse brunette ringlets bounced as she pulled away from hugging me and excitedly jumped up and down. "I'm going to take you to the kitchen. Grandma is in there," she said, smiling from ear to ear.

Busy had gotten so tall. She began to talk nonstop, as Weston tagged behind, eventually ending up in the single-car garage with the menfolk, who were seated on fold-up chairs at a wooden table, drinking out of red plastic cups and slapping dominos hard on the table.

Busy showed me this and that around the house as she grabbed my hand and guided me through the people sitting, standing, talking, and holding their plates full of fried chicken, ham, shaved turkey, dressing, greens, deviled eggs, and Mrs. Elizabeth's specialty — baked five-cheese macaroni. Mrs. Elizabeth may not have been the most stable and loving grandma, but one thing I can say about this woman was that she could throw down in the kitchen. She was originally from the South and was known for her cooking when she was not drunk or in the casino gambling all of their money away. This is what I wish Luke could have had more of on a regular basis — home cooking, nurturing, love, and, most of all, stability. I was hoping that Mrs. Elizabeth had calmed down some from the way she'd acted at the gravesite.

My stomach began to seriously growl from all of the aromas I was taking in as I was being stopped on the way to the kitchen to hug and give condolences to family members in the living room.

Wow, I forgot about all of these pictures. I looked around the living-room walls. It was like a museum. There were pictures of Luke, Lucinda, Busy, and the elders in the family. *I can't believe Mrs. Elizabeth has all of these pictures. They are bringing back so many memories*. There were even a couple of me and my family scattered in the mix of memories. In the hallway, there was a table holding a crystal candy jar that was almost empty. Multicolored hard candy stuck to the bottom of the glass. There was mail scattered around it. There was one particular picture that caught my eye — of Luke in the maternity ward in a gown, holding Busy as an infant. Seeing that picture made my knees almost buckle.

That picture had been taken five years ago. My mind went back to that moment in the picture, when I was seeing patients in my clinic after Weston and I had moved away. I felt the cell phone in my white coat pocket ring. In clinic, I always had it on vibrate mode so that my husband could reach me if he needed to and not interrupt the patient-physician interaction.

I guess that, on the particular day in my memory, I'd forgotten to put it on vibrate so I quickly put it on silent. I took a seat in my office, grabbed an apple, and relaxed my legs before the next round of treating back-to-back upper-respiratory infections, bronchitis, and other acute-care health issues. I was the doctor assigned to walk in clinic today. I remembered I was exhausted; because the baby decided he didn't want to sleep the night before. I was up with him every hour on the hour, and Weston was on the east coast for work. I dared not to close my eyes, but I did, briefly.

Just then, my nurse knocked on the door. "Dr. Mack, I have your next patient ready."

That was my cue. I finished my apple, tossed the core in the trashcan, and went to the sink to wash my hands. My cell phone started to vibrate again. I looked at the number; it was not one I recognized, but answered anyway.

"Hello. This is Dr. Mack," I said, as I stood in the hall.

"You're going to be an Auntie!" It was Luke.

“What?” I said. “Are you kidding me? You and Rachel are going to finally settle down?” I did my jump-for-joy dance in place. “Oh, my goodness. How far along is she and what phone number is this? You got a new phone?” I remarked.

“Ro, it’s a long story. And it is not Rachel who is still very much banished to ex-ville. We’re officially over. It’s Lucinda. She is at the end of her first trimester. She didn’t want to tell anyone until now, just to make sure everything was okay with her and the baby,” Luke said.

“I’m so happy for you and your family. What happened with Rachel? I really liked her. I thought she was good for you. You know what? Never mind — I probably don’t want to know. I just need to know you’re okay. Did you get the money I wired you?

“Yes, Ro. I’m going to get that back to you. I promise. I know I must do better,” he said in a solemn voice.

With a stern eye, my nurse peeked around the corner.

“Dr. Mack, room 100.”

“Luke, I have to go. I’ll call you tonight. Is this the right number to call you back? Remember, this is my late night, but as soon as I get off, I will give you a ring. Cool?"

"Cool. How's my nephew?

"He's good. Getting big. I'll send you some updated pics. I've got to go."

"Thanks again, Ro," Luke said as he hung up the phone.

The remainder of the day was long. I remember I was super exhausted when I got off work. I remembered that day all too well. I had to ship two chest pains to the emergency room, among many other urgent-care similar issues. I got home and fed, bathed, and put the baby to bed. I talked to my husband and heard him recap his day with highlights of his executive meetings before wishing him goodnight. After I fed myself, showered, and got into my pajamas, I called Luke.

Just like we always did, we stayed up until 3 a.m. We talked and laughed about some of everything and a little bit of nothing — but mostly of the excitement and anticipation of Luke being an uncle and me an extended auntie. I had remembered Lucinda being pregnant before, but that was during a time when Luke and I had lost touch, and I never saw a baby, so I did not ask about it. It was not my place. We had shared all of our firsts together, and now this. He was so excited, as if *he* were having the baby.

Luke suffered from a severe illness when he was an infant, and doctors had informed him that his chances of having kids of his own someday were slim to none. When his sister found out she was pregnant, Luke thought of it as if *he* were having a baby. He could rarely keep a steady girlfriend. His own personal demons caused some really great ladies to walk out of his life. "It's going to be a girl!" he said exuberantly. "I wanted to name her 'Sparrow,' but Lucinda wasn't having it! No shade to you, Ro. But, sis keeps saying the baby is moving around so much in her belly. Girl, that baby is on a mission!" Luke said.

"As long as the baby is healthy, that's all that matters — right? Next time I see Lucinda, I'm going to get her for throwing shade on my name!" We laughed. "No, really, I'll plan some time to get up there so we can go shopping!" I was so excited.

From that night on, we would chat daily until the wee hours in the morning about the baby this and baby that. Baby clothes, the baby's room, baby, baby, baby while I was holding *my* baby, little Weston, trying to whisper while rocking him to sleep. There was such great joy. It was like the anticipation of the new arrival gave Luke a reason to get his stuff together. He had held a steady job consistently for three months, which was huge for him. He'd also cut back on staying out late, smoking weed, and drinking. He'd even started going to church. Minister Brown even tried to start mentoring him. As friends, you work up to these moments to be able to celebrate each other's successes and live through challenging moments. I had seen plenty of them with Luke, so I was excited. This appeared to be a good time in his life.

About six months later, while at work, I received an urgent message that was difficult to understand on my cell phone voicemail. It was Lucinda, Luke's sister. She was sobbing throughout the entire message. It was hard to make out what she was saying but something was wrong with the baby.

I frantically tried to call her back, and it was Luke who answered the phone. His voice was heavy with depression.

"Luke, what's going on?"

Whispering, he said, "Ro, let me call you when we get to the car; we're checking out of the doctor's office now. Lucinda is being sent over by ambulance to have emergency surgery. I have to call you back."

"No, Luke, you are going to tell me right now what's going on with Lucinda's pregnancy."

"Ro, it's not the baby. It's Lucinda. Dr. Ernesto just did an ultrasound in his office to check on the baby. He discovered a mass in Lucinda's abdomen right next to the fetus. Dr. Ernesto is going to do the biopsy and possibly remove the tumor. He is working with the OB/Gyn to make sure the surgery is set up. Just pray, Ro — please pray. Momma is in the car with her prayer cloth and anointing oil; she's calling Minister Brown to activate the prayer chain."

"Luke, are you sure it's not a fibroid? They are very common and can grow with pregnancy due to the hormone changes."

"Sparrow, Dr. Ernesto said it is very serious and she needs a biopsy right away."

For some reason, at that point, I thought to myself, *How is the baby's father going to feel about this?* Luke's sister was not married, and no ideas about the father had ever crossed my mind or even been discussed until now.

"Just try to calm down, and keep me posted. Hopefully it's just a fibroid. They can complicate pregnancies, but women deliver healthy babies with them every day."

Just the thought that this could be serious made me a little sick to my stomach. I felt horrible for Luke and Lucinda. They had endured ongoing tragedy after ongoing tragedy in their family. If there were going to be tests, trials, and just plain bad luck, you know they were going to fall on Luke and the Armstrong family.

Damn, I wish I could be there for him, I thought, but I was at work.

It was the longest sixty minutes.

The phone rang when I was taking my lunch break. Luke was upset. All he did was cry and wail in shock and disbelief.

"Okay. Breathe, Luke. What is it?"

I heard him trying to relax, and breathe, but he was finding it difficult. Before I knew what was going on, I began to prophetically speak over the lives of Luke, Lucinda, and the baby.

"You know God is a mighty God. And he would never fail you. He will keep you and protect your sister and baby. Now, tell me what's going on."

In times of trouble, I always tended to reach back to my core; my spiritual roots. I had not been to church in a while, but the truth of God is instilled in your bones when you know who God is and what He can do.

Luke was quiet.

"Luke, what's wrong?" I raised my voice a little.

"We've just arrived at the hospital; we followed behind the ambulance. They just wheeled Lucinda back to the operating room. My sister has an aggressive cancer that must be removed! All I can think about is losing my sister and the baby."

"What kind of cancer? Uterine? Ovarian? I need details."

"Well, you'd have to talk to Dr. Ernesto."

"I can't talk to him without Lucinda's permission. Will she agree to that?"

"Ro, you know you're just like family. I'm sure she would have no problem with that. When she gets out of surgery, I'll ask her."

Without having all of the details, the situation sounded very concerning.

"I'm so sorry, my friend. I don't know everything that's going on with Lucinda or the baby. But let me tell you what I do know. They both are going to be fine and surrounded with love. I want you to rest in that."

"Thanks, Ro. I'll call you when I get more news."

"Here — let me have the phone, Luke," I heard Mrs. Elizabeth say in the background.

Mrs. Elizabeth voice came in loud and clear. "Ro, they told us this procedure was very risky and that Lucinda might not make it. Is that true, Ro? You're a doctor. You should know."

I thought, *Wow — this is a different story than what I was hearing from Luke.* However, I still wanted to be encouraging,

"Mrs. Elizabeth, God has the final say. And Lucinda has always been a fighter. She's tough as nails; she has Armstrong blood running through her veins. You know she's not going to give up. I'll keep my cell phone on. You all keep me posted."

"Yes, baby. I will," Mrs. Elizabeth said right before hanging up.

"God, please let that baby make it," I prayed; as I went on to finish seeing the remaining few of the afternoon patients. I wrapped up my clinic day and made it home from a long day at work. It had been an exhausting and personally emotional for me. I was worried about my best friend and his family. Weston and I had been texting back and forth, but we hadn't been able to talk because he was locked down in meetings and then flying back from the east coast. His flight would land in an hour, and I knew there was no food in the house. The nanny was home with the baby, so I'd stopped to pick up some Italian takeout — Weston's favorite.

As soon as I walked into the kitchen to put the food down, I could tell the nanny had fed the baby when I saw the baby's dish and spoon in the sink. I could hear her vacuuming upstairs, which meant the baby was still up. I walked in; headed to the butler's pantry, and poured a glass of red wine to go with my Eggplant Parmesan, chopped salad, and garlic bread sticks. I sat down without going upstairs to hug the baby. I was spent. I felt that all of the work I had put into Luke was at risk if the baby didn't make it. I knew that would take him over the edge. I started to eat alone, as I was unsure of the exact time Weston was due to arrive.

The nanny looked over the banister at me and turned off the vacuum.

"Dr. Mack, it's good to see you. Little Weston is playing in the bouncy; he has been fed and bathed. I put up the laundry, and I'm finishing up vacuuming. Are you hungry? I can heat up some leftovers for you."

"Thank you. I'm good; I got takeout. I would really appreciate it if you could watch the baby just a little while longer, Mr. Mack will be coming in from the airport soon to handle things. Feel free to come down and make a plate to take home with you when you leave. There is plenty."

"No, I'm good. I'm meeting some friends for dinner. Thanks for the offer. I have a couple more things I have to get done up here, and then I'll put him to bed and come down."

The garage-door sensor went off; it was Weston. I always loved to see him come through the door, see his eyes, and smell his cologne. I missed him in every way.

"Honey, you are home already?"

"Yes, I took an earlier flight because we finished ahead of schedule. Besides, you sounded like you needed me."

"I do!" He kissed me on the forehead and washed his hands. I fixed him a plate, and we ate.

Dinner was over, and we decided to move to the brown leather couch in front of the fireplace. I poured him a nightcap. Although my eyes were puffy and tired, we needed alone time to chat; the nanny had left, and the baby was fast asleep.

“Ro, baby. What is it? You seem like something is wrong.” Weston asked as he rubbed my thigh and sipped his after-dinner beverage.

“You know the issue I texted you about earlier today? That stuff is still on my mind,” I replied while taking my hair down and massaging my neck.

“You know you can’t take on everybody’s problems, Sparrow! Luke is Luke, and he has his own life. It’s not your life,” Weston replied. He put his drink down and massaged my shoulders.

“Baby, you’re uptight. You’ve got to let that shit go. Once you do that, you will feel a lot better.”

“Babe, what does your schedule look like for the next couple of days?” I asked as I grabbed his hands.

“I’m in town the remainder of the week. That one-day trip on Thursday to the east coast was cancelled because we burned the midnight oil this trip and completed everything we needed to get done. So, legal has some minor addendums to make to the contract, and the merger is ready to close. I won’t have to travel until next quarter. What’s up, babe?”

I began to sob.

"Come on, girl," Weston said as he grabbed my hand and led me to the big picture window next to the baby grand piano where the remaining glimpses of the sunset were visible.

"Look outside at everything that is around you. Babe, we are blessed beyond measure. I'm not going to allow you to stress yourself out behind Luke and his family. That is not going to happen in this house anymore. You wipe your tears, you pray, and let God work! You read all of those devotions every day — put that faith to work!"

I hugged him. Yes, those were the words I needed to hear.

"I hear you loud and clear. But I think I need to be there for them at this time. Besides, you know Luke has always had my back. Or rather, our backs."

"Let's not get into that shit again. We said we would never bring that up!"

"Yes, Weston — we did say we wouldn't bring that up again. But you and I both know that, if that crazy bitch Dana was still around, and Luke had not intervened, we would still be looking over our shoulder at every turn."

"Yes, you're right. But let's let that sleeping dog lie once and for all. Agreed?"

"Agreed. But I'm just saying. Crazy and dysfunctional or not, Luke has always been there for me."

"Okay — I get it. Luke has been a good friend to you. So, tell me again — what happened? It was hard to make it out in the text messages. I thought everything was going well with Lucinda and the baby," he said with a raised eyebrow.

I told him all that I knew, and he understood.

"Now if you feel that you need to go out there, I will make it happen for you. But can I be honest about this?" Weston said after hearing the update.

"Yes, I'm listening," I said then took a deep breath.

"Ro, you have made yourself Luke's only lifeline. But, we — little Weston and I — are your family. You have been Luke's crutch all of his life. You can't save everybody. My job is to protect you, to love you, and to take care of you and our son. You are my wife and Lil Wes's mother. Whatever happens — and I hope and pray that it's all good — but whatever happens, that is part of God's will. You've got to let Luke grow up and live. He has to deal with life just as we all have to! But if you feel like you need to go out there, I will make that happen for you. Now, no talking on the phone tonight, which includes no calls or texting with any more Luke updates! You need some rest!" Weston commanded, and he took my phone, turned it off, and plugged it into the charger.

"Come on," he said as he extended his hand, and we walked upstairs.

He filled the Jacuzzi with lavender bath salts. I soaked, and then I went to bed and slept hard.

When I woke up the next day, I was refreshed and well rested. Weston had already gone to work. I looked in the microwave, and there was scrambled egg whites and turkey bacon that he'd prepared. And I could smell the coffee brewing.

On the counter lay a printed airline ticket for me to go and check on Luke, Lucinda, and the baby. My phone was still plugged into the wall. I turned it on, and alerts started rolling in. The most recent text was from Weston:

"Babe, I called Dr. Perry to cover your clinic today due to a family emergency, and I told him you would return next Tuesday. You have plenty of PTO, so he said not to worry and that he would cover your clinic both days. A car will be coming to take you to the airport. The nanny has taken the baby to Gymboree and I will be home early to relieve her. Love you."

I looked to my right, and there were five one hundred dollar bills stacked by my purse, with a note on a sticky:

Love you, babe. I love and support you. But you can't fix the world. We will be fine. Text me when you land. Love, Weston.

Chapter 10

This picture brings back so many memories. I'm standing here at Luke's repast and looking at the photo, and am reminded of the trip that Weston made possible for me to go back home when I came here to check on Lucinda and the baby. I arrived at the same hospital where I'd trained as a medical student and resident. It appeared a lot smaller than I remembered. This was my old stomping ground. I had many a rotation in this hospital.

I made my way to the surgical ward, where Luke had told me Lucinda was.

"Hello. I'm Dr. Sparrow Mack," I said to the receptionist, who had her head buried in the latest Essence magazine. When she raised her head up, I realized it was Candace. She'd grown her hair out and was hardly recognizable.

"Hey, Candace. It's so good to see you. How are you and your family?"

"Oh, my goodness — Dr. Sparrow. It's so good to see you," she eagerly squealed as she got up from her desk and came around to the front to give me a hug bouncing up and down.

"Man, Candace, you helped us out so much back in the day."

"Yes, those were some good times. But Dr. Ro, you were the coldest resident in the game. You gave them Attending Physicians hell when you could answer all of their questions. I always used to stand back and smile, knowing you'd handle your business."

"Candace, girl, I try my best not to dwell on all I went through as one of the only women on the surgical service trying to compete to prove that I was as talented as my male peers. But you kept me encouraged, and I appreciate that."

"What are you doing here? Please tell me you're coming back to work here!"

"No, I'm married now, a mother, and settled in medical practice. After residency and starting out in the collaborative practice with Dr. Ernesto, once I got married, we moved, and I have not looked back."

"Good for you. I'm so proud of you."

"And back to why I am here: I am looking for my friend, a patient named Lucinda Armstrong. She could be on the surgical or on the obstetrics floor."

"Sure, Dr. Sparrow. Let me check and see where she is for you. Man, we sure miss your smile around this place. You were the bright light at this hospital!"

"Thank you, Candace. I miss all of y'all, too."

"I found her. Oh, no," Candace said with a concerned look on her face.

"What?" I asked as I leaned into the counter.

"She's in ICU, up on the sixth floor! Room 612. I know you know where ICU is."

"Yes, I remember. Thanks, Candace!" I said as I hurried onto the elevator.

"I'm praying that everything will be alright with your friend," Candace yelled out as I got on to the elevator.

It seemed like it took forever to get to my destination. I took the time to text Weston and let him know I had made it to the hospital and that I would reach back out to him as soon as I had any news. I finally reached the sixth floor. When the elevator doors opened, I instantly heard the beeps of all of the heart monitors.

I arrived at room 612 and stood at the door. Luke was standing at Lucinda's bedside, holding her hand, praying, with tears drenching the sheets of her bed. Lucinda was on full life support, and she still had the pregnancy bump. I did not know she had taken this turn.

"*Life support?* What happened, Luke?" I said as I put down my bag and took a seat next to him. He was shaking.

"Ro — oh, my God! It all happened so fast. They went in to get the biopsy of the mass, they got the tissue, and the frozen section confirmed it was cancer, per Dr. Ernesto. He performed the procedure himself. After everything, Lucinda woke up and she wouldn't look at me. All she would say was,

'Baby brother, I have a premonition that I'm never going to see my baby.'

"I told her not to say foolishness like that and tried to reassure her. And Ro, I'm not kidding you. Within an hour, while she was still in recovery, she flat-lined. A full code blue, Ro! It all happened so fast. They put her on life support."

"Luke, I'm so sorry," I said as I embraced his tired body and tried to console him.

"Okay — what are the doctors saying now?" I asked.

"The miracle was that the baby was still healthy, per the tests they did. Ro, I've been up for forty-eight hours talking to Lucinda nonstop, hoping she would open her eyes. Just to let her know that I'm here and that she's going to make it for the baby's sake. But she won't open her eyes, Ro. She won't open them!"

"Where's the doctor?" I asked, as I went over to look at Lucinda, who was intubated and not breathing on her own. She was hooked up to life support.

Before Luke could answer, the vitals monitor started to alarm. Lucinda had flat-lined again. I could have intervened, but the code team rushed into the room and pushed us out into the hallway. They increased the drips, brought the paddles out, and started the code. They got her back. Luke and I were in the holding area when the doctor came out to talk us. It was Lorenzo's father, Dr. Ernesto. Lucinda's obstetrician accompanied him. He hugged me.

"Dr. Sparrow Mack, it's good to see you."

"Good to see you, Enrique."

"Dr. Mack, this is Dr. Linn, Lucinda's OB. We both have been involved in Lucinda's care."

They explained that they needed to take the baby right now and that Lucinda was not going to make it. If they didn't act immediately, the baby could sustain anoxic brain injury and could possibly be in a vegetative state. They had conducted preliminary neurological assessments, and Lucinda appeared to be brain dead.

"What should I do, Ro? Grandma Liz is not answering her phone, and I need her and you to help me make the decision," Luke turned to me and asked.

I attempted to explain in layman's terms what was going on with Lucinda and the baby. Luke was torn about the decision he'd been left to make. He was listed as one of two of Lucinda's power of attorneys for medical decisions. Mrs. Elizabeth had just left the hospital moments before I arrived and wasn't answering her mobile phone or responding to texts. And with Lucinda in this dire state and the baby's life hanging in the balance, Luke couldn't wait another moment to make the decision.

They allowed Luke to go back into the room with his sister one last time. He kissed her cheek, whispered some words in her ear, went over to the right side of her belly, and kissed it. He came out the room like he was ready to fight somebody and signed the paperwork. The operating room staff wheeled Lucinda down the sterile hallway on full life support for an emergency C-section.

Dr. Ernesto and Dr. Linn walked away, and, as they did, Luke yelled out,

"Dr. Ernesto, you'd better take care of my sister this time! I'm serious as shit, man!" he said as he flailed his arms angrily.

Dr. Ernesto gave Luke a look of distain, and Dr. Linn looked really confused as they continued toward the elevator.

"Luke, what's going on? Why are you behaving this way? I know you're upset, but you can't be going around the hospital threatening doctors."

"Ro, you have no idea."

"You're right. I have no idea what you're going through. But what I do know is that you are probably about two seconds from getting security on you. And you do not want that in the midst of Lucinda's fight for her life." Luke's comments and behavior had really perplexed me because we'd just heard that Lucinda was brain dead, so how could Dr. Ernesto "fix her"?

A nurse escorted us from the intensive care unit to the maternity ward. When Mrs. Elizabeth returned from going home to get a quick shower and a change of clothes, she was brought to the maternity waiting area, where they put her in a private room. She fell to the floor when she realized the last kiss on the head she'd given Lucinda would be the last forever.

"Oh, Lord! My child! My child! Why didn't I answer that damn phone?"

We did our best to console her until the doctors came to the waiting area to confirm that Lucinda had officially expired and that the baby, miraculously, was doing extremely well. They were throwing the word miracle around as if on some level the baby wasn't supposed to make it. They allowed the family to see Lucinda a final time before they would take her body to the morgue. It was a shame that such a beautiful spirit was no longer with us. The nurse asked the family if they wanted to see the baby.

"Hell, yeah, I want to see my great-grandbaby," Mrs. Elizabeth, yelled out as she pushed Luke and me out of the way. I could smell alcohol on her breath, and it filled the room. It seemed like she'd gotten more than a shower and a change of clothes when she left the hospital. She got flat-out wasted.

I waited in the hall as Luke and Mrs. Elizabeth said their goodbyes to Lucinda's corpse lying on a steel gurney with a white sheet draped over her body. I was expecting to hear a lot of wailing and crying. However, it was surprisingly peaceful. Through the window in the door, you could see Luke kiss his sister's cheek several times, and Mrs. Elizabeth stroked her grand-daughter's lifeless hand. After about ten minutes, they came out and were very angry. There was a chaplain waiting who attempted to console them and offered to say a prayer, but they declined. Embarrassed, I apologized to the chaplain on their behalf.

A nurse took us to the nursery. We stood behind the glass and looked at all of the beautiful babies. However, the most beautiful one was a little girl with beautiful brown eyes, olive skin, and thick, black, curly hair with big locks. If I had to guess which baby was Lucinda's baby, I would say this one was she. The nurse turned her crib around, and it said "Baby Armstrong." Yep, that was she. The nurse moved her up to the window where we saw the baby squirm and wiggle. When she saw her Uncle Luke through the window, she appeared to smile, with a dimple on her right cheek.

"Wow! Look, Luke — she smiled at you."

All of the anger that was in Luke dissipated when he saw his niece.

"Please follow me. I have prepared a room for you all to see the baby up close," the maternity nurse told us.

We followed her and sat down. The maternity room had an empty bed and two chairs. I stood. The nurse wheeled in the beautiful baby. Her eyes were just like Lucinda's and Luke's — big and chestnut brown. She smiled, moved, and cooed melting all of our hearts.

And then the nurse asked, "Does this child have a father?"

"Hell, yeah, this child has a father! How dare you, lady?" Luke yelled out.

"No, sir. I'm sorry. That came out wrong. I wanted to get the father's name," the nurse apologized, attempting to reconcile her previous statement.

"Just leave it blank. Put my sister's name on it only. Lucinda Marie Armstrong!" Luke commanded.

"Do we need to call the state, or will you be taking the baby?" the nurse asked.

"Yes. This is my niece, and I will be taking the baby. And she will be taken care of," Luke replied in an abrupt tone.

"Sir, would you like to hold her?" the nurse asked.

"Yes — bring her to me."

"Would you like me to gown you first?" the nurse insisted.

"Hand me the gown and I'll put it on," Luke responded.

Luke sat down, and the precious baby girl was placed in his arms. The scene appeared so natural. She smiled and appeared to dance in Luke's arms. She was such a beautiful, happy baby, who had absolutely no clue of the circumstances of her birth. I grabbed my phone and took a picture to mark this momentous occasion.

Mrs. Elizabeth sat quietly in the corner, seemingly tired from the day's events or with intoxication as she nodded off in the chair without even taking a closer glimpse of her newborn great-grandchild. The nurse then placed on the table a form on which Luke was to place the name of the baby. He looked over to me and said, "I'm going to name her 'Busy'!"

"'Busy'? Now, wait a minute, Luke. You'd better think about that. This child has to live with that name all of her life," I replied.

"I know, and that is her name. I think that would have made Lucinda giggle. So that's what I'm going to name her. Hand me that paper and that pen. I hear Lucinda laughing right now."

"Are you sure Lucinda didn't have another name picked out?" I asked.

"Nurse, give me that pen!" And just as quickly as Luke said it, it was so.

Her name was "Busy."

"Yes, that's right — 'Busy Lucinda Marie Armstrong,' after my sister, her mother who died trying to bring life into the world." Luke said as he wrote on the birth certificate.

With the mood in the room, I dared not ask about the father of the beautiful baby. I figured Luke would disclose this when he felt good and ready.

For the first time in weeks, I felt Luke was going to be okay. It was different now. He had something to hold on to even with Lucinda gone. I felt that deep in my soul. We had a "fwrin" connection that could not be explained. You know — friends so close they could be twins. I looked at him as he rocked his niece in the chair and knew in the long run everything was going to be okay. I took a picture with my cell phone to capture the moment. I was sure he would cherish the time he'd first met his niece for the rest of his life.

The baby was discharged, which was a miracle in itself. After arriving at Luke's home and walking through the house to get the baby situated in her crib, it was evident this house was not baby ready. Lucinda had not prepared appropriately in anticipation of her new arrival. I decided to take my rental car to do some shopping. I bought diapers, bottles, newborn-baby clothes, and infant essentials.

When I got back to the house, it was quiet and still. There was Mrs. Elizabeth, seated in the kitchen at the table, getting ready to light a cigarette, eating some peanuts, and drinking a beer.

"Sparrow, is that you?" she said as she shucked the nuts and piled them on a napkin in front of her.

"Yes, ma'am. Where are they? Where are Luke and the baby?" I whispered to Mrs. Elizabeth, just in case the baby was sleeping. She pointed up the stairs without skipping a beat, going hard on her peanuts and popping them in her mouth between swigs from the aluminum can.

"I picked up a few groceries to take care of us eating tonight and a lot of items for Busy — bottles and what not. Let me check on them, and I'll come back down to check on you and put the groceries up."

Mrs. Elizabeth could not come up for air from going in on those peanuts and beer and said not a word.

That was my cue to go on upstairs. I looked in the first room on the right, which appeared to be the master bedroom, possibly Mrs. Elizabeth's room. No sign of Luke. I felt like I was going through a maze of narrow hallways and clutter. There was no sign of Luke, and I didn't want to call out his name. Busy needed her newborn rest.

And where was Luke? It was as if he'd disappeared with the baby. At the end of the hallway was what I thought was Lucinda's room. There was a bed and a crib, and that was all. Rays of sunlight beamed across the dim room onto the empty crib. I stood at the door and scanned the area; there were boxes everywhere.

There was Luke, sitting in the rocker next to the window. His head was turned toward the view outside, and he was rocking and holding Busy, who was fast, asleep, sucking on the pacifier she'd come home with from the hospital. I couldn't tell if Luke was asleep or awake; he wasn't moving. I whispered again, knelt beside him, and lightly touched his shoulder.

He turned toward me. His eyes were now swollen with despair from crying.
"Hey, I'm just sitting here rocking the baby and looking out at Lucinda's tree. As beautiful as this all is, it's also sad. Will Busy ever know how breath taking her mother was?" he said, in a faint whisper.

"The baby is asleep. Let me put her in the crib." I gently grabbed Busy from Luke's arms and cradled her.

"She is absolutely stunning, Luke. She looks just like Lucinda." As I placed Busy in her crib, I whispered to Luke, "This baby will be surrounded with love, regardless. We all will make sure the baby has what she needs. We're going to be just fine. And yes, we will make sure Busy knows how beautiful her mother was."

A small smile appeared from the corners of his mouth, and I hugged him.

"Whew, brother! When was the last time you showered? We looked at each other and softly chuckled.

"Luke, you go take care of that smell right now, and then go downstairs and put up those groceries I have on the counter. I will get some work done in Busy's room before she wakes. I'll work on getting things organized," I said, as Luke rose slowly from the rocker and walked toward the door of the room to leave. Before leaving me to work, he looked back and said,

"Sparrow, I'm so glad you're here."

"Man, where else would I be?" I replied.

I placed my hands on my hips and looked around in disbelief at the turmoil this house seemed to be in, especially in this beautiful baby's room. Unkempt and drop the mic, is all I have to say about it all.

"This shit is ridiculous! Who lives like this?" I said to myself.

The next couple of days were filled with laundry, cleaning, disinfecting, burping the baby, changing diapers, and trying to map out a schedule and some normalcy for Luke to get started in his new life as a parent. And in true Sparrow fashion, I set up a dry-erase board where I wrote out a schedule Luke and Mrs. Elizabeth could follow to best care for the baby. I knew Mrs. Elizabeth was a good enough grandmother to Luke and Lucinda, and I was sure she would try to take care of Busy, but she struggled with her own demons, she was getting older, and she still drank way too much.

Many a day, when we were children, she'd left Luke and Lucinda to fend for themselves while she went to the casino. On more than one occasion during our childhood, I heard the doorbell during dinnertime. I automatically would go to the kitchen cabinet to get two more plates so Luke and Lucinda could have a hot meal too. My parents were gracious in that way.

I had overheard the social worker talking to them before we left the hospital, and I realized they could not come up with enough money to bury Lucinda. So they signed the paperwork to donate Lucinda's body to the medical school as a cadaver. At the conclusion of the final semester of this year, the medical center would have a proper cremation burial free of charge to the family. And that was their solution for burying Lucinda, which was heartbreaking.

I worked on Busy's nursery until well past midnight, stopping for a brief moment to make a turkey sandwich. Then I got back to organizing her baby items, folding clothes, and getting her diaper-changing table assembled. Wow — I was tired and had to stop and get some rest. Before I left the room and turned on the baby monitor, I peeked in the crib. Busy was positioned correctly and resting quietly, sucking rhythmically on her binky, after she was fed, burped, and bathed. I gave Luke some newborn-baby training before he took the baby monitor into his room and settled in for the evening. Busy now had infant clothes hung up and in the drawers; her onesies were organized by colors, and diapers were fully stocked in her changing table.

I made my way to the guest room, which was filled with boxes. I plopped myself down on the plastic-covered mattress with no bedding. I was too tired to care. I fell fast asleep in the clothes I had worn to the hospital and had worked in all night. In the midst of my exhaustion as I nodded off to sleep, a loud noise woke me. I rolled over, the plastic on the mattress sticking to my sweaty head. I glanced at the clock on the nightstand. It was 3:00 a.m. What was the noise? It was the electric garage door. Abruptly awakened and startled, I got up and locked the door to my room. Soon thereafter I heard footsteps going to the kitchen. Whoever it was appeared to be getting some water, as I heard the faucet turn on. And then they went up to the master bedroom.

I heard some mild mumbling back and forth. It was Luke's voice, getting louder and louder over the whispers of a stranger. I couldn't tell if it was male or female. *I hope they don't wake the baby.* I couldn't make out all of the conversation. It sounded like something hit the door across the hall. Then the door slammed. Next, I heard footsteps shuffling down the short hallway, down the top flight of stairs and then down the second short flight of stairs. Next, there was a sudden *"Plop!"* Then all movement ceased.

I quietly cracked the door to the guest room to peek into the hallway. Still half asleep, I rubbed my eyes to get a visual or audio on what was going on. It was dark, but I could make out that one of the decorative pillows that were on Mrs. Elizabeth's bed was in the hallway on the floor.

I quietly reached down, picked it up, and listened to see if I could hear any stir from Busy. There was not a peep out of her, thank God. I tiptoed back into my room and gently eased the door closed and quietly turned the lock. I put the decorative pillow down on one of the cardboard boxes. I got back into the guest bed and attempted to go back to sleep, but I couldn't. My desire had been broken.

Instead of counting sheep, I counted cardboard boxes around the room. Man, there were so many of them. *What in the world could be in all these boxes?* They were marked with different labels. However, one stood out to me. It was a cardboard box that had "Safe Contents" written on it in permanent black marker. I pondered for a little.

Would those items in the box be "safe" to be around?

Or do the items in this box belong in a "safe"?

Whatever the contents of this box, I did not have the stamina to try to sort it all out. I was deliriously tired from all the day's events. My eyelids got heavy, and I drifted off to a deep sleep, counting boxes.

The next morning, I rolled over and felt a little more refreshed but not fully well rested, like back in the days when I was a resident physician. I sat on the side of the bed and noticed something a little peculiar. Although I myself had closed and locked it, the door to the guest room I was sleeping in was now open. The decorative pillow I'd picked up in the hallway was gone. I jumped out of bed to see if it had fallen over. This room was filled with boxes, so it would have been difficult to see. I looked all over the room, and the pillow was not there so I looked for it. I was beginning to feel like I'd had one too many and that I'd imagined the whole thing. But, no — I had not had anything to drink last night. I stooped down and looked under the bed as well.

The box marked "Safe Contents" was gone.

Okay, I am truly tripping with jet lag, exhaustion, and grief for the motherless child. That was my answer.

I got up and slid into my sweatshirt and pulled my hair back into a scrunchie. I thought it would be nice for me to cook the crew a good breakfast. We would eat, and then I would check in with my husband. I thought it would be good to get out of the house a little today. I wanted to get Luke's mind on everything positive surrounding Busy and his new responsibility.

I looked in the pantry. There were chips, soda pop, candy bars, more candy, and all kinds of treats. I felt like I was back in college. All this stocked junk food would be the jackpot for later on tonight or even a movie night, but not for good, healthy living. I went to the refrigerator, and there was a half full jug of milk and the turkey, cheese, and mustard I'd bought last night. I pulled the milk out; the expiration date was upon me. I untwisted the top off, and the smell made me gag.

Are you serious? I should have bought a full set of groceries yesterday! This family can't be this *dysfunctional!*

The fridge was pretty much bare, however, I could have any condiment I wanted: ketchup, mustard, pickles, soy sauce, mayonnaise, and yep, hot sauce…but where was the food? Oh, my goodness! When I opened the freezer, it was the same story. "This is ridiculous. Plan B time," I said out loud.

I looked over into the den, hoping to see some life stirring in the house, but there were no signs of movement. I felt like I was in an episode of *Black Mirror*. In the den off the kitchen, I saw some men's socks and shoes on one end of the floor by the couch. I don't know how I'd missed it, but the door that led out from the patio was open. I investigated.

There was Luke, seated out on the patio.

"Hey, good morning. How are you? Did you sleep well?" I was attempting to start a dialogue about what had happened the night before.

"I'm better," Luke replied.

"Are you hungry?" I asked.

He paused, as if he had to think about it, and then stated, with certainty,

"Yes, girl. Can't you hear my stomach growling?"

"Okay. Well, as you know, you don't have any food up in here, so get up and get dressed," I said with a motherly authority and looked at him out of the corner of my eye.

"I do look bad, don't I?"

"Yes Luke, you do. But — thank you, God — you don't smell as bad as you did yesterday."

He reached his frail hand out for my hand. I grabbed it, and he pulled me in for a hug. I pulled him out of the chair, and embraced him before shoving him in the direction of the door leading back into the house.

I yelled out, "Mr. Brush and Comb — here we come! Ten minutes, Luke! I'm hungry. Let's go! While you get ready, I'll give Busy a bottle, and bathe and change her. And we'll leave her with Mrs. Elizabeth."

"Okay. That sounds like a plan."

We had a fabulous breakfast at a diner down the street; we laughed, talked, and caught up, just like old times. Although Luke was distant mostly, I attributed it to all of the issues over the previous several days. But it was like time stood still. We were the same Sparrow and Luke, just as if it were yesterday when Luke had come home from the mall with two sparrow necklaces. This was home to us.

After that breakfast, I finally felt good about leaving and returning home to my family. The Armstrong's appeared to have the start of a new rhythm of life, minus Lucinda.

The next morning, I was getting packed to head to the airport. Although there was some comfort in feeling I'd encouraged the Armstrong family by giving them a blueprint to make it, there was something left undone. We understood Lucinda would have a proper burial when the medical students completed their anatomy course, but how could we honor her life now?

There would be no funeral, and the family was not in the financial position to have a proper celebration of her life. There was a tree out back that Lucinda absolutely loved, and, as a child, she'd called it, "Lucinda's Tree." She would go out to that tree and meditate. Luke and Lucinda had many troubles growing up. They had different mothers, but they ended up living with the same paternal grandmother after their father was killed during a tour of duty in the military. Luke, Mrs. Elizabeth, and I, with Busy in Luke's arms, all wrapped up, went out back beneath Lucinda's Tree and said a prayer as a makeshift going-home ceremony, for the beautiful Lucinda. It was peaceful and honorable.

Luke walked me to my rental car. I rolled my carry-on bag and put it in the trunk.

"Sparrow, thank you so much for everything. There is something I need to tell you. I may need your help. Let me sort out something first," he said as he gave me a hug.

I was so exhausted that I couldn't even imagine what Luke was talking about. I nodded my head and said, "Cool." I turned around and waved to Mrs. Elizabeth, who was sitting in the window, peering out at us holding Busy. As I started the rental car, Luke knocked on the window, and I rolled it down.

"Sparrow, Luke said, "do you think people can be forgiven for something bad, even before they do it?"

I remember that his eyes had tears in them as he reached his hand into the window of the car for me to hold again before I replied to his question or drove off to get back to my life.

I looked him straight in the eyes and said, "Yes, I suppose so."

That was really the last time I spent decent amount of time with Luke. We would video chat with each other to keep in touch, and meet up from time to time, but the distance between us grew when Luke's life seemed to spiral out of control, despite having the responsibility of Busy.

Chapter 11

And now, I was standing before the picture I'd taken with my cell phone of Luke holding Busy for the first time in the nursery at Luke's repast.

Wow! Time goes so fast, and you never can tell how things will end up, I said to myself as my eyes fixated on this picture and those flurries of memories evaporated. *If anyone would have told me I would be standing in Luke's house after his funeral, this early in his life, I would not have believed them.* I sighed in pure disbelief and shook my head.

I felt a tug at my hand. It was Busy. "Auntie Ro, that's Uncle Luke holding me at the hospital. That's my favorite picture in the whole house!"

"Yes, I know. And you know what? Your Uncle Luke loved you so much, you will always feel his love."

Busy's eyes twinkled with excitement as she grabbed me to pull me away from the picture and guided me through the roomful of people dressed in all black, with plates full of turkey, ham, yams, greens, black-eyed peas, dressing, cranberry sauce, and Mrs. Elizabeth's famous five-cheese macaroni and sweet-potato pie.

Busy guided me to the kitchen, and my stomach seriously began to growl. I looked over to the open door of the garage, and I could see Weston seated at the table playing dominos while holding his fork and digging into his delectable plate.

"Mrs. Elizabeth, it smells so good up in here!" I said as Busy released my hand, and I sat with some of the elders of the family at the table in the kitchen.

The aroma of the house reminded me of Thanksgiving, Christmas, and Easter all rolled up in one. And I was hungry — my stomach was rumbling. But Busy was so cute, her curls bouncing and her eyes dancing, as the angel-kissed dimple on the right side of her cheek issued a glowing smile from her face that changed the entire atmosphere of the house. Instead of a going-home observance, it appeared to be a true celebration of life.

"Aunt Sparrow," Busy said with such a sweet, sincere voice.

"Yes, baby," I replied.

"Come on. I want you to see the castle in my room," she said with a twinkle in her eye. She always had this curious look about her. Like she had a secret that nobody else was in on. She was definitely a miracle and had that aura about her. It appeared that the concept that she no longer had her uncle, who cared so deeply for her, had not sunk in yet because her spirit was too upbeat.

"Okay, baby. I'm coming to see your castle," I said as I washed my hands, dried them off, and grabbed a piece of slow-roasted turkey off of the stove.

"Mrs. Elizabeth, you are still the best cook I know. I'm coming back to get some cooking lessons."

"My, Sparrow, you a mess, girl," Mrs. Elizabeth said as she took another sip of her beer and dove face first into her plate.

As I walked out of the room with Busy, I looked around at Mrs. Elizabeth and some of the elders. It was quite unique as she talked and laughed causing the jovial mood in this house to take over. It was as if she had not just buried her beloved grandson several hours ago. *What was supposed to be a repast for her grandson turned into a backyard family reunion that was all the way live*, I thought to myself as Busy led me to see her castle.

Busy pulled me by the hand harder and tugged me from the kitchen, back through the living room, up the stairs, and down the hall to her bedroom. There had been quite a bit of wear and tear on the house since we'd brought Busy home from the hospital. The paint on the walls was now chipped and smudged, and the stained carpet was worn down to the padding in places, but it smelled fresh. As we walked down the dark hallway, Mrs. Elizabeth yelled out to Busy from the kitchen,

"Girl, if you can let your Aunt Sparrow alone now, I need to talk to her!"

"Come on, Grandma! I want to show Aunt Ro my castle."

"*Your castle* — girl, you 'bout really getting on my nerves with this *castle* mess," Mrs. Elizabeth replied.

"Mrs. Elizabeth, I'm fine. Give me about 10 minutes, and I'll be back to the kitchen," I replied.

"Okay, but only ten minutes, little girl." Mrs. Elizabeth raised up both of her hands, signaling the number "ten," and walked back into the kitchen, wiping her hands on her apron and placing more foil on the pots to keep all of her meat and sides warm. She went on to feed her guests and socialize with those who'd come to honor Luke.

As Busy and I walked away, Mrs. Elizabeth said to her loud enough so we both could hear her,

"You can't be in your room when some of your friends from your Sunday School class came over to visit and play with you, so don't be rude, Busy."
Nodding her head, Busy replied,

"Yes ma'am, Grandma, I understand. I promise to be back in the living room as soon as I show Auntie Ro my castle."

Busy and I got to her room, and it was as if time reversed. It looked exactly as I'd laid it out more than four years ago, except the crib was now a day bed, and there were some "big girl" clothes in her closet now.

"Busy, where is the castle?" I asked as I looked around the room and saw nothing resembling a castle.

It was as if, in Busy's four-year-old little mind, she had totally dismissed my question about the castle. She went over, sat on her bed, and patted the area next to her.

"Oh, sweetie. Auntie is too big to sit on your bed. I don't want to break it!"

"Aunt Ro, come on," Busy said, as she continued patting.

“No, sweetie, I’ll sit down here.” I found a spot on the floor near her. With me seated below her, we sat in silence for a minute, and then she said with a serious look on her face, “Aunt Sparrow, my Uncle Luke comes to visit me every night,” she said while bopping her dangling feet together. Her big, beautiful brown eyes reminded me of Luke in the way he was so serious at times. And just as quickly as she’d said that, Busy got off the bed, went over to her closet, and opened the door. She reached into the closet and grabbed something off of the floor. She put it on her head, turned around with a big, beautiful smile on her face, and said,

“See, Aunt Ro? I have a castle. It’s on my head.” Her smile was endless and bright.

“Come here, baby,” I said as I reached for her.

“Well, Busy, it’s phenomenal. But, sweetie, let me tell you something: this beautiful thing on your head is a *tiara*. And many women of royalty who live in castles wear tiaras.”

Her smile shortened, as if she were in deep thought, and she turned her head. She looked at me, went back over to her closet, opened both doors wide, and turned the closet light on as if she wanted me to look inside. She turned her head back to me and winked.

"Aunt Ro, I am going to go play with my friends now. I am a princess, aren't I, Auntie Ro?" Busy smiled, admired herself, and adjusted her tiara in the mirror on the wall.

"Yes, you are, baby," I assured her.

She turned around, closed the door leading to the hallway behind her, and exited her room.

This was cute in a way, but all a little strange. I got up from the floor, dusted some of the carpet fuzz off of my black suit, and went over to the closet to close the door and turn off the light. I stopped a little to admire all of the color-coordinated girly outfits that were hanging there. There were pink, yellow, and purple tutus that were hung on hangers with care. I saw the little glittered slippers and cute patent-leather shoes. It appeared that Luke had learned something from me with the instructions I'd left on how to put up Busy's clothes.

I remembered when I'd bought them and had them shipped to Luke so he could give them to Busy for her birthday; I'd also sent instructions on how to hang them.

I looked down, and something looked out of place in this closet full of fashionable little-girl garments. There was a brown cardboard box. I knelt down to see why this box was in Busy's closet. I turned the box around; written on the outside of the box was the word, "Safe Contents."

This box looks familiar. Damn, could this be the box that had disappeared years ago in the guest room down the hall? I thought.

I pulled the box out of the closet into the middle of Busy's room. I went over to the bedroom door and locked it. I sat down and pried opened the box that had been sealed with tape.

This is probably none of my business, or is it?

I opened the box, and there was a hospital record. The tab on the medical record said "Lucinda," and the last name was blacked out in permanent marker. I opened the file. There was a pathology report that stated that there was a benign ovarian cyst on the impression of the mass of the abdomen. I looked at the date, and it was during the days leading up to the surgery Lucinda had while she was pregnant, before her death.

And then there was an addendum that was provided by Dr. Ernesto, but it was written in pen. It stated the mass was malignant and needed to be removed.

Oh, my goodness — I can't believe what I'm reading. I looked further. I continued thumbing through Lucinda's medical record, and there was a pathology report of a frozen section taken while she was in the operating room. It read, "benign ovarian cyst," just like the original pathologist had said in the report. And then, below the pathology report, there was a typed addendum by Dr. Ernesto, which read, "Final pathology — can not be fully determined to be officially benign."

I sat there in shock. I was horrified. *Why had Dr. Ernesto performed surgery on Lucinda when the biopsy pathology was not cancerous and the frozen section taken in the operating room indicated that Lucinda did not have cancer?*

I thought, *Oh, shit. This is unethical. Why in the hell would he do this? I know Dr. Ernesto, and this does not sound like him. But it does sound like something his wife would persuade him to do. I know she was shady, having a very vindictive spirit. But not him — he'd had his bouts with infidelity, but I would never take him for a murderer.*

I went further into the chart and saw that the post-mortem report had been written as the autopsy. At the header, it stated this was declared a coroner's case. There was the standard sketch of her dead body and an illustration of her pregnant belly. Also there was a notation that there was a laceration of the aorta, which appeared to be an "accidental" result of the surgery. Dr. Ernesto was one of the finest surgeons in the nation. He was known for his stellar surgical skills and for making very few mistakes. Hell, I'd even rotated through his surgical service and even joined a collaborative practice over which he was the medical director, when I first graduated before getting married and moving away.

My heart began to pound, and my hands began to shake as I delved deeper into her chart. The additional records were from when Lucinda was in the intensive care unit on life support, when she was declared brain dead. Also, there were the records regarding Busy and her delivery and all the details surrounding her birth.

I wonder what these were doing in Busy's closet. Luke must have put them there, but for what reason — to sue the doctor for a botched surgery? Dr. Ernesto was now dead himself!

And then there was a birth certificate for Busy. I smiled and picked it up, thinking about how beautiful she was as a little baby. But wait — I couldn't believe this! I thought I was about to pass out: *The birth mother was listed as Lucinda Marie Armstrong, and the birth father was listed as Lorenzo Ernesto.* It was signed by Luke Armstrong and was dated the day we left the hospital.

Are you kidding me? I never knew Lucinda and Lorenzo dated or were even a couple. We all hung out, but it was hard for me to believe there was something more. *This can't be true — a baby together. How did this go over my head?* I said to myself. Lorenzo, Luke, and I always hung out. But Lucinda was kind of in and out of the crew, depending on who could maximize her time. She was always looking to get ahead by any means possible. However, I do recall she did work at Dr. Ernesto's clinic as an administrative assistant one summer.

So, that's why Mrs. Ernesto, Dr. Ernesto's wife and office manager, disliked Lucinda — because Lucinda was after Lorenzo!

I attempted to put the pieces together in my head. I vaguely remember Lucinda sharing that, while she was working as the administrative assistant for Dr. Ernesto, Mrs. Ernesto felt intimidated when the beautiful Lucinda stepped foot in the office they'd built from the ground up. And moreover, she'd turned the head of their son, the heir to the Ernesto throne. This, I remembered Lucinda saying,

"Ro, that old battle axe does not like me."

And now I knew why. Lucinda had hooked up with Lorenzo.

Furthermore, I knew Mrs. Ernesto always kept her fingers and eyes on her husband and her sons. Rumor after rumor was in the air about Dr. Ernesto.

From flirting with the medical students with his Latino skin, water wavy hair, and buff physique, to rumors about him being found in the medication closet with an intern. He was the one who got around, and rumor had it that his sons followed suit.

While Dr. Ernesto was roaming the streets of the city, Mrs. Ernesto, with her blond hair, blue eyes, and neck draped with diamonds and pearls, made sure her boys went to the finest schools, held memberships the elite clubs, and hung around only the upper echelon. Then, here comes Lucinda, from the wrong side of the tracks and mediocre education, trying to infiltrate their perfect family.

I thought, *Damn, Lucinda! We all were close. Why didn't you or Luke tell me about this? I was there when Busy was born. I had absolutely no clue Busy's father was Lorenzo, and her grandfather — before his death and even after — was one of the wealthiest people I had ever met and most renowned physician and surgeon in this area. This is unbelievable!*

Thumbing deeper into the papers before me in the closet, I found another record for Lucinda, an annual physical, taken two years prior to her death. It showed that Lucinda was healthy. The gynecologist who did the exam was in the multispecialty group Dr. Ernesto owned and was medical director over. This exam was before she was pregnant with Busy, based on the date; however, there was something very interesting. The health record said that, several years prior, Lucinda had been pregnant before she was pregnant with Busy.

I knew it! Busy had not been Lucinda's first pregnancy.

But what had happened to that first pregnancy or that baby?

Luke never brought it up, so I never asked. I figured she'd possibly miscarried or had an abortion. It was not my business, so I did not pry.

There was more in this box, but before long, I was sure Busy or Mrs. Elizabeth would come looking for me soon, so I decided to put everything back neatly, just like I'd found it, in the "Safe Contents" box in the closet. Just as I was putting everything back into the box, a bright red envelope caught my attention.

Should I open this? Hell, yeah, I should open this, I said in my spirit.

I opened it. Inside the unsealed envelope there was a key attached to a chain with a number on the back. It appeared to be a key for a Harvey State Bank security box. The number etched on the key was 137.

I think that is a bank in the neighboring town, if I am not mistaken, I thought. I grabbed my phone and looked up the location — and I was right: Harvey State Bank was close by.

I need to check this out first thing Monday morning.

I looked at my watch. *Oh, my goodness — I've been in here looking in this box for almost an hour*! *All this shit is so deep and troubling.* I was shaking my head trying to put everything back like I found it when there was a knock at the door.

"Sparrow, you still in there, girl?" Mrs. Elizabeth asked from the other side.

"Yes, ma'am," I replied.

"Come on down, girl, and eat. Your food is going to get cold. What you doing in there?" Mrs. Elizabeth twisted the knob, but I had locked it earlier.

I returned the box quickly and quietly into the closet and closed the closed door. I pretended I had just awakened from a power nap, stretching my arms as I unlocked and opened the door.

"Mrs. Elizabeth, I hope you don't mind — I had to lay down. This whole day has worn me out," I said, wiping my eyes.

"No, baby. I understand. This day has wiped us all out. I know you're used to high-end five-star hotels and all, but you are more than welcome to stay here. Plus, I need you to help me out with something. Busy would absolutely love it if her Auntie Sparrow would stay over."

"You sure it would not be any trouble?"

"Hush, girl. You're family."

"I would love that. I'll touch base with Weston. He just texted me and said Marcus took him back to the hotel after he'd lost all his money in the garage to Uncle Pete, playing spades. He has a flight to catch later on tonight to get back to our son. The driver is supposed to come back to pick me up and take me back to the hotel. Instead, I can have Marcus bring my bags from the hotel, and I'll have Tabitha cancel my reservation since Weston has to leave tonight, anyway."

"Cool. Well, Luke's old room — you know we haven't changed the sheets since … you know. So, I can bring out the air mattress, and you can sleep on Busy's floor. There are clean sheets in the linen closet. You know where everything else is," she offered.

"Thanks, Mrs. Elizabeth."

"Girl, call me 'Grandma Liz,' like y'all used to."

"Yes, ma'am, Grandma Liz. That would be just fine. What I'll do, if you don't mind, is stay here the rest of the weekend and then move over to my hotel on Monday to get ready for a big interview that my agent set up for me next week here in town."

"Okay, now come on downstairs; let me fix you a proper plate. Girl, you all skin and bones. I can see your clavicles, child. You are going to fly away into thin air. I got some of my famous fried chicken, okra, and five-cheese macaroni waiting for you. Are you ready for that?" she said as she waddled to the door.

"You keep this up, Mrs. Elizabeth, and I won't be able to fit into any of my clothes. I'm on a diet."

"That's what's wrong with you young people today. Y'all so eager to starve yourselves to fit some jeans, you don't enjoy life!" she said as she put her hands on her full waist, turned around, and looked me in the eye.

"You're a mess, Mrs. Elizabeth! And thank you for putting me in the *young people* category! Yes, I'm going to keep claiming that as long as I can."

"Girl, hush your mouth, and come on. The food is getting cold. Come on down here. You know my famous mac and cheese ain't gonna be right cold!"

I turned off the light, closed Busy's door, and followed her instructions. I went downstairs, ate with the family, and fellowshipped with the guests who'd come to the repast to pay their respects. It was nice. It was like a family reunion of sorts. I saw Luke's cousins, aunties, and uncles I hadn't seen since I was a little girl. Mrs. Elizabeth served people with kindness, laughed, and made sure everyone had enough to eat, as she piled more and more food on everyone's plate including mine. I didn't argue.

"Mrs. Elizabeth, I haven't had food this good in a long time. This turkey is so moist — and how did you make these greens?"

"They are sautéed. I bet you didn't know greens could taste that good, did you?" She boasted.

"Oh, my goodness! The ham, yams, and your famous five-cheese macaroni are unbelievable. I won't be able to fit into any of my clothes. You know what? We need to write a cookbook together!"

"Little girl, eat your food. You let me cook, and you do the doctoring and the writing. Ain't gone be no cookbook. I'm taking my recipes to the grave."

This was the Mrs. Elizabeth I loved to see and rarely saw. I'd gotten only glimpses of this side of her when Luke and I were children. She talked about good times with all of us and let out her big, boisterous laugh that was so contagious that you could not help but join in. Busy played and skipped through the house, keeping her tiara — or what she liked to call her "castle" — on her head the remainder of the day, with her cousins and church friends running throughout the house.

"Busy, calm down now!" Mrs. Elizabeth said over and over.

"Yes, ma'am," Busy would respond while giggling with her company.

I touched base with Weston by text. He was going to go ahead to the airport once he knew I was good. Marcus brought my suitcase to the house from the hotel.

One by one, each well-meaning guest and family member left, giving farewells and goodbye hugs.

Left in the kitchen, it was just Mrs. Elizabeth and me putting up food and washing dishes, while Busy was reading a book in the living room after she had taken a bath and put on her pajamas.

"Sparrow, you know you were the sister Luke never had," Mrs. Elizabeth said as she handed me a plastic container to dry with a dishtowel.

"Well, with all due respect, Luke *did* have a sister — Lucinda — and I have never tried to take her place," I replied while putting some food into a container to be placed in the refrigerator.

"Yeah, well, Lucinda gave me a rough go with it after her father died in that war. You know Lucinda's mom got involved with some bad people and got strung out on that stuff and was in and out of jail. You know what? Even when Lucinda was a little girl, she always hated living with me, but I was all she had. She longed to be wealthy and have the finer things in life, and I couldn't give them to her. She took whatever she could from any and everybody. I hate to say this about my granddaughter, but Lucinda was sort of delusional and was all caught up in fairy tales and what not. Thinking that knight in shining armor was going to show up out of the clear-blue sky and save her."

"Luke, on the other hand — that was my sweet boy. He was content with what we had, and he wasn't perfect, but I loved him down to his core! And although he had his own demons to deal with, I knew he genuinely loved me — well, us. Busy and I — we were his family," Mrs. Elizabeth shared as she wiped her wet hands on her red-and-white-checkered apron.

I put the remaining leftovers away. "Mrs. Elizabeth, can I ask you something personal?"

"Yeah, baby."

"What in the world happened at the graveside between you and Lorenzo?"

"It's a long story, Ro." Mrs. Elizabeth's face got tight as she frowned and said,

"That asshole. I wish those people had not pulled me off him. I was really going to give it to that lowlife!"

I was astounded. *What could Lorenzo have done to Luke or this family to make her so angry?* I asked myself.

"Ro, will you take a walk with me?" she asked. I obliged her; I was a little afraid not to.

Leaving the kitchen spotless and smelling of lemon dish soap, with all the food and dishes put away, we walked out of the house to the backyard. She grabbed my hand to help her walk on the graveled rocks out back that led up to the charred, burnt tree, and we stood there hand in hand.

"You see, when the kids were growing up, Lucinda loved this tree. This was her tree. This was the only thing she loved at this house — I would say even more than her brother or me. When my husband, God rest his soul, and I first bought this house, we planted this tree for our son. Oh, we envisioned that we would sit out back and sit under that tree as it got bigger, and we would be able to watch our children play and appreciate the shade it provided. And over time, this tree has rooted itself, and you see how big it has become? Well, it was not so big when we first moved into this house, but it has good roots, the shade is sufficient, and it's strong."

I'm thinking to myself, *What in the hell does this tree have anything to do with the attack at the funeral, and what does this have to do with Luke and his death — other than he hung himself from it and burned himself to a crisp.* But I chose not to interrupt and instead I listened.

Mrs. Elizabeth went on to say, "Lucinda claimed this tree as her own. She would go out back and play every day, just like Busy did after her mother had passed, but it was more intimate. She found the solace she could not find with her mother, who had gotten hooked on drugs, or with her father, who died in the war, or even with me. Strangely, she would imagine she had another life out here with this tree. She would imagine that her parents were rich and that she had the finest clothes and jewelry when she was out here at this tree." Mrs. Elizabeth stared up into the remaining leaves as if both Lucinda and Luke were there looking down on us.

"One day, as she was playing, I heard her imagining she would marry a prince. As she grew older and began to study and work, she would go outside and meditate under the tree daily. Knowing how much this tree meant to his sister, I couldn't imagine why Luke would hang and burn himself to death from this tree! I know what the police said, but it can't be true." Mrs. Elizabeth looked at the charred tree with intense eyes. "Something bad happened to my baby! Both my babies!"

We both stood there silent for a moment. To hear the unimaginable word-for-word about what had happened to Luke made this new reality really *real*.

Luke was gone!

In my mind, while we stood there, silent, I was pondering how or why my best friend could have hanged himself and then set himself on fire.

Something was not adding up. I couldn't believe what I had heard or that Luke would do such a thing. As negative as he was, he loved life. Mrs. Elizabeth had suspicions about how Luke had died. I was thinking it, so, without a filter, I just decided to ask,

"Mrs. Elizabeth, do you think somebody did this to Luke?"

"Ro, that's what I have been trying to tell you. Luke would not have done this to himself — and definitely not herc, at Lucinda's Tree!"

There was an uncomfortable pause as we stood there and looked at each other, tears in our eyes.

I broke the silence with the question, "So where does Lorenzo fit into all of this?"

"Lorenzo is not exactly who you all think he is — he's dirty! He comes from dirty old money and has a downright dirty old family. I hate that bastard."

"What do you mean?" I asked.

"He gambles. I'm not talking about slot machine 'gambling' that I do. I'm talking about big shit. High dollar stakes gambling. And he and Luke got into debt with some loan sharks. This goes years back, before his parents died in that plane accident.

They got into debt with some bad people. Those gangsters would come around here on a regular basis, looking for them both — Luke and Lorenzo — scaring me and Busy half to death. It was probably them who did this to my grandson."

"What does Lorenzo have to say about this?"

"Well, he hasn't said anything. I tried to call him over and over. I felt crazy leaving all those voice messages. He spent so much time over here, and he tried to take up serious relations with Lucinda years back, but his parents weren't having it. You know we come from the wrong side of the tracks for the high-class Ernesto family."

I thought to myself, *What have I gotten myself into by staying here? Are some gangsters going to come to the house? Aw, shit! I need to go pack my damn bags right now and get to the hotel quick!*

Night came, and the house was quiet. I slept on the air mattress on the floor in Busy's room. Still paranoid about the story of the loan sharks, I locked the door, putting my bags against it as an extra barrier for protection. While Busy was in deep sleep in her pink-and-purple pajamas, with her tiara on her nightstand, I decided to go back into the closet and dig deeper into the "Safe Contents" box to try to connect what I'd found earlier with what Mrs. Elizabeth had shared.

Reopening the box, I first saw the key to the Harvey State Bank lock box. I picked up the key and put it off to the side.

I'll check on that Monday.

Also, in the box were old photographs of Luke, Lucinda, Lorenzo, and me.

Back then, no one could tell us anything! We thought we were fly the way we posed and dressed.

I smiled, as memories began to flood my mind. The picture had been taken at the Big Gulp Coffee Hut across from the medical school. We were the wrecking crew, for sure. I gave us the nickname, "L3 plus me." We would tear up this city. In the beginning, Lorenzo and I were going to be big-time doctors. Lucinda wanted to become a model, marry a rich man, and travel the world. And Luke wanted to go into business for himself; he wasn't sure doing exactly what, and it changed frequently. But he had big dreams. Although a little fragmented, we had a plan, and we lived life to the fullest. It seemed times were really simple then.

I looked around and saw Busy was still asleep. I bit my lip and dug a little deeper into the box. I found another key on a key chain. I recognized this key. It was a key to my Uncle Cyrus' condo in the Bahamas.

Damn — how did Luke get this key? I know I hadn't given it to him. And if my uncle found out Luke had this, he would have had a fit. That boy must have gotten a key made. Dammit, Luke!

At the bottom of the box was a leather journal. I pulled it out and began skimming through it. Luke's penmanship filled the pages. The writings appeared to span the past several years, according to the entry dates. The most recent journal entries showed no signs of depression or being distraught. This made calling his death a "suicide" even more perplexing.

I was beginning to think more along the lines of Mrs. Elizabeth: Something surrounding Luke's death did not add up, and we needed to find out what happened. My eyelids were heavy, and I needed some serious rest. I closed the box, turned off the closet light, and fell fast asleep on the air mattress.

The next day, Sunday, a bright-eyed little girl who appeared to have been up for a while awakened me.

"Aunt Sparrow, can you braid my hair?"

"Baby, are you up already?" I said, wiping my eyes and sitting up on the air mattress.

"Yes. We've got to get ready to go to church. I don't want to be late for Sunday School class. I get to lead the worship songs today."

"Wow! That's amazing. I remember your Uncle Luke and I led worship songs — we did that at Sunday School when we were kids, too."

I looked around the room. Busy's bed was already made, and her clothes had been laid out. The navy blue dress with peach accents had matching socks, bows and ribbons beside it.

"Who did all of this, Busy?"

"I did!" She said with a big grin on her face. I could tell by her demeanor that Busy was a kid who'd had to grow up fast and take care of herself, just like Luke and Lucinda did, under the auspices of Mrs. Elizabeth.

"Auntie Sparrow, can you braid my hair? I tried to braid it, but I can't get it right. And when Grandma Liz does it, I don't like it. But don't tell her I said that. She'll be really mad if she knew."

The dimple on her cheek softened her question, and I couldn't refuse. I braided her thick, curly hair and put in the peach bows she requested. I got showered and dressed, and grabbed a Danish for breakfast, and off to church we went.

Busy wanted me to stop by her Sunday School class so I could hear her lead the worship, and I did. She was adorable, her long hair braided with peach ribbons and bows to match, set off by frilly socks and patent-leather shoes, as she led her primary Sunday School class in worship. That brought back so many memories of my childhood.

I really needed this. And the congregational church worship was just as rewarding. Minister Brown's message, ironically, came from Luke 15:11-32. It was about the Prodigal Son. This story resonated, especially with all the questions surrounding Luke. Was this a sign? At the altar, I prayed for strength, discernment, and, most of all, for focus. I asked, *Please, God — keep my family with your hedge of protection around them. And thank you for my wonderful new career as an best selling author. And most of all, please, Lord, give me the wisdom to know which steps to take in finding out what really happened to Luke. Without you, Lord I cannot do this!*

Church was over, and Minister Brown was waiting to greet his congregation as they left. As we approached the good minister, he grinned wide.

"Well, well, well — if it isn't little Dr. Sparrow Jones Mack gracing us with her presence today. It was so good seeing you at the graveside service yesterday, even though we really did not have a chance to chat. You were always a great comfort and resource to Luke. Please, as you climb the ladder of success, don't ever forget where you came from."

Was Minister Brown throwing a little shade on me? I have never forgotten where I come from. I don't get back home often because our parents have relocated. I have sent many a blessing to this community and this church. So, I had no problem responding,

"Pastor, with all due respect, I never left. My roots are here, and I plant seeds at this church and within this community on a regular basis."

Minister Brown looked down and over his glasses at me. And then a little smirk came over his face; he pulled me in and gave me a big hug, and we laughed together.

"Our Sparrow always knows how to keep it *100*! You coming back in the fall for the Church Anniversary?" Minister Brown asked as he crossed his arms in his ministerial robe and looked at me with pride.

"I'll do my best, Minister. My calendar is so busy, but if I can't, I'll send a nice, hefty check."

"I know you will, darling. Give Brother Mack, little man, and your parents my love," Minister Brown remarked as he gave me a high five and then reeled me in for another hug.

"I will," I responded, and the embrace felt like old times in the neighborhood for me.

The next morning, I started packing my bag, while Busy was putting on her socks and shoes and getting ready to go to the zoo for a field trip.

"Auntie Ro, do you have to go?" Busy asked, tugging at my shirt with sad eyes and pouty lips.

"Yes, sweetie. Auntie must get some work stuff done. But I'll be back real soon, and I'll bring you something when I return."

Her eyes lit up as she walked out of the room and was picked up by the church bus to go on a field trip to the zoo.

When Busy left for the zoo, I finished packing all of my stuff and some of the contents that I found in the closet. *Surely no one will miss this*, I convinced myself. I got everything together so I could head to the hotel, to get focused on the big interview with

Abigail Lancaster. It was nice spending time with Busy at the Armstrong home, despite the circumstances surrounding having to bury my lifelong best friend. But Tabitha and Weston were right: It was time for me to take care of business. I worked hard to gain this momentum, and now, being a platinum author with Grace Publishing House, my stock had tripled. This interview with Abigail Lancaster could catapult my career to the next level. Not that I didn't want to help with Luke and all the mystery surrounding his death — but I needed to handle some of my own business.

However, before doing so, I wanted to make sure I checked out what was in the Harvey State Bank lock box, to determine what Luke possibly could have felt worthy enough to secure. So I asked Mrs. Elizabeth to ride with me over there,

"I don't know why you could possibly want to go over to HSB, Sparrow. I haven't banked over there in years. But come to think of it, Luke did have a small bank account out that way," Mrs. Elizabeth stated.

"Mrs. Elizabeth, there is some information I came across that may give us information regarding Luke. And I promise you, after we make that one stop, I'll drop you back home, and I will go over to the hotel to stay there. My reservation has been confirmed."

"Girl, I know there ain't no money in there or anything like that. So I'll gladly go with you and stay all morning over there if you want me to. As long as we are back before my story comes on!"

It was good that she was on board going with me — I might need her to sign the bank registry to get me access to the lock box.

We arrived at the bank, and, sure enough, Mrs. Elizabeth was needed for us to gain access to the box in Luke's absence. She also had to go back with me into the vault, where the lock boxes were. Once we were back in the vault, the clerk left us alone. There was one chair in the vault, where Mrs. Elizabeth sat; she was disinterested in the contents of the lock box. She complained about her feet and how her ankles looked like they were a little swollen.

"Sparrow — look at my ankles, child. I've been eating too much salt. I think those greens got me, girl," she said while sitting and raising her legs to get a better look at her ankles.

"Yes, sodium can do that, Mrs. Elizabeth. You need to cut back on all that salt, Mrs. Elizabeth. And when you get home, elevate your legs," I said as I was looking around for box 137.

She nodded and continued to tell me how hungry she was and how she needed a beer and a cigarette.

"I could really use a smoke right now."

"I thought you were cutting back," I replied.

"I am, but not today," Mrs. Elizabeth chuckled to herself.

Ignoring all her foolish joking, I walked up to box 137, put the key in, and turned it. The box clicked and opened slightly. I grabbed the metal box; it was surprisingly light. I brought it over, placed it on the table in the vault, and completely opened the box. Inside the box, there was another, smaller box that could be removed. I took out the box and laid it on the table.

I withdrew the top item, a newspaper article that appeared to be a little weathered. The headline read, "Prominent physician and spouse die in private-plane crash; community mourns." In that newspaper clipping, there was a beautiful picture of Dr. and Mrs. Ernesto in their living room at the top of the article. I remember that living room very well from when we visited their home during their over-the-top-opulent annual Christmas party, to which Dr. Ernesto invited only the chief residents, esteemed faculty and staff. It was definitely a *Who's Who* event to attend. Those invited, were expected to write a big check toward the Children's Hospital Cancer Ward development, which appeared to be one of the Ernesto's' passions. They were a very pretentious but genuinely philanthropic family in the community.

Why would Luke have this article in a security box in a bank? This was in the public newspaper — everyone from this area knew about this tragedy.

Under the newspaper article was a bottle of diabetes medication. These were pills that were prescribed to patients to normalize their blood sugar.

That was strange, too. *Why would Luke have diabetes medication in a lock box in a bank?* I turned around and asked Mrs. Elizabeth if Luke was a diabetic.

"No, he wasn't a diabetic He did not have *the sugar*! Girl, you need to hurry up — my stories are about to come on!"

When I shook the bottle, it felt like it was full. The label on the bottle read it was a 90-day supply. Something made me open the bottle; there were only 30 pills in it, so 60 were gone.

I don't know how I'd missed it initially, but the name stood out this time. I wondered who it was.

"Mrs. Elizabeth, did Luke know a Michael James Parker?"

"Hell, naw, girl — hurry up!" Mrs. Elizabeth said as she crossed her arms and looked as if she were positioning herself to take a nap sitting up in the chair.

Ignoring her, I put the pill bottle on the table and dug a little deeper into the box. I pulled out a binder of paperwork. It appeared to be a contract for a residential facility in Florida.

"Mrs. Elizabeth, do you have any relatives in a nursing home in Florida?"

"Girl, I'm getting really tired of you! What are you talking about? No, we don't have any family in those parts. And we don't believe in nursing homes. So, no! Now, if I miss my stories, Sparrow Jones Mack, you are going to get it!"

Ignoring Mrs. Elizabeth's foolish ranting, I read the document further and noticed more specifically there was paperwork regarding someone named Eric with the last name blackened out. It didn't say if this was a relative or someone Luke knew. But I did see a invoice with Luke's name on it for a payment of $650 per month.

Now, wait a damn minute: This is the amount I secretly sent to Luke monthly for automatic withdrawal from my private bank account. What in the hell? Have I been paying for this person to live in a residential facility? That can't be. Luke told me he needed that money to refinance a loan they had on their house. I need some answers right now!

"Mrs. Elizabeth, do you have a mortgage payment, or have you had your house refinanced within the last several years?" I asked.

"No and no! My house has been paid off since my husband died, God rest his soul. And we are still getting my son's military benefit check since he was killed in that war. We don't have much, but one thing we do have is that house. And it is ours, outright. We don't owe anybody anything!"

I paused, as it appeared that Luke had caught me up in a web of lies and deceit.

Why would he ask me for $650 a month? Like a fool, I'd set it up to be automatically drafted from my separate checking account. And who on earth is this Eric person to Luke that he felt like he would have to take care of him? I had so many questions, with absolutely no answers. I had to figure out what in the hell was going on.

"Grandma Liz, do you know an Eric?"

"Little girl, if you don't hurry up."

I pulled out the next paper in the vault box, and it was a flyer from the Big Gulp Coffee Hut.

What is this doing in a bank lock box? This had to have been put in here by mistake. I remembered this place all too well. This was the coffee shop that was across from the medical school. This is where Lorenzo and I used to study until the wee hours of the morning before he dropped out. On top of the flyer was the name, *Sophie*, and it was not in Luke's handwriting. So, I presumed someone named Sophie had written her name on the flyer. I knew nothing about a "Sophie" or about the significance of this flyer.

The last item was a postcard of the islands Luke and I used to visit in our childhood and early adulthood. Luke fell in love with those islands and had become acquainted with them due to the fact that my Uncle Cyrus had a condo there. He'd made Weston and me the secondary entitlement persons on his contract with the condo and even willed it to us as a part of his estate. This postcard was not an unusual find, since I knew Luke absolutely loved the islands. However, just like the flyer from the coffee shop, I thought, *Why would you have this in a bank vault lock box, where most people store their most valuable items?*

I stared at this postcard for a while, as it brought back so many memories, while Mrs. Elizabeth snored, sleeping while sitting straight up in the chair in the bank vault. I picked up the beautiful postcard, and the white sands and deep blue water seemed to jump off of the postcard at me. I turned it over, and, on the back, in Luke's handwriting, was one word — *Home*.

This was significant because I knew from the first time I'd met Luke as a child and all the challenges he and his sister had been through, they never felt truly at *home* anywhere, even though Mrs. Elizabeth did the best she could. I knew the closest thing he felt to having a home was when he was at my house or hanging out with me and my grandmother. I invited him on what started out as family vacations to the island and then turned into friend vacations to the condo, as we got older. I could see how Luke would feel so comfortable with this space that he would seem like it was "home" to him. He was able to go up to the water's edge and be free from all the worries and woes of his reality, which was filled with dysfunction and fear.

I looked around, positioned my back to the cameras, and put all the contents from the lock box into my purse. I don't know why I felt the need to acknowledge the security cameras in this moment, but I did. I closed the number-137 bank vault lock box, locked it, and put it back where it belonged. I tapped the sleeping Mrs. Elizabeth's shoulder.

"Grandma Liz, it's time to go."

She jerked herself awake, wiped her mouth, looked at her watch, and said, "Girl, you have about 30 minutes to get me back to my stories."

It was clear that she was focused on her soap operas and that I was focused on figuring out the mystery surrounding her grandson's death, so I needed to get her home quick. However, on the way from the bank, I took a different route to see if the Big Gulp Coffee Hut was still in business. I hadn't been there in years. Sure enough, it was, just like we had left it. I smiled; there were a lot of memories in that place. I would come back later.

"Sparrow, you're going the long way home!" Mrs. Elizabeth said as she crossed her arms in the passenger seat.

"Mrs. Elizabeth, I will have you back home soon."

I took Mrs. Elizabeth home. She made a sandwich, lit up a cigarette, and turned on the television. Busy was still on the field trip. I picked up my luggage and asked Mrs. Elizabeth if I could take some of Luke's trinkets with me that were in a box up in the closet.

Mrs. Elizabeth said, "Girl, please take *all* of that stuff. It's cluttering up my house. It ain't nothing but junk."

Junk or not, I put it all in my car. I believed beyond a shadow of a doubt that this junk held some clues as to what had really happened to Luke. After I loaded up my car, I went back into the house, where Mrs. Elizabeth was still intrigued with her shows, talking to the television, deeply involved in the daytime story drama. She had no idea I had even come back into the house. I left an envelope with one thousand dollars cash on the kitchen counter. I walked in the living room where Mrs. Elizabeth was zoned in on the soap opera.

"Grandma Liz, I left some bill and food money for Busy and you. Now I don't want it all spent up in the casino!"

Not peeling her eyes away from the television, she absently said, "Thank you, baby. I know I can always count on you," while trying to look around me at the TV screen, as I obviously was in the way.

"Give Busy a kiss and hug from her Auntie Ro. And I will be getting some new princess books to send to her."

"Yeah, baby. I'll let her know. You be careful now, you hear."

Chapter 12

On the way to the hotel, I decided to circle back by the Big Gulp Coffee Hut to see if I could get any more information about Luke and why he had this flyer in the Harvey State Bank lock box. I went in, and it was like a time warp. I looked over to the left and smiled at the booth in the corner. That is where, many years ago, Lorenzo and I would study until the sun came up. Luke would come by after he got off at whatever job he was working that week, and we would hit up a happy hour afterwards. Lucinda would join in sometimes. This is truly where we all became connected. Most of the content of my new book, *Step 1*, was based on my experiences while in medical school, and some of those experiences occurred right here at the coffee shop. Those were some of the best and some of the worst days of my life.

"Hello, ma'am. May I help you?" a polite strawberry-blond-haired lady asked from behind the counter. My eyes zeroed in on her nametag. Her name was Sophie. It matched the name on the flier. *How ironic.*

"Does this place still serve chai tea?"

"You've been here before, haven't you?" Sophie asked.

"Yes, I was a medical student across the street years ago. Why do you ask?"

"Because only people who have a history here know we are known for our delicious chai tea."

"Yes, I know. It was my favorite when we used to come here and study. This was kind of a second home for me and my crew. Do you still stay open 24 hours?" I asked, as I looked over at *our booth*.

"Oh, no. That changed with the new management. It's hard to get good-quality staff to consistently work those shifts," Sophie said as she punched in my order. "We close at ten." She smiled. I liked her warmth.

"I'm putting in your order now. What's your name?"

"Sparrow."

She wrote my name on the cup, and I smiled while she was writing it. *Wow! My name written on my cup! This was new. Look at the Big Gulp Coffee Hut catering to the millennial's*, I thought to myself.

"Well, Sparrow, did you finish medical school across the street?"

"Why, yes. I did, thank God."

"There are a lot of people who say they went to medical school there, but something happened, and they did not finish. Just curious."

"Not sure about who you are used to seeing up in here. But no, my dear. I finished — and with honors." *Oh, no — this girl didn't just question my credentials! I hated to have to flex on her, but how dare this chick question me? Maybe I am overreacting, with everything going on. I just need to go over to the old booth and sit down.*

"Well, Dr. Sparrow, there are some delicious pumpkin bars right over there. Feel free to take one, and I'll get your chai tea right out to you." Sophie pointed to the desserts on a table to the left.

I walked by the pumpkin bars. I was just going to take a look, but the spicy aroma was so strong and warm, I had to indulge. I took one bar and placed it on a napkin. It was fresh out of the oven. The white cream-cheese icing was topped with candied pecans, and the made-from-scratch icing oozed down the sides, soaking into the white napkin.

I sat in the booth near the window with a non-restricted view of the medical center. This view was my constant motivation. That building used to seem so big and tall but now appeared to be just another building. I took a bite of what I was certain was the best pumpkin bar I'd ever had. Between Mrs. Elizabeth's cooking and this pumpkin bar, I was sure I'd picked up ten pounds since being back home.

"Dr. Sparrow, here is your chai tea. I put a little something on top for you!"

"Oh, my goodness — it's a heart. Thank you. I needed that."

Sophie pulled out the chair opposite me, sat down, and said,

"And I am truly sorry if I offended you about asking if you completed your education at the medical school."

"Oh, no. No offense taken." *What else could I say to her apologetic gesture?*

"I see you got a pumpkin bar. Aren't they yummy? They are made from scratch and my grandmother's recipe. My long-term goal is to become a full-time baker and open up a sweets shop," Sophie said.

"Well, Sophie, they are absolutely delicious. And if you put your mind to it, I'm sure you can accomplish your goal." I tell her this in my true Sparrow fashion – trying to inspire wherever I go.

"Why, thank you, Dr. Sparrow," Sophie said as she started to get up.

"Please, keep your seat, Sophie. Do you have a moment? I'd like to ask you something."

"Sure. What can I do for you?" Sophie asked with a serving look on her face.

"Did you know a gentleman named Luke Armstrong?"

Her eyes widened as she grabbed her heart and said, "Why, yes — that was my man."
"*Your man*?" I replied.

"No, not in that type of romantic way. He was a regular here, and we became acquaintances, buddies in a way."

"Really?"

"Yes. And I was so shocked about his death. You know, Dr. Sparrow, I didn't know him all that well, but he didn't strike me as someone who would take his own life," Sophie said. Her voice held as much genuine concern as her eyes. She was sincere.

"I know — it surprised us all," I replied. Even though I felt the exact same way as Sophie, I'd just met her and could not share my private inklings. But there had to be some significance to Luke keeping this flyer in the lock box with her name on it. I wondered what message Luke was sending to me about this place and, more specifically, about Sophie.

She smiled more and made herself quite at home at *our* booth, and luckily, I was the only customer in the coffee shop.

"You know, Luke was a very giving person. He volunteered down in the bottoms at the homeless shelter. I don't know if he was a part of a homeless ministry or something like that, but he would ask to take our day-old baked goods we were going to discard, so he could give it to people in need."

"Wow, that is phenomenal." Now, that intrigued me. I didn't know this side of Luke. I had no idea he was involved in a homeless ministry.

"Dr. Sparrow, were you and Luke friends?" Sophie asked.

"More like family," I replied.

With a puzzled look on her face, Sophie asked,

"Did Luke talk about me, since you asked me if I knew him?"

"Well, kind of. In Luke's belongings, I found this flyer with your name on it." I showed it to her.

"Yes, I remember this exact flyer," Sophie said as she picked the flyer up off of *our table* and held it close to her eyes.

"This was an advertisement for one of the fall promotions we were running. I gave it to Luke when he came in to buy some pastries. And you know what? Come to think of it, it was the same day he bought a gallon of coffee with that order. I thought it was so sweet for him to do that for his former boss. Luke was such a kind person," Sophie said as she sat across from me and smiled.

"His 'former boss'?" I inquired with a raised eyebrow, perplexed. Since Luke changed jobs so much, I had no idea who she was referring to.

"Yes, you may have known him: Dr. Ernesto, the big-time surgeon in the city!"

"Oh, really?" I said as I thought to myself, *I had no idea Luke had ever "worked" for Dr. Ernesto. I knew Lucinda, his sister, had, but not Luke himself.*

"Yes, and as a matter of fact, you know what? Hold on," Sophie said as she looked up something on her phone. I continued to eat my pumpkin bar and, totally without class, lick my fingers. And I needed to down my chai tea before it got cold, but I attempted to process the fact that Luke had a boss.

Her eyes were fixed on her phone. I noticed they widened in a discovery she was yet to share.

"Yep, I knew I remembered that right. I gave Luke the flyer the same day Dr. Ernesto and his wife were killed in that awful plane crash. It was later that very same morning. See here," she said as she showed me her phone. On her phone was the news release on the untimely deaths of a prominent physician and his socialite wife. It mirrored the newspaper clipping that was in Luke's bank vault lock box at Harvey State Bank.

"That's awful," I replied, as I was still taken aback at the connection I had just learned about Luke and Dr. Ernesto being his former boss — and now this!

The bell on the coffee shop door chimed as a group of customers entered. Sophie stood up, put her phone in her apron pocket, and headed back to her post.

"Dr. Sparrow, I have to go. Well, it was great talking to you. Once again, I'm so sorry for your loss."

"Sophie, thank you for your time. You have been such a great help. Have a nice day."

As I was walking out of the coffee shop to my rental car, I was dumb-founded, as it appeared the more I tried to find out about what happened to Luke, the more I received disturbing information. And I for damn sure wasn't ready for where this story was leading.

I headed to the hotel with all the mental and emotional baggage quickly mounting up in my being. When I arrived, I gave the keys to the valet; he unloaded my car, and I went up to my hotel room.

As soon as I got to the room, I went straight into organizational mode, which was my MO to deal with my thoughts. I unpacked my clothes and laid out all the findings I'd discovered — all the information from the box marked "Safe Contents" I'd rediscovered in Busy's closet, the items in the Harvey State Bank lock box 137, and the information Sophie had just shared with me at The

Big Gulp Coffee Hut. As all of this was laid out on the coffee table, the one thought that kept lingering in my mind and baffling me was Luke volunteering in the bottoms at the homeless shelters. He'd never told me about that. And although Luke was kind, this seemed so out of character for him. *This does not sound like Luke*, I thought over and over in my mind.

On a separate table, I laid out everything I would need for the upcoming interview with Abigail Lancaster. Tabitha had been texting me all morning to review the press kit she'd emailed to me, but I had gotten sidetracked.

Tabitha, I will be reviewing the press kit in a couple of hours, and then I'll email you back with any questions I have, I replied.

Once everything had been laid out, I stood back and realized how blessed I was in this space, despite all that was going on. On one table, there was pure dismay, confusion, and disconnected dots. And on the other table, was an example of hard work, tenacity, and predestined future that lay before me. I existed in both worlds at this very moment.

This hotel room was a deluxe room and had a separate living-room quarters and butler's area adjacent to the king master suite. It would have been so nice to have Weston here with me. I missed him and could have used his shoulder to lean on now, for reassurance before this big interview and to help sort out all that was going on with Luke, post mortem. And I knew that he would be furious with me for allowing even a morsel of my being to be distracted by the puzzles surrounding Luke.

I took a shower and put on some lounging clothes to lay down and relax in this gigantic, beautiful hotel room and take a breather from those hectic last couple of days. However, I knew I could not rest easy until I got a little more clarity around Luke's community service at the homeless shelter.

I can't believe he'd been volunteering at a homeless shelter. Why did he not share this with me? I thought. Before it got too late, I figured I would go down to the bottoms and see what I could find out, because my entire day tomorrow would have to be dedicated to preparing for the interview.

"Sparrow, you need to go check this out!" I said to myself.

I grabbed my jacket and a snack bar because I was starving. The pumpkin bar was good, but the sugar high that it had provided was now wearing off. I jumped in my rental car and headed out. This area of town had the nickname, "the bottoms," because it was a rough part of the city. There was trash everywhere, liquor stores on every corner, and an abundance of people walking around who looked like all the hope had been sucked from their souls.

I looked up the address of the only remaining homeless shelter in the city, and it was easy to find. When I drove up, it looked like a refurbished old warehouse. I parked in the front, even though there was no actual sign that said parking was allowed. I was going to have to take my chances on getting a ticket or getting towed. It was starting to get dark, I was alone, and, to be honest, I was a little scared and uncomfortable with my surroundings. I knew what went on in this area. On a regular basis, it was a part of breaking news segments — and not in a good way. And to top it off, most of the gunshot victims that I triaged and worked on in the emergency room and trauma service, when I worked in this town came from "the bottoms."

I got out of the car, looked around, locked the door, and saw no one. I cautiously ran up to the front door from the parking space.

Damn, I should have my mace or my nine or something! I thought, as I waited for the door to open after I rang the buzzer, while I cautiously looked around into the night; every noise seemed magnified. Without being asked a single question or even announcing myself, I was buzzed in. I opened the door and walked down a short hallway, and I could see a table in what appeared to be a dining area, where people were eating. They appeared to be homeless. Right along the wall, there was a table piled with small black leather Bibles with a sign in front of them that read,

"Free Bibles. Take one. God has a blessing in store for your life!"

"Hello. May I help you, sweetie? You need to eat or shower?" a polite lady asked as she approached me and gently reached out her hand.

I thought, *Well, damn! Do I look that bad? Do I look like I have been living on the street?* However, I maintained my cool and politely responded, "No ma'am. I don't need your services at this time. I'm a doctor who graduated from the medical center up the road." I pointed in the general direction of the medical school.

"Oh, I'm sorry, doctor. I didn't mean to imply that you were homeless. Pardon me — I've had a long shift. Then, how may I help you, dear? Would you like to volunteer? I am short-staffed, and we need some help around here."

"I am so sorry to barge in this late in the day, and I really appreciate your time. I came by to inquire about something."

"What is it, doll? I don't mean to be rude, but please get to the point. I have to get back to work because my relief is no longer here to help me out." She was an older, fair-skinned petite lady with tapered salt-and-pepper hair and bright-red glasses; I could tell right away she had a lot of spunk.

"I was informed that a friend of mine used to volunteer here."

"So, who was your friend, dear?" she asked.

"Luke Armstrong," I said without hesitation.

"No, we've never had a 'Luke' here! Ethel, have you heard of anybody who has volunteered here by the name of 'Luke'?" she asked as she held her hand to her mouth and turned her head toward what appeared to be the kitchen.

In the distance, someone said, "No, Katherine. I've never heard that name before."

"Ma'am, I have his picture pulled up on my phone here." I showed her a picture of Luke.

She grabbed my phone and pulled her glasses hanging around her neck by a chain, up to her eyes. She turned toward me, our eyes locked, and she said,

"This is our 'David'!" And you say his name was 'Luke,' sweetie?" she said as she frowned.

"Yes. That's Luke, my friend."

"Well, I wonder why he told me his name was 'David'? She asked with a curious look on her face.

"Well, ma'am, 'David' was his middle name. His proper name was Luke David Armstrong. We were childhood friends," I replied.

"Around here, we even had a little nickname for him — 'King David' — because he was always walking around here quoting scriptures and carrying his weathered black little Bible," she said as she smiled and chuckled.

"Oh, really?" I was dumbfounded. This was not the Luke I knew.

"Well, honey, can you tell him to come back to work? I've been swamped since he just disappeared off the face of the earth." The lady started to get up, so she could go back to the kitchen, as she straightened out her apron, dropped her glasses off of her nose, and handed me back my phone.

"Well, ma'am, you might want to stay seated when I tell you this. Luke — or 'David,' as you knew him — has passed away," I said.

“Oh, my God!” She plopped down into the chair against the wall.

“Are you okay?” I asked as I naturally went to her aid and braced her arm against the chair.

“He was such a nice young man — and so helpful. The regulars here really took a liking to him.” She seemed really distraught as she asked, “What happened to him?”

“It was unexpected. That’s all I can say about it at this time,” I responded.

“Michael would have taken this news really hard,” she replied.

“Who is ‘Michael,’ ma’am?” I asked.

“Michael slept many a night here at the shelter. David and Michael were like peas in a pod. Every day when Michael showed up, they spent a lot of time together.”

“Okay.”

“Yes, they developed what seemed to have been a real genuine friendship. They played cards, laughed, and talked all the time. David really tried to make

Michael take better care of himself, since his health was failing him."

"This is interesting. Tell me more," I inquired.

"Well, you can choose to believe it or not, but Michael looked up to David and really tried to get himself together because of the mentoring David gave him. And, oh, boy — you should have seen Michael when David gave him a haircut a couple of weeks ago."

"Really?"

"Oh, yes. That made Michael feel real good about himself. That haircut alone built up his self-esteem. You know, after that haircut, David and Michael almost looked like brothers, or even twins. Everybody thought so! We gave them the nickname around here of 'The Twins.' And they got a kick out of that."

"Oh, really. Where is Michael now?"

"You know, he disappeared about the same time David did. We also run Street Ministry, and I have been asking a lot about him and his whereabouts in the streets. We found some of his belongings where he would sleep on the street, when he's not here at the shelter. But, strangely, no one has seen or heard from him."

I stood there, frozen. This was beginning to sound all too familiar. I almost dared not to ask this question, but suddenly, I blurted it out without hesitation: "Would you happen to know Michael's full name?"

"Why, yes. It's Michael Parker. You know what? I stand corrected. His full name is Michael James Parker."

I stood there with a blank stare on my face, thinking back to the medicine bottle that I saw in the Harvey State Bank safe deposit box with that name on it.

"And would you happen to know what type of health issue Michael James Parker had?"

"Yes. He struggled with drug addiction. But he was also a diabetic. David helped him get set up with a doctor to get his diabetes medication."

Gathering myself, suddenly, I felt a little sick to my stomach. This was all too much, and I guess it was written all over my face as I began to fan myself with my hand.

"Sweetie, are you okay?" she asked.

I kept my composure and said, "Yes, I'm good. You know what? I'd better go. Do you have a card, ma'am?" I asked.

"No, little lady. Does this look like an executive high rise? I'm Ms. Katherine, and when you call here, I am the secretary, the treasurer, the president, and the CEO of this here establishment. You call here and you are going to get me! It was nice chatting with you. If you run into Michael out there in them streets, let him know he can always get a hot meal and a shower here. And sweetie, I am so sorry about David — or, rather, 'Luke.' He meant a lot to us," Ms. Katherine stated.

I went to my car, held the steering wheel, locked the doors, and began to cry in the dark night of the parking lot. I felt like I'd been thrust into a bazaar movie. *What in the hell is going on? This is getting crazier by the day.*

Flustered, I drove back to the hotel in the dark of the night. And when I got back to the hotel, all I wanted to do was climb into bed, check on my baby back home, and go to sleep. I ordered room service from the Chateau Restaurant & Bar in this five-star hotel. I had a nice filet mignon cooked just right, baked potato with Gouda cheese, sour cream with fresh chives, and the Chateau's famous caramelized Brussels sprouts. And to wash it down, a German bottle of their finest Riesling. *On some level, I know*

I'm trying to flush today's news from my system with food and alcohol.

After dinner, I stepped foot into the luxurious rainforest shower provided in the master suite and let the water massage my weary, tired neck and shoulders. As the water hit my head, I just let loose and cried my eyes out. I could not believe what I had just found out. I was connecting the dots, and I just knew in my gut that the picture I was going to end up with was not going to be a good one.

How in the hell did all this shit that was going on with Luke get by me? Luke claiming that he worked for Dr. Ernesto and volunteering at the homeless shelter? And, why in the hell was Luke's bank lock box filled with the shit that it was filled with — newspaper clippings of cryptic life tragedies, flyers from the local coffee shop, and, most of all, why did Luke have the homeless man, Michael James Parker's diabetes medication? And where in the hell was Michael James Parker now? As everything was unfolding, my spirit shuddered at what the final outcome could possibly be. I got out of the shower, put on my robe, and wrapped the towel around my weary head.

Sparrow, Luke has really put you in a bind this time! And you will find out everything that happened to him. But now you have got to focus on your upcoming interview with "the" Abigail

Lancaster! So stop all of this crying, girl, and get your shit together! Now it is time for you to focus on your business. Take care of that, and when that is over, then connect the dots regarding Luke! These were my thoughts.

I put on my lavender lotion, got into my silk pajamas, and sat at the hotel table digging into my dessert assortment while looking over my cue cards for the Abigail Lancaster interview.
Before I knew it, I fell asleep, with the television watching me. I jerked myself awake with the cue cards and fork still in my hands, still seated at the table. I realized I had forgotten to call my husband to tell him that I had made it to the hotel from Mrs. Elizabeth's house and to check on our son. By the time I called, he informed me that little Weston was fast asleep. My husband and I chatted about his long, busy executive day, and he highlighted all of the adorable things that the baby had done since I had been gone. I was missing so much. He turned on the video camera to show me his precious little sleeping face. And that was just what I needed to make this crazy day fizzle.

"You ready for your interview?" Weston whispered.

"Yes, I'm getting there," I responded.

"Babe, you don't sound ready. Don't let this Luke stuff get your head all messed up. This is your purpose. Luke made his decisions, and you can't undo the things he has done, Sparrow. Call me in the morning before you head out, so we can pray,"

"Okay, my love," I said with pure confidence, knowing, despite anything, this man had my back beyond the shadow of a doubt.

"Yeah, that's the Sparrow I know. You got this. Get some rest, and we'll talk in the morning."

That was just what I needed to put everything in perspective.

After tossing and turning a little bit, I drifted off to sleep. When Weston was not sleeping next to me, I never sleep through the night. All of a sudden, I felt wide-awake again. I decided to get up and get a glass of water. From the butler's pantry, I grabbed a glass, put some ice cubes in from the ice bucket, and poured myself full glass of bottled water. Drinking the water not only quenched my thirst while I sat on the edge of the bed, it hydrated my spirit and, most of all, my curiosity.

I wandered over to the desk where my purse was. Still nestled comfortably inside was Luke's leather journal. I sat down at the hotel-room desk and stared at the book for a moment. I was hesitant to open it. These were Luke's private thoughts. I always knew he kept a journal, even when we were kids. A sudden glimpse back to our childhood showed me times when I was playing in the dirt or riding my bike, and he would be sitting on the curb with his pencil in hand, writing about his complex life of being in elementary school. I believe it was his way of coping with all the losses he'd experienced at a young age and with his life of tyranny under his Grandma Elizabeth.

Many times I felt that, when I decided to add "writer" as one of my talents, Luke was a little jealous of that gift that I had, because he was the one who was always writing when we were kids, not me. Holding his journal now, since he was gone, I felt perplexed. *If I look into this book, I would be infringing upon Luke's innermost thoughts — and what right did I have to do that? I am not God! Also, in the last days of his life, when he was in dire need of a friend, I was preoccupied with my own life and career. I chose to put myself as a top priority for once, and I purposefully ignored him. Shame on you, Sparrow!* Those thoughts infiltrated my mind.

In that moment, I felt a warm sensation in my hands holding the journal, and I put it down in shame. I felt like I was an awful, selfish person.

Would God ever forgive me? I asked in my spirit.

I took a deep breath and got up enough courage to open the first page of the journal. On the inside of the front cover was his name - Mr. Luke David Armstrong. He never would write out his whole name; he always said he didn't like it. To see his handwriting and realize he was no longer a part of the air we all breathed was almost too much to take. Despite my apprehension, I went right in to read the words of my deceased best friend. The first sentence read:

I don't think I can make it another day.

I was taken aback at the first line of his writing. The words were heavy and deep, and they cut to the core. I went on to read,

The decisions I have made and the actions I have taken are too much to bear. I have been hurt all of my life and have intentionally caused too much pain. When I think back on my life, I wonder what the purpose was. Why was I the magnet for every possible bad thing to happen to me?

I kept my hand on the page of the book and closed it. I was confused and could not fathom the perils Luke could have been going through to write such words. There was no doubt about it — Luke did not have much, but what he *did* have were people who loved him dearly. And after all of the time and effort I put into him, it was disheartening that he did not feel that love, for whatever reason.

I looked back down at the book, with my thumb marking the page. I sat in disbelief at the thoughts of my very best friend — thoughts I'd known absolutely nothing about. *How could I have missed all of his misery?* I wondered. I re-opened the book and was mortified by the dark spirit that clouded the words of this journal of sadness. Page after page was replete with the abyss of dismay.

Chapter 13

After hours of reading and wiping heavy tears from my eyes, my mouth dropped when I got to the part about Lucinda, Lorenzo, and what Luke referred to as "The Monster".

Luke had become very descriptive when he wrote in his journal about these three individuals.

Years ago, there were a lot of rumors going around about Lorenzo and Lucinda, however, Lorenzo's mother was not having it.

"The Monster" already had a hold on our family; it had abused my sister and ripped out her soul.

"My goodness! What is he talking about? And what in the hell is 'The Monster'?" I said to myself. My mind was overloaded. These words were like a sword piercing through my soul. I looked at the clock; midnight had come and gone, and I needed to get some rest. I thought that, if I truly could get a good night's sleep, it would help me sift through these clues to figure out what in the world had happened.

I marked the page of the journal, put it on the table, and lay down in the plush, high-end hotel's master-suite bed, rolled over and looked at the nightstand, where I had placed the postcard of the islands I'd taken from the Harvey State Bank security box. When I glanced at the postcard propped up against the lamp, a light bulb appeared in my head. I don't know why, but I had a gut feeling that, if I could get away for a moment, back to our island getaway, I could sort some things out — there might be some answers there.

Sparrow, go to bed! I kept telling myself. I needed rest so I could nail my interview tomorrow. Abigail Lancaster was a tough cookie — and I needed to represent! I placed the journal on the nightstand, rolled over, and drifted off to sleep.

The next morning, a driver picked me up from the hotel, and I was headed to the radio station for my interview. On the way there, Tabitha called so we could go over every question Abigail might throw at me. Despite not getting a full night of sleep, and all the emotional waves of energy, I was spot on with my responses. Tabitha was always super organized but even more so when she was not going to be with me in person for my event.

"Sparrow, what are you wearing? Did you get that rack I sent you?"

"Tabitha, girl, this is a radio show, not live television. They won't know what I have on. I was thinking of wearing my gym clothes and sneakers," I responded, with a little smirk on my face. I loved getting under her skin even though I was already wearing the fine threads she'd picked out and had shipped to my hotel room.

"Are you kidding me? I don't have time for that. Ro, I know you are pulling my leg. Anyway, by the time you get back to the hotel from your interview, your bags will be packed. On the desk in your room is an envelope that has been over-nighted with some contract paperwork in prep for the upcoming events. You can review them on the plane, but you will need to have them confirmed and signed off on as soon as you land. I am really working hard on this for you, and you have a good shot at this new opportunity. Are you sitting down, Sparrow?" Tabitha asked as if she were going to do a drum roll.

"I am in the back seat of the town car you scheduled to pick me up. So, yes. I am sitting down."

"It is not final, but Lifequest Network would like to make *Step 1* into a Lifequest movie. I sent the paperwork to you for review. We need to act fast and get these documents over to your attorney for review ASAP!" I could hear Tabitha's excitement over the phone.

"Are you serious? That has got to be the best news I've heard in a long time," I said, clapping my hands, looking upwards, and saying, *Thank you, God.* It was at that moment I felt the need to call Weston and then Luke to tell them the good news. Then it hit me: I no longer had a best friend to share these great moments. I began to cry.

I had to regroup — and quickly. There was a pause on the phone.

"Dr. Sparrow Mack!" Tabitha demanded, as she always does.

"Yes, I'm here!" I said as I sniffled and patted my eyes with a Kleenex, trying not to smudge my makeup.

"Now, I need you to keep yourself together. I know you've been going through a lot lately, grieving and all the while trying to get as much work done as you possibly could. Ro, the AP went over the wire about one hour ago, regarding the movie first-look, and I say, talk about it, if Abigail asks. They have given you the green light, and the network is very excited about the project. Let's get the word out. This can be huge for us, Ro!"

I arrived at the radio station. It was more like a studio, one of Abigail's satellite stations that she worked out of as she traveled throughout the country. It appeared to be a nice radio station but a little cold — not in temperature but in the atmosphere that resonated through the demeanor of everyone who worked there that I came in contact with. An intern, who appeared to be scared of the interviewer, led me to the sound booth.

Damn, I thought I would at least get to meet Abigail before going live on the air. But I guess not! I thought to myself, while being escorted directly to the sound booth by the intern. And there she was in the flesh — Abigail Lancaster. She sat and looked me up and down.

"Hello. I'm Dr. Sparrow Mack. How are you? And thank you for granting me this interview," I said in an attempt to open the conversation in a friendly way.

"Sit. I know who you are!" Abigail exclaimed.

Well, damn! I thought as I sat on the edge of my seat. My palms and my armpits became a little sweaty. I tried to position myself and adjust the microphone; it gave back reverb and feedback.

"Don't touch anything until I tell you to," Abigail said as she situated her big-framed eyeglasses comfortably on her face.

Oh, no, she didn't. My eyes bucked. I had to keep in the forefront of my mind that this woman had at her fingertips the potential to blow up my career, so I had better play it cool. I just smiled and remained calm.

"I have been looking forward to this all week. And finally, you're here. Sparrow, I don't use titles, so don't get your panties all in a bunch," she said in a dramatic, over-the-top tone. She pointed to the guy in the corner, and the green on-the-air sign lit up. Just like a shark that was headed for its prey, all at once she came right in for me with the questions.

"As I promised my faithful listeners, I am sitting here with Sparrow Mack, author of the little book, *Step 1*. So, first, I'm so sorry for your recent loss. Is this the friend that you reference in *Step 1*, who died a couple of weeks ago?" Abigail asked.

"Well, this is a fiction book. And the character in the book is a fictional character."

She interrupted. "Yeah, yeah, yeah. Just in case you didn't get the memo, this is reality talk radio. We get down and dirty and all up in your business. The people, my listeners, and all my followers want to know the truth. Are you the truth? Are you real? That's why I have you on my show, because you're real, right? And we have only real people on my show!"

She leaned toward me and asked again, echoing in the microphone,

"Sparrow Mack — are you real?"

I could feel my blood pressure rising.

"Yes, I am real. My followers know I am real. However, out of honor and respect to my late, recently deceased friend, I am going to allow the readers to read the book and gather what they wish from it. It is about the power of true friendship. Now, please, out of respect, can you please move on to your next set of questions and focus on the book and not assume it's about my personal relationships?"

Damn! I really messed this shit up, didn't I? I thought as beads of sweat started to gather at my temples. I attempted to wipe the sweat off discreetly, so as I would not reveal how much *The Abigail Lancaster* got to me and got under my skin. *Or was I just truly insecure? Or was I indeed not really real as she put it?* I could feel Abigail looking me up and down in distaste. My neck and cheeks felt hot. I was embarrassed, confused, sleep-deprived, and disgusted with myself. *Why did I just lose my cool and possibly fumble what I had worked so hard for?*

I took a deep breath and proceeded to answer her questions. However, they seemed to get tougher and tougher. I knew I had all the answers to the questions; she just got me rattled, but I hung in there. I had even heard of her making some of her interviewees cry, and not in a good way. I was not going to go down without a fight, besides I knew God was on my side. *And no weapon formed against me was going to prosper,* I kept telling myself over and over.

It had been about an hour of heavy questioning, not so much about the book, although I kept redirecting my responses back to the reason that I was invited to the interview in the first place, and that was to talk about *Step 1.* The interview started out a little rough, however I was steadfast, nimble, and quick with my responses in true Sparrow fashion, determined with all of my might not to let her break my spirit and put a halt to what I had worked so hard for. *This was my time to shine, and I claimed it!*

After what I can truthfully categorize as the longest forty-five minutes of my life — question upon question — there was an uncomfortable pause in the room while the man in the corner motioned to Abigail to keep the conversation going. She looked at me with one eyebrow slightly raised, and the pregnant pause lingered in the air. You could hear crickets. If Tabitha were here, she would be climbing the walls in disapproval at the delivery of my brand. However, it was too late. This was it. I'd probably bombed the interview, but I wasn't going to let anybody, even *The Abigail Lancaster,* run me over.

The interview was finally over, thank God. She was a genuine straight shooter, and I can honestly say that everything that I had heard about her was absolutely true. She was a tough woman, a true critic, intelligent and crass. She did not bite her tongue and just downright did not give a shit if she hurt my damn feelings or left me feeling like I wanted go into the corner curl up in a ball and cry my eyes out. We were polar opposites. I continued to sit still, afraid to move, in pure shock of the words that had come out of my mouth, let alone the tone that I'd relayed to her.

You know what? To hell with it. Let me get my shit and get out of here! I thought as I got up to leave, gathering my belongings, including my self-pride, to get the hell up out of here quickly.

Breaking the awkward silence, Abigail stood up from her position across from me, moved her eyeglasses up from her nose and smirked while she pulled the microphone off of its stand and said to me and her listeners,

"I knew I was going to like you. You have spunk. You have zeal." She came over to the side of the table that I was on and reached out and gave me a shoulder hug. She concluded the up-and-coming author interview segment by saying, "There — you've heard it from the author herself, Dr. Sparrow Mack. She has written the soon-to-be-best-seller, *Step 1*. To all of my listeners, go out and support this awesome, dynamic woman!" She signed off her segment, looked at her cell phone, and responded to a text.

The paid-programming commercial came on, and Abigail leaned into me and said,

"Sparrow, the interview is over; you can relax now." I felt a huge weight lift off my shoulders. I'd survived *The Abigail Lancaster,* and it had turned out better than I could have ever imagined. This was nothing but the Lord's doing, and I was grateful.

"Sparrow, do you have a moment? Can you follow me down to my office?" Abigail asked as she signaled me to follow her.

This is unbelievable! I kept thinking to myself, taking it all in. *I can't believe, despite everything I am going through and feeling, that God has shown me so much favor.*

As we walked down the hall, everyone in Abigail's path jumped out of her way, and I could see the fear in the eyes of her employees.

Oh boy, what is this woman really like? Should I be glad I have her endorsement if everyone is afraid of her?

All of the individuals in their cubicles held their heads down to prevent eye contact and pretended to do busy work as we passed.

In the hallway leading up to her office, there were pictures of Abigail with all of the living presidents during our time and every celebrity imaginable in gold frames. And those fabulous pictures were alongside stellar crystal achievement awards mounted on the wall.

"Wow! Abigail, do all of these awards belong to you?" I asked, acting all new, but I could not help it.

She just ignored me and walked toward her office door.

We arrived. I looked in, and the area was modern and sleek. There was a strong aroma of jasmine present as soon as I entered the room. Abigail walked in, hung up her fine knit jacket, took a shawl off the brass coat tree in the corner, and draped it around her arms in a hurry. She sat down behind her desk, made of white quartz, and peered at me over her glasses.

And then, all of a sudden, she relaxed and began to chat. We talked about our careers and families, and we got so carried away that we were virtually both talking at the same time. It was as if the Abigail in the booth and this Abigail in her office were two different people. To be honest, it was a little bipolar. It was like having a much-needed girls' day with one of your best girlfriends as opposed to the prolonged bout with tyranny that had occurred just moments before in the radio sound booth.

This side of Abigail Lancaster and I had so much in common. We were both mothers, wives, and highly functioning career women who were at the pinnacle of success and who had accomplished so much, with so much more ahead of us to achieve. We got along so well that we even planned to connect again for lunch soon and possibly a spa day. To top the day off, Abigail informed me she would like to set up the book signing in Florida.

"Oh, my goodness, Abigail. Are you serious? Thank you so much. I'm honored and truly humbled by this opportunity."

As we walked out of the building laughing and talking, everyone at the radio station was in awe of seeing this side of Abigail and the joy that exuded out of her face. You could tell the radio employees in this satellite station were not familiar with this side of Abigail. It was as if, in true Sparrow fashion, I was able to encourage Abigail to get down to her core and be her true self — a genuinely happy person — not at all the miserable tyrant that she played in real life.

And more so, it was amazing to see that, if you are true to God and yourself, the divine will work things out for you. God was definitely smiling on me in the midst of this horrific storm. It appeared I had lost so much — my best friend, my history, and a part of me. But, right in the midst of the storm, it felt like the clouds were finally rolling back and God was putting me back on track.

After my interview with Abigail in my hometown, Luke's funeral, and my detective work, I hopped on a plane to go home and get back to work for the time being. Now that the book signing would be coming up soon, I had to put my detective hat on the shelf for a minute to get through taking care of business. I was transitioning out of my medical career, and my writing career was all over social media and the AP after the successful interview, with my books flying off the shelves, per Tabitha. My plane landed, and I arrived back home. I could not wait to see my family. I had missed my boys.

As soon as I landed, Tabitha reached out let me know that she had already received correspondence from Abigail Lancaster regarding the book signing she'd offered to set up in Miami next week and confirmed that the book sales continued to consistently catapult.

When I got the confirmation of when the book signing was going to be, a light bulb went off in my head: *The book signing is going to be in Miami! Man, I can kill two birds with one stone. When I complete the book signing, I can go check out that home for the disabled that I found out about in Luke's belongings. I need to know why in the hell the money that I was automatically drafting out of my personal account and wiring to Luke was going toward taking care of this mysterious person in the home for the disabled!*

I'd finally made it home. It was so good seeing my family and getting a good night's sleep. The next morning, I lingered a little bit in my own bed in my own home. This was nice. It was great to sleep next to the love of my life and also get a chance to spend time with my son. My life was starting to feel a little normal again, minus Luke. There were things that I still needed to figure out regarding him. But I was in a place of balance and transition and needed to regain my total focus on what was at hand today. In getting started with my day, I realized I had several missed calls from Tabitha. In addition, there was a text message she'd sent:

"Ro — call me ASAP. I have some news for you!"

"What's going on, Tabitha?" I replied

"Girl, you will not believe this, but 'The Abigail Lancaster' set you up with a premier book signing!" she replied.

"I know — Abigail said that her assistant would contact you once she'd confirmed all the details," I replied.

"Okay, since you know so much, I bet you didn't know this: the one and only Abigail Lancaster has set it up where you have a guaranteed 300 books sold at this book signing," Tabitha replied.

I almost hit the floor. I could not believe what I was reading.

I looked toward heaven and hollered, "Thank you, Jesus!" and let out a big scream that startled the baby, causing him to whimper some. But the nanny was already in the house; she soothed his crying and took him upstairs to get him dressed, so mommy could talk business.

"God is so good, girl!" I typed back to Tabitha.

"All the time, girl — all the time!" Tabitha typed back in agreement.

My phone rang, and it was Tabitha.

"Sparrow, enough with all the text messaging. This news is too good to be texting about. And since you know so much, I bet you didn't know this. Are you ready?" Tabitha said in a curious tone.

"Tabitha, get to the point. Quit playing with me!"

"Sparrow, come outside."

"What are you talking about?" I said as I slipped on some shoes, went to the front door, opened it, stuck my head out, and looked. There was Tabitha in her car, parked in my driveway, with a big grin on her face.

"Girl, have you been out here all the while?"

"Just come here. I have something for you to see!"

What in the world is Tabitha up to? She always has something up her sleeve, I thought to myself as I walked toward her drop-top yellow Corvette with 24-inch rims.

"Tabitha, girl, I see you in this ride!"

"Sparrow, I'm trying to keep up with you!"

"No, you're not, because I'm keeping it humble and still roll in my paid-for classic *hoop tie*." We laughed as she handed me an envelope that had already been opened.

I glanced at who it was from; it was from Grace Publishing House.

"This envelope is addressed to me, but it's open!"

"Yes, I know. I couldn't help myself. Besides, I had to make sure it was legit and up to our standards!"

I looked at her with the side eye as I pulled the documents out of the envelope.

Staring at the contents, I could not believe my eyes. Attached to the proposal was my first check from the publishing house — for $100,000.

I let out a deep breath, as I could not believe it. I was so grateful, but still, this was nowhere near what I needed to fully retire and focus on writing full time.

"Yes!" I said, as I clutched the check in my hand and raised it to the heavens in gratitude. I could not wait to call Weston at work and let him know.

I hugged Tabitha through her hot-rod car window.

"Now, who's your girl?" Tabitha proclaimed.

"Girl, you are!" I responded.

"And who's got your back?" she asked again, filling up her ego tank.

"Sistah — you do!" I said as I waved the check in the air.

Tabitha confirmed she would get the details ironed out for the book signing. And out of curiosity, I questioned her about how she came to know about the signing so quickly.

"Ro, that's my job. No, seriously — I called Abigail Lancaster a couple of days prior to the interview to go over the potential questions. She requested a preview copy, and I sent it to her."

"For real?" I said in excitement.

"Yes, I knew you were busy with the funeral and everything, so I didn't bother you with those details. However, once she read the book, she was sold on it and was a Sparrow Mack fan. She loved the concept of the book and what it stood for — the perils of friendship. She insisted on using her influence to help set up a book signing, and her team also helped me work out the details of the requirements of the contract. So in having your back, I went for the gusto, and they agreed to our terms. I knew your heart's desire was to have a guaranteed-book-sold book signing, and Abigail's influence was able to make it happen. I know all that has been going on has been really hard to process. Now that the funeral is over and your clinical obligations have slowed down, we appear to be on the backside of all of the distractions. You are now able to focus on making some dividends in the literary world."

"Thank you, Tabitha!"

"No thanks needed. It's my job!" Tabitha said as her yellow Corvette drove off and she turned on her beats in my neighborhood, playing loud music all the way out of the subdivision.

She better turn that music down, or the HOA is going to be all down my throat!

And truth be told, I was right behind her headed to the bank to deposit that large check, while the nanny took care of little Weston. As I signed the back of the check, I kept saying, "God, you sure are good. You sure are good!"

I left the bank and headed back home with a smile on my face. Weston was at work, and I sent him a text regarding this abundant blessing.

I arrived home still on cloud nine.

Damn, if Luke were here, we would be catching a flight, on my dime, of course, to meet up with me to celebrate. That is how we used to roll. That caused me to want to find out a bit more about what had happened to him, but I would need to handle business first. I looked through the emails detailing the particulars of the book signing Abigail had set up for me, and I was floored. The set up exceeded any and everything I thought I could have asked for. I was so grateful for God's favor!

I saw where Tabitha had forwarded the contract to my legal counsel for review, as I was carbon copied on the email. And the lawyer felt that the contract looked good and recommended we agree to the terms. It was a blessing and relief.

Leading up to the book signing, I had an overwhelming sense that my literary career was off to a great start. I had to hold off on the puzzle pieces of the mystery surrounding Luke until I got through the book signing in Miami. My focus needed to be on my business and career goals. I wanted to make sure my commerce and legacy wealth was a priority for my family. Even though my focus had been redirected, I kept the journal and all of the mystery it held in safe keeping while I prepared for my upcoming literary events.

Later that night, after we read a bedtime story to our son and put him to bed, my husband and I enjoyed a nightcap together. We had a nice conversation about the upcoming book signing, and I told him all about the interview that I had with Abigail and how I represented. Before we knew it, he fell asleep, and I sat in the bed, restless. I decided to get up and retreat to the study. I sat in the chaise lounge to reflect on the blessing of the upcoming book signing.

God is always lining things up for me! I said to myself. Next to the chaise lounge was a wood end table with the leather journal — Luke's journal.

"Oh, my. I forgot I put this here!" I said as I reached toward it and allowed my hand to graze across the embossing. I picked it up and went right in reading it. With each word, the more I read, the angrier I got. Luke wrote:

I can't continue to go on like this! It is time for me to do away with myself, because I cannot live with myself any longer.

How could Luke not value his life? I had stuck with him through so many trials and tribulations. Those words angered me and riddled me with guilt at the fact that I, his best friend, had missed all that he was going through.

It was late that evening, and I was tired. My phone was on the end table next to the chaise lounge when I got a text. It was Abigail Lancaster. I sat up and looked at my phone. *OMG, Abigail Lancaster is texting me! Who would have ever guessed this would happen?*

"Hey, Sparrow. This is Abigail Lancaster. I'll be in town tomorrow. Let's touch base over dinner. How's eight?"

It was late. I could see by looking at the clock on the desk across the room that it was near midnight, however, I could not help but respond. Besides, this was *The Abigail Lancaster* texting me. "I'm free. Let me know the place," I responded, trying not to sound too eager, although I was.

"You live near the Meadows Country Club, right?" Abigail texted.

"Yes, I do. That's my neighborhood!"

"How about the clubhouse? I love their food. See you there," Abigail replied.

"See you then!" I stated enthusiastically. With Luke's leather binder on my chest and all of the issues written on every page of this book, I felt a little refreshed communicating with a possible new friend who was already an established person and needed nothing from me. And this was a person who had already planted a great seed into my life.

Chapter 14

The next night I arrived at the Meadows Country Club at 7:45pm so I would not be late for girls night out dinner with Abigail.

I needed this break, just to unwind a little. I was looking forward to this.

I thought, as I stood at the door of the Meadows Country Club, hesitant to go in without Abigail. I figured that would be rude. While I waited, I grabbed my compact and refreshed my lips with that slamming coral lip stain I'd gotten from Dean Baby in the green room. Out of the corner of my eye, I saw a speeding car drive into the circle drive of the country club, almost hitting the curb. It was a fully loaded Maserati with black-bladed 22-inch rims. You could tell the driver did not have a good handle on the car, but the car was fire.

My, that is a nice whip! I thought as I put my compact back in my bag and reached in to grab my phone so I could unassumingly take a picture of this beautiful car.

I am going to put this on my vision board! I said to myself, as I snapped the photo, trying to be discreet, then quickly put my phone down by my side and attempted to look away.

The butterfly door opened, and the valet quickly went over as the other patrons waiting on the curb and I stood there with our mouths open at this beautiful, drop-dead-gorgeous car. A svelte leg swung out of the car door, and it was Abigail. She hopped out of that fierce ride, tossed the keys to the valet, came over to me, and we hugged. She said,

"I'm starved. Let's go eat!"

"Aren't you going to check your car in with the valet?" I asked with naiveté.

"Girl, they know me!" she said as she grabbed my arm and walked me around the front of the car, so I could see it in its full grandeur.

"Girl, I see you! Nice ride," I said, as we greeted each other casually.

"Yep, it's beautiful isn't it? Black on black — you can't go wrong with that! I picked it up just today. It's custom. I flew in to get it, and I'm driving it back home tomorrow. It is an early b-day present I bought myself. Happy Birthday to me! I earned it! You like?" Abigail asked as she wiped off the hood with her bare hand and blew the car a kiss.

"Yes, it is gorgeous. That's what's up!" I replied, giving her a wink.

I'd called ahead for VIP seating, so the wait staff showed us to our table.

I had on my skinny ripped blinged-out jeans, couture t-shirt, Italian slip-on shoes, my oversized bag, shades, and a wrap for my shoulders. Abigail must have gotten the memo too, because she was dressed casually chic as well.

The waiter showed us to our seats, and we sat down. We were already seated and had begun a superficial conversation when the waiter came to take our drink order. Out of the clear blue, Abigail demanded,

"Let's go sit over there by the window. I would love to look out at the pond while I drink — well, I mean eat and drink. Waiter, I want that table right over there!"

The wait staff was a little taken aback, as they presumed they'd seated us at the top table in the establishment. However, they obliged her, and we moved. As Abigail walked in front of the waiter and me over to the table she wanted, I mouthed in silence to the wait staff, "Sorry," as I shrugged my shoulders and smiled. I was not sure how this evening was going to go, but I was here now, so I might as well make the best of it.

"Abigail, do you like this country club? I think it is one of the nicer ones in my city." I was hoping that Abigail would be impressed with the venue and the food. Even though I had apparently sealed the deal with her, she was a tough cookie, and I felt like she was still impressionable and could change her mind at any moment about her generosity.

To my question, Abigail looked around at the marble floors, mahogany wood paneling, magnificent crown molding, and tables accented by columns everywhere.

"This place is kind of cute," she said as she sipped her slightly dirty martini with blue cheese stuffed olives and I sipped a chilled Riesling. As the drinks kept coming, the conversation continued, and this was turning out to be a nice outing. *Who would have ever thought little ole' me would be schmoozing with Abigail Lancaster, the mega-celebrity of the literary world?* I thought to myself.

We ordered stuffed mushrooms, lamb sliders, and sautéed chicken skewers with grilled vegetables.

We talked about where we grew up and our college years. As the evening wore on, Abigail asked me a multitude of questions. It was almost like an interview for a new-best-friend role. It appeared she had a void to fill in the friendship area, and I *definitely* did, with the loss of Luke.

She shared that she had an older daughter from a previous relationship and a son in elementary school. She and her soon-to-be-ex-husband still lived under one roof. They were in the process of divorce. They had not been happy for years. While she was off living out her dream of becoming a big-time radio personality, establishing her career as a literary critic, and now a well-known celebrity in her own right, he was a stay-at-home dad raising their son. He went to all of his school functions, helped him with his homework, took him to soccer practice and made sure Abigail was free from any parental duties that got in the way of her profession. She confided in me, as she sipped on her drink,

"My soon-to-be-ex-husband is living in the basement," she explained as she finished off one martini, wiped her mouth with the white linen napkin, and sucked down the olive stuffed with blue cheese. She waved over the waiter for another.

"Okay. I thought you were separated."

"We are."

"Okay. Well, how is that working for you and your children — him still living in the home?" I asked, wanting to know more but trying not to pry, since we had just made acquaintance.

"Well, my daughter is out of the house, and it works great for me. It's so good, at times. It's as if he is just a nanny taking care of our son," Abigail shared as she signaled for the waiter to bring another round.

Wow! That's pretty deep, I thought to myself. She went on to say,

"We're like roommates, and we rarely cross paths. Our son just thinks daddy is in his man cave all the time when he is home. My little boy has no clue, and I'm going to keep it like that."

"Pardon me for infringing, and please tell me if I am out of line. But how long do you plan on living like this?" I was concerned, trying not to pry too much.

"Not too much longer; he's really insecure. I'm rich now. He thinks I'm going to become wealthy and super famous and leave him high and dry. I am ready to make this divorce final, so I can start dating. Sparrow, I am so ready to move on, and I'm going to break the news to him real soon," she shared.

Before I knew it, in true Sparrow fashion, I let it slip out of my mouth: "Be careful, what we plan and what God plans are two different things." I advised with a grave, look on my face. She nodded her head in agreement, took a sip of her freshly made martini, and licked her lips as she grabbed another appetizer and devoured it like she had not eaten in a week.

"This food is fire. If I had this chef, I would not be able to fit into any of my clothes," Abigail said, and we both gave a small laugh, as it was obvious to me that she was deliberately changing the subject.

We downed our fair share of cocktails and ate enough food to last a week. And most of all, we appeared to bond over deep conversation. The dinner was over, and the chef got word that Abigail Lancaster was in the restaurant and came out to make sure that the cuisine was to her liking. He announced that the delicious meal was on the house, after he took a picture with her. *God is good*!

"Wow, I can get used to this," I said.

"Don't worry, Dr. Sparrow Mack. This is the life you are walking into soon with your talent. You have a gift."

"Why, thank you, Abigail. I must say that I can't let this evening go without showing gratitude for your endorsement and arranging the books-sold and book signing, Abigail. No one has ever done anything like that for me."

She grabbed my arm so we could walk our heels on the cobblestone walkway to avoid falling, as we both were a little tipsy.

"I see a lot of me in you. It's time for me to pay it forward. Besides, you deserve it!" Abigail replied as we arrived to the valet area like long-time sister-friends.

"Abigail, are you ready to head back to your hotel? And are you good to drive?" I asked.

"Girl, I am nice. I am good. The hotel is just down the street. I'm familiar with this area," Abigail replied as she reached for me to give a surprising embrace. I obliged and returned the gesture.

As I began to walk away, she yelled out to me, "Hold on, Ro."

"Yes, Abigail?"

"Come here, girl, it's selfie time! I would love to post this on my site in preparation for the upcoming book signing."

We came in close, I tousled my hair, she adjusted her glasses, and we pouted our lips and took our picture. We chuckled afterwards like schoolgirls. This felt like a natural beginning to a long friendship, and I welcomed it.

We were at the curb, and George said, "Goodnight, Dr. Ro. I hope you and your guest had a good time tonight. We'll see you soon. Hey, are both of you alright to drive?"

George took one look at us laughing and swaying on the railing at the valet station and said, "Nope — y'all are not alright. Alex, you get Mrs. Lancaster's keys, and I will get Dr. Sparrow's."

We made it to our perspective destinations safely due to my valet buddies at the clubhouse.

When I arrived home, Weston was sleep, and so was the baby. I took my shower and was putting lotion on my arms when I received a pic and text message from Abigail:

"Dr. Sparrow Mack, you are truly a superstar! I am so excited about the future that lies ahead for you. I may not see all that you become, but I know it will be great!" Abigail also sent the pic we took outside of the clubhouse.

I was still in awe that I was getting a personal text from Abigail Lancaster. I texted back,

"Thank you from the bottom of my heart. I had a great time tonight, and I look forward to all that the future holds for both of us!"

The house was quiet, and my husband rolled over once and asked me if I'd had a good time. I assured him I had as he rolled over and went back to sleep.

Still inebriated with spirits, I was up and wide awake, so I decided to look at the documents I had gotten from the box marked "Safe Contents" in Busy's closet.

How did I miss this? I asked myself when I picked up an official document from a private detective that was an analysis of the plane crash that Dr. Ernesto and his wife were killed in.

Regarding the plane, the investigation of the engine and mechanics of the plane were certified, and it was determined that the plane was working properly. There was no engine failure, no gas leakage, and no structural compromise of the body of the plane. Based on the analysis of the plane's integrity and radar plotting, what appeared to have happened was that the plane, operated by physician and seasoned pilot Dr. Enrique Ernesto, suddenly banked left and crashed. The bodies of Dr. Ernesto and his wife Mrs. Ernesto were burned but intact. The autopsy report showed both of their blood sugars were significantly low, at 20 and 35 respectively, which is alarming. And that was thought to be the root cause of the crash — hypoglycemia. The investigative synopsis was that the pilot suffered a severe hypoglycemic episode, causing the crash that resulted in the pilot and his wife's death. This was determined to be a tragic accident due to a medical emergency. Additional toxicology studies were recommended. However, the son, with power of attorney, refused to have additional testing. They were made aware that the window of opportunity to determine if there were any additional drugs found in their blood system was closing. The children declined any additional testing be completed. Signed, Detective James Stroud.

My soul cringed at what I read. Dr. Ernesto was a mentor during my medical school years and residency. I knew his wife; she was not a warm-and-fuzzy type of lady, but they were a powerful couple in the community and were always in the newspaper, handing out big checks to charity. I sure hated that they'd passed away in that manner. That was awful.

"Babe, you need to get some rest now. Go ahead and turn out the light," Weston said as he pulled the covers over his head to shield himself from the beam coming from the lamp on my nightstand.

"I will, sweetie. You want me to go into the other room? There is a little reading I need to do before I call it a night." By the time I finished my sentence, Weston had gone back to sleep, so I finished reading right where I was. I decided to pick up Luke's journal and read a couple of pages.

I'd bookmarked where I'd left off in the journal. I took a deep breath and dove right in to this lengthy journal entry that was written many years ago:

After I am gone, my work is still not done. I have a lot of unfinished business, and I pray I am forgiven. There are people who have betrayed my family and me in such a way that I cannot let that shit go. My spirit will not rest until I do what I need to do. There are those who are closest to me who have betrayed me beyond belief. I have taken note of that. I feel so cheated and abused. I have always come in second or no place at all, and I am tired of this feeling.

I will never forgive myself for allowing people to take advantage of my caring spirit. The Monster will no longer reign! It is my time up to bat, and this is only the beginning. I am my own demise.

Those words put me in full contemplation mode. I could see the words, but what were their underlying meanings? I was baffled at what Luke was going through, and moreover, I asked myself,

"What is Luke trying to tell me?"

It felt like I was truly trading my physician/writer hat in for that of detective.

I needed to write out a plan and looked around for some paper, but there was none. I thumbed to the back pages of the journal, where a few blank sheets were. What better place to write out a plan to get to the bottom of the mystery surrounding Luke?

I decided to write out a timeline of the information I knew. The timeline laid out my finding out about the passing of Luke, to finding all of the contents in the box, to the discovery at the bank. I realized beyond a shadow of a doubt that *I* needed to figure out what had happened and no one else could get to the bottom of this but me. God was speaking to me by giving me this duty to fulfill.

I felt there was more information to be had, and I decided the best next step was to get my paper lined up, so I could have the money in my hush account to do what I needed to do. I could make moves without tipping my hand to anybody. Neither my husband nor my parents would approve of me getting involved in any of Luke's indiscretions, even from beyond the grave.

I would go to the next stop on my tour, the book signing Abigail set up for *Step 1* in Miami. And while I was in that area, I would check out that Florida Residential Care facility on the outskirts of Miami to understand the relevance of this place Luke felt so inclined to put into a vaulted bank lock box. I could swing by there to see if I could square up any answers to the questions I hadn't even fully developed in my mind yet. I had a plan. I placed the journal in a secure place, and I went back to bed.

The next several days I spent preparing for a once-in-a-lifetime opportunity, the book signing Abigail Lancaster had set up. I was excited. The way this book signing was arranged was sure to catapult my writing career and take it to the next level.

I battened down the hatches on the clinic that I worked locums in periodically and then packed to head out for the book singing. As soon as the plane landed in Miami, I began getting alerts. The first one was from the driver, letting me know he had gotten the updated flight information and knew the flight was going to be late. He would be waiting outside of baggage claim since I only had a small carry-on per the information from my agent. I had several texts from Tabitha but decided to check them once I got to the town car because I didn't want to make the driver wait any longer, since I was running behind schedule. I would love to have gotten my favorite chai tea over at the food court, but I did not have time, and my stomach was surely mad at me, as it had begun to growl. Those peanuts on the plane had definitely not been enough. I would get a bite to eat at the hotel.

I walked out of the airport toward the black town car with the gentleman holding the sign with my name on it. Miami was as beautiful, sunny, and relaxing as I remembered. I felt relaxed just by breathing the air; it was so delightful and refreshing. Tabitha was able to adjust her schedule to be present for this book signing. It was going to be nice, as we would be meeting at the hotel. She had taken an earlier flight to get here before me to iron out any last minute details.

Since starting off representing me, Tabitha had developed quite a notable roster of clients for herself, which caused her to miss some of the appearances she'd lined up for me as one of her premier clients. However, I supported her growth. And even when she was not able to be there in person, she took care of business. Sometimes, it was a little overwhelming trying to figure everything out, even with a well-laid itinerary. It was going to be so good to have my agent here in person to walk me through the event and be my onsite ace in the hole.

In the back of the town car, I scrolled through my texts, and there were several general ones from Tabitha to call her ASAP. I called her, and it went straight to voice mail:

"This is Tabitha, Celebrity Broker and Agent to the Five Star Elite Personnel. If you have a mission of excellence for your career and are ready to go to the next level, I can make it happen!"

"Tabitha, call me! I just landed." I called several more times, but there was no answer.

I guess I'll connect with her at the hotel, I thought to myself, *as she should already be there*. It was going to be so good having her here, and I was getting a little excited about the event — with guaranteed book sales, who wouldn't be?

I arrived at the hotel, and I could see Tabitha standing in the lobby with her back to me while the bellman retrieved my carry-on bag to take it to check in.

"Tabitha, I've been calling you," I proclaimed as I walked up to her.

She turned around with tears streaming down her face.

"Girl, what's wrong?" I asked as I put my purse on the end table next to the leather couch in the lobby and reached out to embrace her.

"Sparrow, I have been trying to call you! You won't believe this!" she said frantically.

"Tabitha, what happened?" I asked.

"It's Abigail!"

"What happened to Abigail? Did she back out of the book signing deal? I knew this was way too good to be true."

"No, no! Nothing like that! They found her dead in her home this morning!"

"Are you serious? What happened?" I had to sit down. I pulled Tabitha toward the couch to sit.

"Tabitha, I am not understanding. Start from the beginning. What happened?"

"They think it was her estranged husband. A murder-suicide."

"Oh, dear God. What about her son, or rather, her children?"

"Her son was with her parents at the time. And the older daughter did not live in the home. Thank God the children weren't harmed."

A vision of how Abigail and I had had a chance to bond at dinner flashed through my mind. And truth be told, I had a bad feeling about what she was telling me regarding her husband. It seemed he didn't want to let her go, but *he didn't have to kill her*. I did a web search while in shock, and Tabitha continued to wipe her eyes. I was inundated with newsfeeds about the death of famed radio personality Abigail Lancaster.

"Tabitha, did they arrest him?" I asked as I scrolled through my phone, skimming the information.

"Girl, didn't you hear me say it was a murder-suicide?"

"This is awful. I'm having trouble wrapping my head around this. I was just with Abigail."

"So, Sparrow, this brings me to the change of events. I already spoke with Abigail's publicist, and the 100 books have already been purchased; you should see the direct deposit into your account later today. But, the book signing has been put on hold."

"Girl, my goodness — this is awful. I just can't believe this. I just had dinner with her the other day.

And now she's gone. Tabitha, what can we do for her kids and her parents?"

"I don't have any information on that, but I'll keep you posted."

I pulled up a picture, the selfie that Abigail and I took before we left the restaurant. Her smile lit up the picture. We looked like lifelong friends. I showed it to Tabitha, and she gave a half smile while shaking her head in disbelief.

"Tabitha, you know what? Let's scrap the book signing here altogether. Let's not put it on hold or anything like that. And the deposit that was put in for the 300 books — let's donate half to Abigail's children's memorial fund when they establish it and the other half of the monies to a domestic-violence charity in her name. I'm sure Weston would not have any problem with me doing that."

"Ro, that is so thoughtful. You touch base with Weston; then give me the green light, and I'll make that happen!" Tabitha said while wiping her eyes and typing on her phone, making modifications to our plans.

"Tabitha, what are your plans now since you flew out here and the book signing is cancelled?" I asked.

"I have already booked another flight out tonight. I have some work I really need to get caught up on. What do you want to do? I was going to go ahead and book your flight too, but I wanted to check with you first. But, as usual, you didn't have your phone on airplane mode, did you?"

"No, I did not. Girl, you know I am not good with this tech stuff. You know what? I'm good. I have some things I need to look into while I'm here. I will text you later to let you know when to make my travel plans back home."

Tabitha got in a car headed to the airport. I looked further online to see what else I could find out about Abigail and the tragedy. I found a press release with the details surrounding her premature and tragic death. On the news feeds, there were several photos. There was her solo picture, in which she gave her signature Abigail Lancaster look. Effortlessly, in the picture with her two kids, she exuded joy. However, contrarily the wedding picture with her husband showed her looking more alarmed than happy. He held her tight. The article below shared that she was a huge philanthropist toward domestic violence charities. The article talked about how she was a no-nonsense radio personality and how all of the up-and-coming radio personalities attempted to mimic her harsh and straight-to-the-point tactics in interviewing.

Weston was in meetings, so I texted him the newsfeed article online. He couldn't believe it, just as we all couldn't. When I got into my room to unpack and take a shower, it was all over the national news, on every channel and social media.

While Tabitha was in the air, we texted back and forth about the next steps regarding the book tour, the recent cancellation of this one in Miami, and what I should do next. I sent out a tribute to Abigail Lancaster on social media and asked for prayers for her family. I notified the fans of what the plans were regarding the books sold. I got my pen out and signed the 300 books, which, strangely, did not take that long. When I'd finished, a man came to get the books to take them to the venue.

"Dr. Mack, do you want to hand deliver them? The venue is down the street."

"Sure. I would love to."

There was a boatload of people already there for the official book signing. A lot of them were just now finding out about what had happened to Abigail. I wanted to at least make an appearance and thank everyone for the support for my newly released book, *Step 1.* I showed up, and the crowd was welcoming; many people were very tearful, as they were huge fans of Abigail Lancaster's, and had shown up to support me because of her prompting. And all who showed up were very grateful.

Instead of the normal type of book signing, I decided to have a candlelight vigil for those affected by domestic violence. The owner of the boutique bookstore had some candles; we passed them around and had a moment of silence. I honored Abigail in a brief speech, and we had a moment of silence. And then I announced that a portion of the proceeds from the pre-sold books would go to a local domestic violence foundation. Although she was not there, Tabitha was glad I had still shown up and delivered, and had been there for my new fans. I could feel their emotions surrounding the loss that they were experiencing — I could identify.

After that emotionally draining event, I made my way back to the hotel, unpacked my carry-on, and decided to relax. I poured a glass of water and decided to pull out the journal. One of the first papers I pulled out was the paperwork regarding the Florida Residential Care.

I was still very perplexed as to why Luke had this individual's residential policy in his security box. And who could "Eric" possibly be?

I looked up the address and the distance from the hotel, and the facility was about 30 miles north. I grabbed a snack and called down to the concierge for a car and driver. I gave the driver the address. The 30-mile ride seemed to last an eternity. I arrived at the building, which looked like an old colonial house. The lawn was perfectly manicured, with square, short hedges that lined the house and sidewalk with the sign out front. The door was red with a gold footplate and a doorknocker sign that read,

Please do not ring the doorbell. Come right in!

I walked in and smelled the strong aroma of gingerbread. There was an elderly gentleman who greeted me with a red-and-white-checkered apron wrapped around his waist and his sleeves were rolled up. He wiped his hands on the apron and glanced at me with a smile.

"Hello, young lady. What can I do you for?"

"Hello, sir. I am Dr. Sparrow Mack, in town on business, and I thought I would visit one of your residents."

"Oh, okay, Dr. Mack. Follow me to my office. Let me see if we can make that happen for you. Are you on the guest list?"

"Not sure," I replied as I followed him down the hall. The place was immaculately clean. It smelled very sterile. The gingerbread scent tickled my nose and my stomach.

"My name is Mr. Norton. We opened this facility 30 years ago, and this is my passion — providing a home away from home for the disabled. Today is cookie day for the residents — their favorite day of the week! Gingerbread cookies are on the menu today. Now, that is my specialty — well, actually it was my late wife's famous recipe. Okay, my dear. What is the name of the resident you are wanting to see?" he said as he entered his office and sat behind his desk, opening a file folder.

"Eric," I stated. Since the first name was really the only name I was sure of, that is all I said as I crossed my fingers.

"Oh, you know Eric? Well, he is the only Eric who resides here. And it has been a joy to take care of him. You know, when we first got him, he was a baby, but I'm sure you know that. He was the first baby we agreed to take here. My wife, God bless her precious soul, when she was still alive, nursed him through many an ailment. We got him to walking when he was about five, and he can now make a short sentence with words. After my wife passed away from heart disease, he stopped making much progress with his speech. But I think we have him back on the right track now. Now, Dr. Mack, let me see if you are on the visitors list for Mr.

Eric," Mr. Norton stated as he thumbed through Eric's file.

I knew I would not be on the visitors list in his chart. *What do I say then?* I pondered, but I continued to smile confidently.

All of a sudden, a lady ran in, looked at me, and then frantically turned to Mr. Norton.

"Excuse me, Mr. Norton — and pardon me, ma'am — there is a little problem in the kitchen. There's smoke everywhere! Come quick!" Mr. Norton quickly excused himself to attend to the emergency, leaving me in the office with Eric's open chart. I stood up, and my eyes could not help but notice the room number located next to his name: 201C. I looked at the approved visitors, and saw Luke's full name, he was listed as 'uncle.' However, there was a pencil line drawn through that name. Then there was another name — Lucinda Armstrong — she was listed as 'mother', and apparently she had visited last week. I was stunned.

This is Lucinda's son? Okay, I knew I remembered she had been pregnant before. However, the real question is how did Lucinda visit Eric last week when she has been dead for years? I thought.

I could not help but to quietly turn to the next page. It showed the demographic paperwork of the resident. It gave his diagnosis as Mental Retardation and Mild Cerebral Palsy due to traumatic premature birth. I don't know how I missed it, but at the very top of the page, there was Eric's full name, Eric Paul Ernesto.

Eric is an Ernesto? Aw, shit! What in the world? Lucinda from the wrong side of the tracks had a baby with wealthy-beyond-measure Ernesto? So why was Luke paying for this resident care here? I was truly perplexed.

And then there was a listing of Eric's parents' names. There was the name of "Lucinda Marie Armstrong," Luke's deceased sister. And Eric's father was listed as "Enrique Apollo Ernesto."

You have got to be kidding me. That's Dr. Ernesto! I quickly grabbed my phone to take a picture of the document.

I couldn't believe this! Dr. Ernesto and Lucinda had a baby together? I knew that she'd hung out with Lorenzo, Dr. Ernesto's son, but not the *Dr. Ernesto. This is crazy, and if Luke knew this, why did he not tell me?*

My heart now racing, I turned the page, and it was the billing information. The residential information listed for Lucinda Armstrong was in the Caribbean.

Wait a minute: The address listed here is to my Uncle Cyrus' timeshare condo. Luke often visited there with me, and I'd just discovered that Luke had made keys to the condo behind my back. I can't believe this!

And the change of address had been updated two weeks ago.

I was trying to hurry as fast as I could to obtain as much information as possible. I could hear people running around down the hallway, trying to contain the smoke. They were opening the doors, and I could hear Mr. Norton talking to attendants in the hallway.

"Everyone calm down. It's just a little smoke, no fire," he said in a calm, reassuring tone.

Interestingly enough, no fire detector had gone off. However, the fire trucks' sirens approached shortly after.

I need to get out of here! I thought. I decided to slip out of his office before Mr. Norton got back. I closed Eric's chart, as the rest of the contents seem to be demographic-type documents that served me no good. I snuck out of the office and walked down the hall.

The firemen came into the building, determined the all clear, and made the announcement that everything was fine; however the staff were still scurrying around, attempting to calm and reposition the residents they had started to evacuate.

As I was exiting the office, I looked at the wall and noticed the hallway to the right was the 200 hall and that the rooms were A through H. There appeared to be two wings to the facility; this place was a lot bigger than I thought. The smoke was all clear, and the residents were back in their places.

I had come too far to turn back now. I am going to take a chance and venture down the hallway to try to see Eric, if he was in his room, I thought to myself.

I stood in the doorway of room 201C. The smoke had cleared; however, the feeling of the room was dark and destitute. I saw what appeared to be a grown man sitting at a table, drawing with crayons — nothing specific, just coloring on white paper. He pressed hard on the paper to make an impression of his art. I was not expecting this person to be so big and grown. I don't know what I was expecting — possibly a kid or something. I walked in quietly, not knowing how he would take me or what type of reaction to anticipate.

"Uhhh!" he screamed out as he heard my footsteps walking toward him.

"Eric, how are you?" I asked softly keeping my voice gentle. He continued to color and grunt. The closer I got, I realized he looked just like Luke and Lucinda's side of the family, with beautiful olive skin. And I could definitely see Dr. Ernesto in him, as Eric had deep, big curly locks of hair.

"Eric, I'm Dr. Sparrow."

He turned around and looked down at my shoes; then he turned back and began to color again. "Shoes loud!" His voice boyish but demanding.

Compelled to connect with Eric, I took my shoes off, held them in my hands, slowly approached the table, and sat down across from him in a non-threatening way. In my natural parenting way. I said, "Eric, that is a nice drawing." He pressed harder with the crayon, and replied, "Green, green." And then he gave a half smile. I smiled, too, and he continued to color. He was a well-taken-care-of person. It appeared this facility was doing well with him, as he was clean and appeared to be groomed, although I was curious about why he'd been left alone, especially since there had just been an evacuation. I sat there for a couple of minutes and observed.

Eric had Luke and Lucinda's walnut-brown eyes, his skin was flawless, and his hair reminded me of Busy, with big dark curls. And ironically, he looked identical to Dr. Ernesto, which was extremely eerie. He was a very handsome young man who had the capacity of a five year if not younger. I looked at my watch and realized I needed to get back to the hotel. I had enough information about who Eric was and who his presumed parents were, and why Luke — or, rather, I — had been paying the bill here. This may explain why Mrs. Ernesto absolutely hated Lucinda and treated her with such disrespect. I had witnessed it with my own eyes on multiple occasions.

I looked into Eric's clueless eyes. They were totally oblivious to what had happened to his beautiful mother, Lucinda, or that his father, Dr. Ernesto, was thought to be one of the most brilliant medical minds of our time before his tragic end in that private-plane crash years ago. Or that he even had a little sister, Busy. And moreover, to what happened to his beloved uncle Luke, who made sure he was taken care of by any means necessary.

I got up to leave. Eric stopped coloring, turned toward me, and said, "Mama?"

I replied, "No, Eric. I'm not your mama."

Just then an attendant appeared from a closed door in the room that appeared to be a bathroom; she was drying her hands off.

"Ma, am, can I help you?"

"No, I was just leaving."

I quickly left the room, making my way to the foyer, in my bare feet with shoes in hand, running down the hallway like I was a convict on the run. I stopped at the foyer to put on my shoes, and I could see the fire trucks leaving the parking lot. I turned around and was startled to see Mr. Norton standing right there. He was chuckling to himself, as he said, "False alarm, false alarm. We'll have another batch of gingerbread cookies on the way. Now, let's get back to that visitor's list for Mr. Eric."

"Mr. Norton, you have been so kind. Thank you. I really have to go. I'll come back some other time to visit."

"Are you sure, sweetie? In about twenty more minutes, you can have a batch of warm gingerbread cookies to go!" he said, kindly.

"Really, Mr. Norton, they smell absolutely delicious, and if I had more time, I would stay," I said as I walked out the door and waved.

I got back into the waiting car and sat in the back with tears in my eyes for the entire ride back to the hotel. I think it was a combination of learning of the tragic death of Abigail today and now connecting the dots of who Eric really was, and the compounding deceit I was seeing unfold.

I was kicking myself, because I pride myself for being in tune to what is going on around me and I was out of tune with most of Luke's life.

I cannot believe all of this was going on right under my nose, and I was not aware of it. How in the world did this happen? I thought as I wiped my eyes.

"Ma'am are you okay?" the driver asked.

"Yes. I just have a lot on my mind."

"Okay. Let me know if you need anything."

My mind was spinning but focused on the fact that the condo address was being used for billing for the residential care for Eric Ernesto.

I needed to get to the islands to check the mail and see what other clues I could uncover, with God's direction.

"Lord, please help me get some understanding about all that is going on surrounding Luke," I whispered.

I got back to the hotel; I had a lot of time to spare, since the book signing had been canceled due to the tragedy surrounding Abigail. I needed to get over to the islands, to get to the condo to see what, if any, more information was there. *But what do I tell Weston? I know he would not approve of me going there for that reason. So I decided not to tell him.* I called him,

"Hey, babe. How are you and my baby? I'm going to put you on video so I can see his face!"

"No, no. Don't do that, Sparrow. We are good. Where are you?"

"In Miami." I continued to eat lunch and fill him in on everything else I had heard about Abigail's untimely demise and what I had decided to do about the proceeds from the book, and he was agreeable. I heard background noise with hustle and bustle and overhead announcements,

"Weston, are you at an airport?" I asked.

"No, that is just the TV. Hey baby, I have to go. Can I call you back in a few?

"Sure thing love. Talk to you soon, " we hung up. I was glad because I really needed to get into a neutral zone to get my head together and put the pieces of this puzzle together, and that was going to be in the islands. And Weston would not agree with the reason that I was going. Not by far. I sent Tabitha a text of some items God had placed on my heart that I may need so she could get them to me as soon as possible while I was still in Miami. She was okay with my requests, however was all up in my business as usual as she sent a text back,

"Ro, what on earth do you need steel-toed boots for, especially in Miami? I am confused."

I didn't know what I might be facing as I tried to uncover more and more of what now appeared to be a tangled web of lies. Besides, I might need to kick a door down or something.

"Tabitha, just get them for me!" is the best I could reply to her text and not tip my hand too much.

This was the first time in a long time that I made my travel arrangements to the islands on my own. I wanted Tabitha and Weston to think I was still in Miami taking care of business. Even though it was a hunch, I figured I would tip toe over to the islands, check out a few things that could be at the condo, and slip on back to Miami before either of them noticed. That was my plan. By the next morning, just like I knew she would, Tabitha had my request sent up to my hotel room.

I dropped the top on the rental car early the next morning and headed to the airport with my oversized carry-on bag with my steel-toed boots inside. Although it was still dark, early morning breeze tasseled my hair and settled my spirit as I decided to put the pedal to metal and flexed on this rental coupe bending the rims with each corner I took.

I hope I don't get a ticket. I thought, as everybody always knew I had a little speed demon in me.

The airport was like a ghost town, and parking was plenty however I still decided to valet. I was hungry and wanted to get through security quick in hopes of grabbing a bite to eat. Me venturing off to the islands was going as planned so far. Tabitha and Weston had no clue, my baby was being taken care of, although the book signing had to halted due the tragedy surrounding Abigail we were able to honor her legacy and make a contribution to her children and her cause; my literary career was exceeding all that I hoped for, and now all I had to was get over to the Bahamas see what the heck could possibly be up there and get back to Miami before any one noticed. *No problem, Sparrow you got this!* I thought.

The line for security was short, and I chalked that it up because it was too early, in fact — there was hardly anybody there. But it made it good for me, so I could get through security easily — or so I thought. The damn boots caused me to have to go through a security check in a private room, which was not a part of the plan!

Are you serious? I muffled under my breath, or so I thought.

"Yes, ma'am we are serious. Come this way."

After being frisked and body-searched in the airport security room, there was only one store open this time of morning. I quickly thumbed through a couple of magazines and found one that intrigued me with an article about how bookstores are trying to make a comeback in the technological age.

"I need to read this," I thought. As a nice distraction and impart some wisdom about the next steps in my career. I bought some gum. I loved to chew gum during my flights; it soothed my nerves and helped with popping my ears.

My ticket said my gate was 15; however, at this time of morning, I had to go way past my gate to the food court by gates 37 and 38 to get some much-needed breakfast. Little did I know, that while waiting devouring my breakfast, my morning jolt would not come from the chai tea, but from saving a life.

Chapter 15

I had arrived in the Bahamas and was now on the white sands right next to the water's edge; my mouth was full of blood, and my head was confused from the powerful blow to my lower jaw. I was actually seeing stars, while trying to catch my equilibrium.

Can this really be happening to me? And, at whose hands? I could not even imagine the answers to the questions, which I continually asked myself, over and over.

I balled up my fist in retaliation and faced my assailant, as I licked the blood that I could feel oozing down my chin.

Before I knew it, against my wishes, I had downed a shot of tequila. I looked directly at the person who was holding me hostage, and I reached toward his face. I pulled at the wig that adorned his head, and he pleaded with me,

"Not here, Ro."

It was Luke, my best friend, whom, we'd thought, we had buried just two weeks ago.

"Luke, what's going on? Why did you do this?" I asked, wiping the blood on my hand and checking my inner lip that felt cut as my bottom lip pulsated in pain.

With a calm disposition, Luke asked, "Sparrow, how is Busy? I know you have been making sure she has everything she needs."

"Busy is fine," I responded in a high-irritated fashion. "Answer my question."

"What about grandma?"

"Mrs. Elizabeth is fine, as well! Luke, don't play me! Why did you do this? I am baffled and, frankly, mad as hell at you, man! You can't go around faking your death! And then popping back up and acting like everything is okay! Do you know what I've been through, behind losing you? We buried you just a couple of weeks ago, man. What's going on? Are you hiding from somebody? Tell me now!" I demanded as I pounded the blood-soaked napkin onto the wicker table.

"Yes and no," he stated as he rubbed his hand on the tote on the table between us holding the gun.

"What do you mean — 'yes and no'? And stop with the idle threats. I know you are not going to shoot me!" I said with authority.

Luke grabbed a napkin from beneath the shot glass with tequila overflowing and began to rub the red lipstick off his lips while shaking his head.

"Ro, just stop. Please let me think! You always have to know the mother-fucking answer to every damn thing. And it is annoying as hell!" Luke protested.

There was a significant moment of silence that was unusual for us. And then Luke turned toward me, after placing the napkin on the table. He looked me square in the eye.

"Ro, do you remember when I began to get close to Lorenzo? When we started to party and hang out together at the Big Gulp and in the clubs?" Luke said as he invited me on this nostalgic journey that did not seem welcoming at all.

"Yes, back when Lorenzo and I started medical school together. Yes, I remember. What's up?"

"Well, during that time, Lucinda was really acting out and wanted to do anything she could to get out of the grasp of Grandma Liz and her drunken outbursts."

"I remember Grandma Liz's actions — well, borderline abuse. My parents did their best to help y'all out. But what does that have to do with you faking your death? Get to the point — I'm waiting!" I said in a frustrated tone as I massaged my lower jaw.

"Be patient. I'm getting to the point. It's a long story, and I know being patient is not a virtue that you have," Luke said as he moved himself to the edge of his beach chair, looking around as if he were making sure he was all clear to speak.

"Man — bye with that. I need to know what in the hell is going on — *now*," I demanded.

Luke grabbed another shot and looked around again, clearing his throat to proceed with his story.

"Lucinda got a job in Dr. Ernesto's clinic as an administrative assistant to earn some extra money, so she could leave home. Lorenzo hooked her up with that gig, as a favor to me."

"Okay."

"As you know, Lucinda always wanted the finer things in life. So much so, that, in her past, she got caught with some girls boosting from high-end boutiques a couple of times. After she spent a short stint in juvie, she realized going against the law was not the ticket. So, she was trying to take the straight-and-narrow path, but saving up money was taking way too long in her mind. She became downright desperate."

Tears began to well up in Luke's eyes. I grabbed him a napkin and placed it in his hand.

"Dear God — I knew Lucinda went through it, but I did not know about all that."

"I don't know if you know this, but Dr. Ernesto always had a wandering eye. You may recall Lorenzo used to joke about it sometimes, talking about how his daddy was a player."

"Yep, I remember."

"As soon as Dr. Ernesto laid eyes on Lucinda, he hired my beautiful sister right away as his new receptionist, despite the fact that she didn't have even the skillset to carry out the job. What she did have was allure and the ability make people smile. And she made Dr. Ernesto smile everyday as soon as she stepped in the room, and that got under the skin his office manager/wife's, Mrs. Ernesto's, mean, hateful-ass."

"I think I remember something about that."

"Well, one day after Lucinda and Grandma got into it, she went to work. It was like a light bulb went off in Lucinda's head, and she orchestrated a horrific plan. Dr. Ernesto invited her into his office to dictate some notes. When she got home that night, she started talking crazy, Ro. She was saying how she was going to have Dr. Ernesto by any means necessary."

"You have got to be kidding me! That does not sound like the Lucinda I knew."

"That is just the half of it. One night, when Dr. Ernesto was going away for a medical conference, Lucinda was able to find out all of his information and logistics about the medical event and lodging because she had access to his personal calendar. Girl, she had the login information and passwords to the most prominent surgeon in the country's computer. Can you believe that, Ro?"

"Most administrative assistants do. But what does that have to do with you faking your death and having us bury your ass?" I spit back.

"Just listen! As Lucinda told it, she showed up to the hotel and got Dr. Enrique Ernesto totally blasted. I mean really intoxicated, at the bar of the boutique hotel lounge. And the next thing I knew, she was telling me she was pregnant with his baby! Ro, did you hear me?"

"Yeah, I heard you alright!" I sat there stunned. I had put two and two together based on what I had discovered, but I had no idea about all of this. However, I still had a lot of questions.

"So, Luke, let's cut to the chase. Who is Eric Ernesto?"

"You know about Eric? Damn, Ro, you're good."

"Yes, you know I don't play. But level with me — who is Eric Ernesto?"

"Well, when Lucinda began to show, she went away to live with a retired midwife who used to work with Dr. Ernesto at the hospital. Or rather she was forced to do so. The retired midwife moved to a neighboring town after she retired. Dr. Ernesto tucked my sister away in hiding with this woman while she was pregnant with his baby and made many discreet — and false — promises to my sister."

"Luke, I'm going to ask you to get to the damn point!" I said as I sat on the edge of the beach chair, looking around for any and everyone in case I needed backup.

"Well, that Monster provided her with hush money to live with the midwife and be totally quiet about the pregnancy and who the father of her baby was. Lucinda's food and shelter were paid for, and there would be a guaranteed deposit in her bank account after she delivered the baby. Lucinda, not in her right mind, thought this was a great deal. It was unclear what was going to happen to the baby after the delivery.

"To be honest, Grandma Liz did not even know where Lucinda had disappeared to. She just thought Lucinda had run away again to be with relatives on her mother's side of the family like she had done so many times before. The midwife, I forget her name, was an elderly lady, and she took good care of Lucinda until she went into labor. At about her thirty-second week, Lucinda started having contractions, and she felt like something was wrong. Lucinda kept calling and texting Dr. Ernesto and begged him to allow her to go to the hospital to get checked out.

However, he did not respond to her, meanwhile instructing the midwife over the phone on what to do for my sister. Ro, he's a surgeon, not an obstetrician," Luke said with an infuriated look on his face.

"If what you say is true, Luke, this is unethical! Are you sure he did this? That does not sound like Dr. Ernesto to me. I've known him a long time. He used to be my attending when I was in residency. He taught at the medical school. Luke, you're making some pretty strong allegations. I know he had a reputation for being very flirtatious with the ladies, but this does not sound like him at all," I replied.

"Yes, my friend — trust me. This man — I hope his soul is burning in hell every day — was a monster! Wait — there's more. Lucinda was really scared. As she was going into premature labor, she felt she needed to go to the hospital. And that son of a bitch would not let her!"

"Luke, this is awful!"

"Lucinda was so gullible and felt that monster and the midwife had her best interests at heart. The midwife, I'm sure, at one time knew all about childbirth, but when she was taking care of my sister, she was feeble and possibly on the verge of having Alzheimer's."

"Did you ever talk to Dr. Ernesto about this, Luke?"

"No, Lucinda had sworn me to secrecy, so I couldn't. I could not betray my big sister. Besides, Dr. Ernesto paid for everything by cash and needed to keep Lucinda and the baby a secret, so he had to keep her out of a hospital setting, and Lucinda seemed to be okay with that approach."

"My goodness, Luke! Why didn't you tell me while this was going on?"

"Ro, I couldn't. I was already in your pocketbook and business enough. Besides, Lucinda had bound me to secrecy!"

"So, what happened to that baby?"

"You are really going to need another drink when you hear this. When Lucinda went into labor prematurely, she was in labor for 72 hours without her cervix truly dilating. The midwife should have taken her to the hospital, but under strict instructions from that monster, he insisted on having my sister suffer through this childbirth without proper medical care. Ro, she was in so much pain. She called me and screamed continuously into the phone. I was trying to calm her to let her know I was coming, but the midwife hung up the phone. I can still hear my sister's shrill voice in my head to this day and can't shake it. I can hear it just as if it were happening right now. *'Luke, please help me! Please come and help me!'* Lucinda begged me.

"And there was nothing I could really do for her. I got a ride and made it there as soon as I could the same day she called, but it took me a while. And Ro, when I finally got there, Lucinda was a sick girl. All of the color had seeped out of her beautiful skin. She looked like a shell of the gorgeous woman we all knew she was. She was pale, weak, and in deep agony. Ro, my mind cannot erase all of the blood that was around her. I begged that lady to call the ambulance. But she wouldn't!"

"Luke, I can't believe this!"

"Ro, after I had been there almost a day, the baby finally crowned, and I saw it with my own eyes. The baby was born blue — he was not breathing. The midwife cleared his airway and gave him a couple of breaths, and he had the strangest cry. Not like a normal baby would cry. It was an *angry-to-be-here* cry. It was like nothing I have ever heard before."

"So, is that Eric?

"Yes, that is Eric. When the midwife began to really examine him, his body was very weak, and he had no body tone. She called Dr. Ernesto, and he had one of his doctor cronies come by and see his son. I stood by helpless, praying for this sick child."

"What was the doctor's name who came to the midwife's house?" I asked.

"I can't recall; however, he was the one who broke the news to Dr. Ernesto. I overheard the conversation when he said that Eric had cerebral palsy and some anoxic brain injury. The midwife cleaned Eric up and wrapped him in a blanket. It seemed that this baby needed to be in a neonatal intensive care unit. I did not know much, but I did know that this baby was very sick. The midwife and I cleaned up Lucinda, and she lay there pale, clearly sick and curled into a ball. She refused to even hold her son. 'Take him away — I don't even want to look at him!' she said, as she was weak, delirious, and seriously depressed. But I held my nephew, and I named him Enrique Apollo Ernesto, Jr., after his low down no good father, so the world would know. I kissed his forehead and said to him, 'Enrique, I am your Uncle Luke. I love you, and so does your beautiful mother, Lucinda. You are going to be loved and well cared for — don't you ever forget that. And just like it had been planned all along, within the next couple of days, there was a very nice couple that arrived at the midwife's home and took Eric. They had a home in Florida for special-needs kids. Their name was Mr. and Mrs. Norton."

"Yes — Mr. Norton?" I said, thinking back on the nice man that almost burned down the lovely facility trying to bake gingerbread cookies for the residents.

"They were a lovely couple. The nicest people you would ever want to meet, Ro. And even in the midst of that horrible situation, I felt some relief in knowing Enrique was going to the Norton's. I knew they would take good care of him. I saw firsthand the type of love and care baby *Eric* would be getting. When the Norton's first arrived, Enrique cried inconsolably. 'Now, now, little baby boy. I'm going to call you 'Eric' because you are your own person, and you are going to be loved unconditionally,' Mrs. Norton said as she cradled this parentless child. And without missing a beat, Mrs. Norton picked Eric up and held him closely to her chest like he were her own. She soothed his unusual cry, and rocked him to sleep. That couple took Eric and nursed him while he was a baby up until how he is now, and saved his life. Without them, I'm not sure what would have happened to my nephew."

"Man, Luke, this is a lot! And I am glad that you got Eric the help he needed — but just level with me. Was I paying for his care at the facility?"

"I did what I had to do."

"But, at whose expense, Luke? Mine, as usual! And I'm sick of it! You know what? I have a family now! I know you think I'm rolling in dough, but you can't go around lying and causing people to sponsor different issues in your life without letting them know. That is just plain down-and-dirty wrong! Luke, you have always been like a brother to me, and I have treated you like family, and I just can't take any more!" I said, as I began to get up from the beach chair, trying to stand steady in the sand beneath my feet in the steel-toed boots.

Luke got up, grabbed my arm, and said, "No, wait, Ro. It's me — Luke" as he pulled off his wig.

"Sparrow, you are my sister, and I know I was wrong, and you are absolutely right. I should not have lied to you, of all people. But be prepared — there's more. And all of what I told you is not the half of it. Please sit down. There is a lot I have to get off my chest."

"You've *got* to be kidding me. There can't be any more." I sat back down.

"I have done a lot of bad things — really bad things! Just downright awful things. Unforgivable things. I could not let everything that happened to me and my family go with out getting vengeance for them," Luke said as he placed his head in his hands as they trembled.

I sat there in disbelief of all I had just heard and in fear of what was about to come out of Luke's mouth. He motioned for me to get up and follow him. I did. I had not realized it, but it was now night, and the tiki lights were the only brightness on the beach as far as you could see. The roar of the ocean seemed more intense, as the throbbing of my bottom lip eased up a little. I followed Luke along the shoreline toward the condo, with the dark water's edge in the distance.

"Luke, where are we going?" I asked while looking around at the beach, even more barren than before.

Should I follow him? I'm not sure where his head is at this present time. I am not sure how safe I really am with this dead man walking, I thought in my inner spirit. But we were walking toward the light, so I felt some sort of solace.

He downed his last Tequila shot. "Back to the condo. It's getting a little chilly out here. Don't you agree?" Luke stated as he continued to walk putting the wig back on with his tote bag that had his black, weathered Bible and gun tucked inside, as we walked toward the condo. It seemed the last shot of the liquor settled him. "Whew, that hit the spot!" he remarked.

Not totally convinced of Luke's sanity, I recommended we go up to the *Cocina*. I knew they would have night heaters on the outside dining area that would shield us from the ocean's cool nighttime breeze, so it would not be so brisk. It would be the perfect environment for us to continue our conversation.

I was still extremely curious about the explanations Luke would need to share with me, as I felt like I did not have all of the answers to all of my questions. I felt like now I had just enough information to go a little deeper with Luke to get to the bottom of why he faked his death.

The *Cocina* was filled with vacationers eating to their heart's content. The only seats available were the ones near the bar — pub tables. We chose to sit at one of them. We placed an order for a round of waters with lemon slices. I could not take anything else, since the tequila shots still had my head spinning, hydration is what I needed. And I absolutely did not have any appetite, which was so not like me. While we waited for our water, Luke leaned across the table and grabbed my hands,

"Ro, I must tell you: It's so good to see and talk to you, and I really needed this. You have been so busy, and I have been so crazy minded — all I know is that it has been way too long since we have had a heart-to-heart, sit-down talk like this. Besides, I know if I'd had a chance to discuss some of this out with you, I would have made better decisions."

I abruptly let his hands go, and, boldly raising my voice, said, "Luke, don't you dare place any blame for your actions on me! And lest you forget, we just had your funeral. Who does that? Not a person in their right mind!"

"Ro, lower your voice; people are looking at us. Don't make a scene like you always do. I'm keeping myself in a low profile. But, please forgive me, Ro."

"Luke, you're asking a lot!" I said as I crossed my arms.

"Ro, I figured you, of all people, would be the person who would figure out what was going on. The only caveat was, I didn't think you would figure out everything so quickly."

"Luke, you have known me since way back — long enough to know I don't give up without a fight. And I'm nosey. Once I was tipped off, I had no choice but to seek answers."

"I've been so on guard — which explains the gun — I didn't know who to trust or who was coming after me," Luke said as he hung his head low.

"Speaking of trust, tell me more about Lucinda, Dr. Ernesto, and their relationship," I inquired as I leaned in across the table.

"It was only a relationship to my sister. That monster didn't care about her. He used her. After the delivery of Eric, it took a while for Lucinda to recover at the midwife's house. She was so depressed her plan had not worked out like she thought. In her sick mind, she actually thought she could waltz right into the good doctor's life and make him fall madly in love with her, and he would leave his beloved wife and family. But what she did not know or realize, was that it was Mrs. Ernesto who really had the legacy wealth. She had raised Dr. Ernesto up by her own bootstraps, and she was not going to let a little girl from our side of town come in and destroy anything. Dr. Ernesto was her arm candy, and Dr. Ernesto knew that he was nothing without his wife's support and monetary strings. Not to mention, the hefty prenuptial that she made him sign before they got married years ago. He wasn't going to leave her."

"Of course. We all know the origins of their wealth."

"Yep, so he was never going to leave his wife, and that is not what Lucinda thought in her delusional little mind when she plotted out her scheme — that she and the good doctor would run away into the sunset and have their family together and live happily and wealthy ever after. And now you know how that worked out. That monster made sure Lucinda's life would never be the same."

"So I get their story. So what else did he do?"

"When Lucinda returned to the city after healing from almost dying after giving birth to Eric, in her naiveté, she showed back up at work and thought everything would be back to normal, just like before she left. She was wrong. Although she was just trying to get a paycheck, after Mrs. Ernesto found out about Lucinda and her husband, she immediately terminated Lucinda."

"Wow!"

"Yes, he paid her and Grandma Liz's bills with that pitiful amount of hush money that did not last long thanks to Grandma's gambling habit and Lucinda's love for material things. Instead of stacking the cash, Lucinda went out and bought new bags, red bottoms and shit like that."

"Oh no."

"Yes girl, the monster even paid for the first couple of months of Eric's stay with the Norton's, and then the bills started coming to Lucinda, and there was no way she could pay to keep her son, who she never even held, in that rehabilitation facility. That's when I asked you for the money for the mortgage. Sparrow, Dr. Ernesto single-handedly destroyed my sister's spirit, and she was back to the humble beginnings she despised. She moved back with Grandma Liz and me. I guess it was postpartum depression and separation anxiety from her baby for years, but she fell into a deeper depression. Until…"

"Until what?"

"You remember how beautiful Lucinda was?"

"Yes, she was gorgeous. Everybody knew how beautiful she was, beautiful skin and hair, with deep, long curly ringlets. And I remember Mrs. Elizabeth used to keep that bat by your front door for all the boys who tried to come over and take her out back in the day."

"Yes, she was. Well, she was in a pit of despair for years, until one night at the coffee shop long after you had moved away. When Lorenzo and I were hanging out, she came by one night after work to grab a cup of java before heading home to cook for Grandma Liz. And over the course of the evening, Lucinda and Lorenzo, over a cup of hot coffee, really connected. It seemed so natural."

"And?"

"And as they began to get close, Dr. Ernesto and Mrs. Ernesto heard about it in the streets and were not happy. Keep in mind, Lorenzo never knew the details of the history of his father's infidelities, especially that Lucinda had played any part in it. Nor did he know that his father had fathered a child with Lucinda. He had no clue about his half-brother Eric."

"Luke where is this story going?"

"When Lorenzo's parents found out he was fond of Lucinda and that they were spending time together, those evil people did everything to try to break Lucinda's spirit and fill Lorenzo's head that Lucinda was the devil. But it backfired," Luke said as he hunched toward me and leaned in to whisper.

"What happened?"

"Lorenzo found a confidante in Lucinda. He finally felt like he'd found someone who would not judge him and be supportive of him and his goals. And in turn, he was good to her, and I could see that Lorenzo manage to make the dark cloud over Lucinda disappear. Ro, her spirit was full when even though they were dating on the down low. I had never seen her smile the way she did. It was as if all of the terrors of her past were forgotten."

"So, what happened? Get to the damn point!" I demanded.

"Lucinda found out she was pregnant with Lorenzo's baby, and she was over the moon."

"And then here comes Busy," I said.

"Yes, here comes Busy! You see, Busy was conceived out of love. And the Ernesto's were not happy about it, when they found out this wrong-side-of-the-tracks girl, my sister, was pregnant with their royal heir, Lorenzo's, baby. They felt that this chick had tried to infiltrate their family twice. And they were losing ground with this scandal on the horizon as Lucinda began to show and there were murmurings around town."

"Are you sure?"

"Yes, I'm not only sure, but I believe Dr. Ernesto killed my sister because he thought he had gotten rid of her once in the past. And there she was again, trying to destroy their wealthy, perfect little family," Luke said as anger filled his eyes.

"Luke, that's a harsh allegation."

"Dr. Ernesto performed surgery on my pregnant sister to remove a tumor that he knew, all along, was not there! He purposefully cut into her aorta while in the operating room. That's what happened Ro — that's the damn truth!" Luke said as he crossed his arms and sat back in his chair.

"Luke, how do you know that?"

"I did some investigating. The only 'tumor' that Lucinda had was Busy inside her trying to live."

"And what did Lorenzo have to say about this? And about Lucinda's death?"

"Lorenzo was crushed by Lucinda's passing, and he was infuriated with his father. He had no clue of the possibility of cancer in Lucinda; he was completely in the dark. They kept this grown man totally secluded from the woman he loved."

"What do you mean?"

"I found out from a reliable source that, while all of that was going on with Lucinda, the Ernesto's made up a fake story, to tell Lorenzo about some land back in Mexico that he would inherit if he went there to take care of some deeds to the land."

"What is so wrong with that?"

"While he was away, they murdered my sister, Ro!"

"I am so sorry, Luke. I can't believe all of this!" I said.

"That monster thought he had the final say by killing my sister, but I got his ass!"

"What do you mean, 'you got his ass'?" I asked.

"Hello. Here are your drinks. Will you be dining with us this evening? We have some appetizer specials." The waitress attempted to go on and give us menus.

Luke snapped. “Don’t you see us talking?”

I looked at him sternly and then turned toward the waitress, who had a puzzled look on her face, with her cheeks flushing. I said,

“Thank you, Miss. Can you give us a minute?”

“No problem. So sorry to have disturbed you. I’ll be at the bar. Let me know when and if you are ready to order,” she said as she walked away, shrugging her shoulders.

“Thank you. We will.” I looked disapprovingly at Luke. “You did not have to be so rude to her.”

“I’m sorry, Ro. Do you realize I’m a dead man walking? I don’t have time for any distractions. Just like you found me, somebody else is going to find me. I am sure there are a lot of puzzle pieces being put together back in the States. And when they do, Boom!”

“What do you mean, ‘Boom’?”

“Let’s go back to the condo. I’ve got some crazy stuff to tell you.”

“Not sure I can take much more,” I said while shaking my head and sipping my water.

"No, it's my soul that can't take much more. I need to get it off my chest," Luke said as he stood up and put down a couple dollars' tip for the wait staff. I guess he was attempting to make up for behaving so badly.

"Come on, Ro," Luke said, walking toward the walkway from the restaurant toward where the condos were.

We walked side by side. We were strangely quiet, which was so opposite from how we used to be. Luke had keys to my condo and walked ahead and opened the door.

Oh, no, he didn't! I said to myself.

He walked in, looked around, saw where I had placed my belongings, and turned to me with a stern eye when he recognized the contents of the "Safe Contents" box from Busy's closet and the bank security box.

Sucking on his teeth, he looked me in the eye and said,

"Ro, you've got skills."

"I had no choice. Since you want to go all in, let's go all in," I responded.

"Are you ready?"

"Yeah, I'm ready," I replied.

"Can you handle it?"

"Boy, talk!"

Luke and I were in the living room of the condo. We sat down on chairs opposite each other, with a coffee table between us.

Luke positioned himself in that chair as if he were on the witness stand in a courtroom. He looked so serious and ready to plead his case.

"Sparrow, I feel like all my life I have let people run over me. And, truth be told, you've been the only one in my life who has ever stood up for me. However, after Lucinda's cruel murder, I felt like I had to get vindication on my own. And the worst of it is, I did something so awful, I still can't believe I did it," Luke said.

"Luke, what did you do?" I asked.

"Sparrow, I knew Dr. Ernesto was going by his office before flying his private jet to a medical conference, based on the information Lorenzo shared."

"Luke — no. Whenever you keep calling me 'Sparrow,' I know you're going to tell me something beyond awful."

"Sparrow, just wait for it. I can't believe I'm telling you this. I went by the Big Gulp and got some coffee and Danishes for Dr. Ernesto, for his trip. I knew he always had coffee and a Danish from the Big Gulp while flying to his satellite clinics, and I didn't think this trip would be any different."

"Luke — please, no! What did you do?" I said as I sat on the edge of my seat.

"I put crushed pills into the container of coffee. It was a medication that controls your blood sugar that I'd found. I took the coffee and pastries to the front desk of Dr. Ernesto's clinic and left them with the new receptionist, labeled specifically for Dr. Ernesto."

"Luke, how could you?" I asked.

"I knew there was a 50/50 chance he would actually get the coffee. But evidently, he did. I believe his wife did as well, but, Sparrow, I swear, I didn't know that his wife was going to be with him. I did not like Mrs. Ernesto, but that demise was meant only for Dr. Ernesto. Hell, that monster caused my sister to plummet into a deep despair, and I figured

'An eye for an eye.' I was going to make his ass plummet to his death!"

"Luke, you're not God. 'Vengeance is mine, says the Lord.' It's in the Bible!"

"And I am paying for it every second I'm alive. And Ro, you're sitting here all high and mighty. We can't forget what I did not too long ago for you and Mr. Weston Mack, your beau!"

"Luke, we said we'd made an oath to never speak of this. And once you make a commitment to family, you keep your word."

"All I can say is that you act all perfect, Ro, but your shit stinks as well, family or not!" Luke looked at me with disgust, turning his body sideways, distancing his eye contact from me.

"Let me tell you something with your ungrateful ass. I have put my neck out for you all of your life. I took you under my wing, so you could have a sense of belonging from the very first day I met you. I have loved you through so many ups and downs I can't even count. So, don't you even fix your lips to say, 'family or not.' I am all the real damn family you got! And I promise you that I am the true meaning of 'family' to you. And if you don't know that by now, I don't know how else anyone could care for you more other than God himself!"

"Bitch, are you comparing yourself to God?"

"Absolutely not, Luke. You know good and well that's not what I'm saying."

"Well, Ro, speaking of family and the Christian way to do things, while you are judging me and my dysfunction and reminding me of how you saved me from my pathetic upbringing and life, don't you forget about Dana is all I'm saying."

"Boy, you better fall back. Luke David Armstrong, you chose to do what you did in the name of true friendship. Let me make something crystal clear, and this is the last time I am going to say this. I promise before God, I never asked you to do anything crazy. You acted on your own accord. That was your decision!" I said as I began to tear up, thinking back on all of the ups and downs that I had experienced in my friendship with Luke and to that horrific day he was referencing.

"Hell, we were family! Most people don't have a choice of what family they're born into, but from day one we have always had each other's back. And that is what family does for each other." The angry tears that were streaming down my face baffled me. And I didn't realize that the wound was still fresh from when Luke told me what he had done for us!

I got myself together, wiping my eyes and taking a deep breath. "Now, let's focus on you and your trifling issues." And I thought back to the contents of the bank lock box,

"Boy, are you diabetic, or not?" I said in a demanding tone.

"No!"

"Then how in the hell did you get of all of that diabetes medication that was in the bank safe lock box?"

"Sparrow, I can't believe you got up in my private bank security box!"

"Luke, I need you to be 100 with me. Where did you get the damn diabetes medication?"

"I had gotten in a little trouble with the law and had to do some community service. To comply with the probation office, my probation officer set me up with this homeless shelter in the bottoms. It was very rewarding."

"And?"

"And, I met this young man who was homeless and had started coming to the mission for meals at first. And then he would stay overnight from time to time. We instantly connected. He reminded me so much of myself. He was an army kid, just like me, got strung out on drugs, and dropped out of school, just like me. His family had turned their back on him, and he ended up on the street, just like I had one point in time. It was like he was a lost soul, and it seemed like I'd stepped into his life, like you'd stepped into my life early on, and became like an extended family. Sparrow, I tried to help him by cleaning him up, but his addiction was too strong, and I couldn't always relate. To make matters worse, he was diabetic. On many occasions, he would not take his 'sugar' medication because he was high on drugs or just forgot. One day, while doing some street ministry, I found him unconscious on the street, unresponsive. I got him to the hospital, and the doctors said that he was in a diabetic coma. The doctors said that, if I had not found him, he would have surely died."

"And?"

"And we nursed him back to health at the mission, but he refused to totally come off of the street. We took baby steps in getting him back on track. I got him set up with a doctor, and he got back on his diabetes medications. But it was like a yo-yo. He would do well for a minute, and then he'd fall off the wagon and get back on the needle. Although I was really angry with him for his relapses, I saw a lot of me in him. And, to be honest, Ro…."

"What, Luke?"

"Ro, for the first time, I really saw how you must have felt sticking by my side all those years while I continued to mess up on a regular basis."

"Yes, you put me through a lot of shit, Luke. So, what happened to the guy?" I asked.

"Well, he didn't show up for a meal and shower for two days back to back, and this was out of character for him. And all of us at the shelter were concerned. So, I took it upon myself to go out and find him. I looked in his usual spots, and…"

"And what?" I asked as I leaned forward.

Luke hung his head and, with a tear rolling down his cheek, said,

"Sparrow, you are going to need another shot of tequila for this."

"What is it, Luke?"

"I found him with a needle in his arm, his eyes wide open and glazed over. All of the teeth were gone out of his head. It looked like someone had busted him up."

"Oh, no. What did you do?"

"There had been a detective snooping around my house, per Grandma Liz. His name was Detective Stroud, and I was getting nervous since the plane crash. And the bookies were coming by on a regular."

"And?"

"Well, I figured someone had started connecting the dots regarding the plane crash, and so I was ducking and dodging in these streets. In and out of the homeless shelter volunteering, trying to lay low and not be found out. Spending less time at home so I would not put Grandma and Busy in harm's way, trying to dodge detectives and bookies that Lorenzo and I were indebted to for a stack of cash. And then that one day when I found my poor friend on the street dead from an overdose with a needle still stuck in his arm, it was as if a light bulb went off. He was my way out!"

"How in the hell would he be your 'way out'?

"When I looked down at him lifeless, I saw myself."

"What?"

"In my sick warped desperate mind, I saw this as a way out. Ro, Grandma had taken the bus with the senior group to go to the casino for the weekend with the ladies in her spades group. And Busy was spending the night at the church for a lock-in with the children's ministry. Ro, I can't believe I'm telling you this."

"I'm listening!" I said.

Luke's head hung low, and his facial expression was very flat.

"Sparrow, I began to drag his body down the cold dark alley. And then out of nowhere, this homeless man jumped me. Before I knew it, the homeless man hit me in the head on my right temple with a wrench." Luke turned his head to the right, so I could see the wound that was now healing.

"That's crazy. What did you do with your friend that you found? Did you take him to the hospital and get him help?" I asked.

"Sparrow, you're not listening. He was already dead when I found him. I hid the body. I figured I would came back later, when I got off my shift. I used the homeless shelter's van to take the body to my house. I told them I needed the van to get some donations. I hid the body at home and took the van back to the shelter."

"That is insane. Keep talking. What happened next?"

"After I got home, I took the body out back, put my driver's license in his pants, and hung him from Lucinda's tree in the back of our house."

"Luke, this is sick."

"I then did the unspeakable!"

"What?"

"I set his body on fire."

"Dammit, Luke. Why?" I said. As I rose off the chair, he grabbed my hand and beckoned me to sit down again.

"Ro, please. I need your help. Let me finish telling you what happened," Luke's voicc cracked.

"Luke, this is just awful. I have gotten you out of many predicaments. But this — are you serious? I have no idea how I am going to help you out of this one!" I said as I sat there holding my head.

"As the body burned, I watched while hiding behind the bushes."

I sat there trying to process everything Luke had revealed. I was used to fixing his issues, but I can't imagine how in a million years I could fix anything he'd told me today.

"Ro, I had to do this. I just had to. So, I made sure I took care of some business, and then I vanished."

"Luke, we had your funeral, and now you are telling me that we buried some homeless drug addict? Listen to me — all this craziness and this dark vengeance are not okay! Regardless of his background, he was a person too and deserved more respect. We are all God's children, lest you forget. Do you know how many lives you have single-handedly destroyed? You have been through a lot — I know you have — and so have we all. But, Luke, you're better than this. I know you are."

"Ro, I don't know how good I am or not. But I felt like this was my way out. I would rather disappear than be locked up for life for the deeds I carried out. I knew everyone would assume the charred body hanging from the tree was me because of my photo ID in his pocket. People at the homeless shelter used to mistake us all the time. Everybody thought we were brothers." He attempted a small laugh. "They called us twins, sometimes. There was such a strong, uncanny resemblance. And I knew there would be no dental records and little if any substantial DNA to verify that it was or was not me.

In my own crazy distorted way, I felt this way, I would be able to get vindication on the Ernesto's and disappear into the flames."

I began to sweat all over and felt a sense of paranoia shroud me, "Luke, or who ever you are, I just can't be around you anymore. I just can't. Do you realize, by telling me this, what position you put me and my family in? Typical Luke always looking for the easy way out, at the expense of every one around."

"Ro, I am the thorn in your side — I know I am. But can you forgive me?"

"You need to be asking God that! I will seriously have to think about your request."

"Ro, I'm exhausted. Can we finish this discussion in the morning? Would you mind if I slept on the couch?" Luke asked as he took off his shoes, made his way to the linen closet, and pulled out a blanket.

"Well, why don't you make yourself at home, then?" I said while grabbing a candlestick holder off one of the end tables, holding it in my hand tightly, still unsure if this was my brother who was in the condo with me or the cold-blooded killer he professed to being.

"Ro, don't be afraid. It's still me, Luke, your best friend. Little Weston's Godfather…"

It was if he wanted to go on and on telling me about all of the kinships that we had, but I cut his ass off. "Yeah, yeah, yeah. I know who you look like, but I no longer know who the hell you are!" I went over to the table and gathered the leather journal and articles of discovery into my arms, with the candlestick in the other hand, and turned around and went into the master suite. Luke had not been joking as to how tired he was, because before I knew it he had quickly drifted off asleep on the condo pullout couch on top of the blanket. I went to the master suite, put all of the contents down, went back into the linen closet, grabbed another blanket, and draped it across his body. As he lay still, breathing slowly, he seemed at peace. *This was the Luke I knew.* He was out of the disguise, and I recognized him. For a quick moment, it was as if we had been to this condo many times on vacation, but I could not forget today's events, and any moment of peace was fleeting.

Who is this person lying before me on the couch pullout bed that could do such horrific things? This was a downright cold-blooded murderer! My heart skipped a beat as my brain pondered over this.

I need to call the police, however. Personally, I need to figure out a little bit more and set up a strategy as to how to get Luke back to the States safely, so he can confess his crimes. And most of all, I need to do this now, because I'm not going to wreck my career, being named as an accomplice to this serial killer's disappearance. Especially after I found out I was paying for some of his secrets and he was now hiding out of the States in my condo! This does not look good at all, but I needed some rest to figure out methodically what next steps to orchestrate. I really needed Weston's advice on what to do next. But he has no clue that I am here, and he would be furious that I allowed myself to be a silk thread in the web of demise.

I went into the master suite in the condo, locked the door, put a chair up against the doorknob, and put the heavy candlestick on my nightstand. *I wish I would have never convinced Weston to ship that gun back to the States after we had the baby,* I thought to myself as I felt very vulnerable and without a sound weapon to keep me safe. I looked over at my arsenal on the nightstand.

A damn candlestick, Sparrow? You have got to be kidding me! How is that going to protect you? You've got a grown-ass crazy man who faked his own death and killed others, with a sawed-off shotgun by him; the only thing between you and him is a wooden door with a four-legged chair as your extra security, and all you got is a candlestick? Girl, are you out of your mind?

Even though, before I left the living room, and I looked down at Luke sleeping on the couch, this person looked like my lifetime best friend. But the image of him, in disguise, pressing a gun into my head and striking me in the face could not be easily erased. As the adrenaline of today's events still pulsed through my body, my mouth continued to throb from the powerful blow to the jaw that had occurred earlier in the day. As I sat up in bed in the secured master suite, I could not help but to think,

Sparrow, you have done it this time. You have definitely bitten off more than you can chew. If I could only rewind time, I would not have been so curious and always trying to figure shit out. "If you go looking, you sure will find," is what my grandma used to always say to me. And yep, this time I sure in hell did find. And I was now on a tightrope with no balance left in me.

I grabbed the journal with the intent to get some more reading done to orchestrate more conclusions on my own. I knew what I was hearing from Luke, but how could I confirm that it was the truth? I set the alarm on my phone, to get up a little early so I could delve more into the contents that I had found. Luke always liked to sleep in, and I wanted to get up before him so I could get to my detective work.

The next morning came quickly as I was awakened by the ring tone on my phone.

I wiped my eyes and stretched my arms toward the ceiling. I rolled over on the journal and picked up my cell phone and unplugging it from the wall.

"Hello."

"Hey, it's me. Just checking in. How's Miami? I hate that I had to leave you there, but I had to get back to some business. "

"What time is it?" I asked.

"Sparrow, I'm surprised you are not up. It's 6:30 am! You are usually up working out by now," Tabitha said.

"I know. I set my phone alarm, but I guess I slept through it."

"Well, get up, girl. You got to get on the ball this morning. I emailed you your new electronic press kit to review last night since your interview with Abigail and her endorsement posted, God rest her soul. However, you didn't respond, and I know you have had a lot going on, but we still have to keep our momentum, Dr. Sparrow Mack!"

"Tabitha, can I call you back in about 30 minutes? I'll look at the email and give feedback ASAP. There are a couple of things I need to take care of first," I said as I made sure that the door was still secured by the chair that I'd placed in front of it last night to *protect* me.

"Cool. I'll be by the phone. And remember, Sparrow, you need to get back into full throttle, we have some tight time lines to adhere to!"

"Tabitha, I get it! Geez!" I hung up, wiped my eyes, and stretched my arms to heaven even bigger, took the journal that was on my chest, and placed it on the nightstand adjacent to the bed. All of the contents from the "Safe Contents" box and the bank security box were just as I had left them the night before. The door was still closed and securely locked.

Thank God I survived the night. I did not know if Luke was going to kick it down in the middle of the night and finish me off. In the movies, right after the killer confesses, he offs the one he confessed his crimes to!

I knew more than ever I was grateful to be alive. I went to the bathroom, washed my face with cold water, and brushed my teeth.

Grabbing the candlestick, I went to the door, unlocked it, and stood in the doorway of the living room.

"Luke — you up?" I whispered, so I would not startle him. I walked into the living room and up to the front of the couch. He was not there, nor was the blanket I'd placed on him the night before. And the couch was back in form, no evidence that it had been pulled out the night before.

He must be in the bathroom.

"Luke — you in the bathroom?" I yelled out louder.

I walked to the bathroom, and he was not there. There was no sign of the gun, his beach tote, or any traces of Luke David Armstrong. He must have gone down to get some breakfast in the condo lobby. He'd always liked the breakfast buffet in the *Cocina* because it had a robust spread.

Totally baffled at where Luke could be, I went down to the lobby and over to the *Cocina*; I scanned the dining area that was filled with beach-ready people piling their plates high with scrambled eggs, bacon, Belgium waffles, and other delectable pastries. The aroma made my empty stomach growl, as I had not had anything since the morning before at the Miami airport, but I would wait to have breakfast with Luke, once he showed his face. I walked through the restaurant.

"Ma'am, would you like a seat?" the waitress asked.

"No. I'm looking for my friend. But I don't see him. I'll come back later."

"The breakfast buffet ends at 11:30 am. So, you have plenty of time."

"Thank you. I'll be back."

There was no sign anywhere of Luke. I needed to get back to the condo, so I could check my email and get back with Tabitha to handle business. "Then Luke and I can connect," I said to myself.

I went back to the condo and logged onto the computer to review the electronic press kit. As I pressed "Send" to forward my approvals to Tabitha, there was a knock at the door. *It must be Luke. But why is he knocking? I knew he had a key!*

"Luke did you forget your key?" I said as I opened the door. It was a man dressed in a suit, with salt-and-pepper hair slicked back.

"Can I help you, sir?" I asked of the stranger, as I pushed the door slightly closed, leaving only a crack to communicate.

"Yes, ma'am. I am looking for Dr. Sparrow Mack."

"And who is asking?" I insisted.

"I am the Coroner for Nassau County. Are you Dr. Sparrow Mack?"

"Yes. How may I help you?

"I have this urn for you!"

"Excuse me — an urn? I think you have the wrong person. I was not expecting this."

"As you can see right here on this document, you are supposed to be the recipient for the remains of Luke David Armstrong."

I looked down at the document, and it read just as he said. And I guess the look on my face was a cause for concern, when the Coroner asked,

"Ma'am, are you okay?"

"Yes, I just need to sit down."

"Here, let me help you. Is the couch okay? The Coroner insisted making his way through the door.

"Yes. But I don't understand, sir. Who sent this to me? He did not pass away here in the islands!"

"It was a part of a jurisdiction and execution of a last will and testament."

"What was the cause of death, may I ask?"

"Doctor, as you can see right here, it was a suicide-hanging and burning himself to death. Do you feel well enough to sign that you received this?"

"Yes." My hand was shaking, but I signed the document and handed it to the Coroner. He put the urn on the table and left.

I sat on the couch in the living room and stared at the urn in a trance. The urn's presence filled the room.

Damn! What in the hell is going on, and who is in there? Is that Luke's friend from the homeless shelter in here? And where in the world is Luke? I am so overwhelmed, confused, and almost frozen in angst. I grabbed the envelope that was taped to the urn.

Sparrow,

Thank you for honoring my wishes by taking my remains. I have always felt one with the islands. This was my home. I have always felt safe and loved here. So please, if you would scatter my ashes into the ocean at the water's edge, I will truly be at home.
Your brother,
Luke

I held the letter in my hand and paused for a second in disbelief.

From everything I had heard the night before, what I had been reading in the journal, what all of the souls I uncovered in my journey toward the truth told me about my best friend, from Busy leading me into the closet to find the clues, from Sophie at the coffee shop, Mrs. Katherine at the homeless shelter, and Mr. Norton in the Florida residential facility, I realized that this entire reality was distorted. And where I am now — this uncomfortable reality of the matrix — and even after all of this, I felt I was no more closer to the truth than when I started on this journey. I put the letter back on the coffee table next to the urn.

I really need to call my husband to get his sound advice, but I'm not supposed to be here in the islands trying to solve a murder. He thinks I'm still in Miami wrapping up some business after the canceled book signing due to Abigail's passing. And he would be beside himself if he found out that Luke was still alive. I can hear him saying, 'I wish that leech would just get out of our lives so we can live in peace.' I cannot call Tabitha. She never really understood Luke's and my friendship from her privileged upbringing. She'd always thought Luke could bring me down, and she was right. I could not call the police over here or back home, unsure of what I would tell them.

I did not know what to do next, but what I did know was that I was in a bad way and that I had pried too much and uncovered a rock that I wished I could turn back over.

Sparrow, get up and get dressed. You need to go and find out where Luke is! I said to myself as I went to the bathroom to take a shower to wash my body and head to cleanse away this nightmare. The more I thought about the request for me to scatter the ashes, the more delusional it sounded. But I decided to go along with it. I had come too far to turn back now. I felt like I was in a game or maze, and somehow, with all that had led me up to the climax of what was going on, I knew that Luke would surface and that he was the puppet master in all of this. I blow dried my hair while talking to myself in the mirror.

Luke you want to play, crazy? I'll show you crazy! I thought as I went to my closet that was always stocked with clothes that I left here at the condo. I pondered what to wear. There was plenty of black that seemed fitting for the dark cloud that complemented what I was feeling on the inside to go and scatter the ashes. However, there was one white blouse in the closet, and my eyes and spirit were drawn to it. I needed to be uplifted. I refused to wear black for this ceremony of the unknown.

Still unsure of what I would be facing, I put on my combat boots, which definitely did not go with the beach attire that I was wearing. But I was beyond caring at this point. I grabbed my bag and placed the urn in it. It was still bright and early, and the beach-goers had not made it to the white sands yet. The only things moving were the tides that ripped the beach shoreline. I walked through the white sands up to the water's edge on the rocks that lined the beach. Standing on the rocks, I grabbed the urn out of the bag, took the lid off, and sprinkled the ashes into the crystal-blue waters.

"God, please forgive me for whatever I have not done for my friend Luke. I know I am a vessel, and I have not allowed you to use me like I was supposed to. I now ask you to accept this person and their soul back to you and forgive all those involved — the perpetrator and even me, Lord. And help me, Lord, and most of all help Luke. Amen."

The ashes dissipated into the ocean and seemed to coalesce together slowly migrating into the edge of the sea. I watched them for as long as I could see them, from Luke's favorite spot on the beach - the water's edge. Which was truly home to him. I knew that, by doing this and granting his wish, regardless of whose ashes they were, this was going to allow

Luke to finally be at home. To escape the life that had given him nothing but despair. *If it was Luke in those ashes, then I was good with my decision because he was finally at peace. And if it was not Luke, and what had occurred was truly a means for him to start over in life, then I was at peace as well. Right or wrong, I was just the vessel honoring his wishes. And I hope that God could forgive me for getting involved in this mess. Even though everyone thought of Luke as a leech off of my life. If it was not for Luke and him sticking his neck out me nor Weston would be alive today. And that was the truth.* As uncomfortable as this was, doing this for Luke made us even. I felt that I had finally paid him back for what he had done for my family and me. Still uneasy and a little livid at him for putting me in this position, this was just like any other day all of his life, thrusting me into the midst of turmoil to clean up his mud.

Still at a total loss for what to do next, as I risked being an accomplice in getting rid of evidence regarding a faked death, I needed some help figuring out what to do next. I reached into my oversized bag to pull out my key; a card fell out of my purse. I picked it up off the sand. It was the card of that detective. I guess it must have fallen out of the journal.

I went into the condo, dusted the white sand off my feet, and for the last time yelled out, "Luke are you in here? Please show your face."

I got no response. He was not here.

Damn, I cannot believe this shit. Where is Luke?

I picked up the phone and dialed the number on the card. It rang.

"Hello, you have reached the voicemail of Detective Stroud. Please leave a message."

I hung up the phone, nearly choking. *Dammit, why did I do that? I didn't block my number.* I felt I was truly coming apart at the hinges and making sloppy moves, partly, because I was famished. I got up and went to the kitchen to get a snack and a glass of water. I grabbed a couple of almonds, then looked over the mail. It was all junk except one; a letter in a plain white envelope addressed to Lucinda Armstrong care of the condo address. I opened the envelope, and it was a check written to Lucinda dated two weeks ago for fifty thousand dollars. I almost fainted when I looked down at the bottom and saw that the payer was Weston Mack.

As my mind spun and rewound, how could this be? My Weston? Not the man I said vows till death do us part? *Did Weston know all along about Luke, him faking his death, and him taking on the new identity of his dead sister, Lucinda!* I grabbed my cell phone to call my husband to go in hard on getting his side of the story, but there was a knock at the door. I rushed to open it, my temperature rising with each step as I snatched the knob and turned it, figuring it was Luke. I was ready to ballistic on him for putting me in the middle of this mess.

"Luke, you've got a lot of explaining to do!" I said with aggression that came from the depths of my soul.

The door opened. I gasped in shock.

"No, I'm not Luke. But yes, baby, I know I have a lot of explaining to do. Just know I did everything in your best interest," Mr. Weston Mack said as he stepped inside and reached down to kiss my cheek, as I stood there speechless.

When most people think of true friendship, they think of a comfortable place to exist, but not me. I can't relate. My journey with my best friend was not pretty; it was raw, jagged, and downright horrifying at times, erasing all possibilities of comfort. It had the potential to rip apart the fabric of all that was good in my life. But it was what it was.

The End

CPSIA information can be obtained
at www.ICGtesting.com
Printed in the USA
LVHW021746130619
621133LV00026B/469